Right Wrong Guy

ATTENTION: ORGANIZATIONS AND CORPORATIONS
digital of the books may be purchased for educational, business,
or sales promotional use. For information, please e-mail the Special
Markets Department at SPsales@harpercollins.com.

Also by Lia Riley

Last First Kiss

Coming Soon
Best Worst Mistake

Right Wrong Guy

A BRIGHTWATER NOVEL

LIA RILEY

AVONIMPULSE
An Imprint of HarperCollinsPublishers

Excerpt from *Last First Kiss* copyright © 2015 by Lia Riley.
Excerpt from *Close to Heart* copyright © 2015 by Tina Klinesmith.
Excerpt from *The Maddening Lord Montwood* copyright © 2015 by Vivienne Lorret.
Excerpt from *Chaos* copyright © 2015 by Jamie Shaw.
Excerpt from *The Bride Wore Denim* copyright © 2015 by Lizbeth Selvig.

EPub Edition AUGUST 2015 ISBN: 9780062403780

Print Edition ISBN: 9780062403797

10 9 8 7 6 5 4 3 2 1

To Nick,
sorry I flood the kitchen, stick frozen peas in the pantry,
and can't park the car to save my life—
but hey look, I wrote another book!
Love you.

To M.L.

...I'll flood the kitchen, that you'n need in the pantry
...and can't get ... the car to start or fly—
...but hey, look, I wrote another book!
love you

Acknowledgments

GRATITUDE, AS ALWAYS, to my brilliant editor, Amanda Bergeron, who makes everything I write way better. Special appreciation is also due to the fabulous and patient Gabrielle Keck. To my lovely agent, Emily Sylvan Kim, you always know when to give the perfect pep talk and it's so appreciated.

Love to my dear writing compadres: Jennifer Ryan, Jennifer Blackwood, Natalie Blitt, Jules Barnard, Megan Erickson, and A.J. Pine.

Super special thanks to my family for putting up with me. When I grunt an answer or stare off into the distance, what I'm really saying is "I love you."

To my readers, I couldn't do any of this without you. Your support means the world.

The Legend of Hidden Rock Ranch

(excerpt from *Brightwater: Small Town, Big Dreams*)

FIELDER KANE, THE youngest son of a Rhode Island textile worker, ran away to seek his fortune during the Gold Rush. He arrived in the Brightwater Valley's first wagon train, one of the thousands of adventurous young men flocking to California. Slowly but surely, the rugged town began to thrive despite the harsh weather. A merchant arrived with a raven-haired daughter, Margaret, rumored to be the most beautiful woman in the region. He made it clear that his beloved child would settle for nothing less than the man with the most land, the greatest potential.

For five long years, Fielder put his head down, gathering a sizeable cattle herd, a loyal cadre of working men as well as land, position, and power. At long last, when he had amassed his fortune, he purchased a ring as elegant and beautiful as the woman he loved.

Margaret joyfully accepted the handsome young cattleman's proposal. They were soon wed and she bore him three healthy sons. But alas, consumption also migrated to California, and the pernicious, deadly disease soon found home in her lungs. All too soon, she wasted away, leaving behind a grief-stricken husband.

Fielder vowed never to love again. Instead, he secreted that hard-won engagement ring on his property, never telling a soul of its whereabouts. He claimed it was a gift of true love and only another with equal grit and conviction deserved to discover such a prize.

To this day, though many have tried, no one has ever found the hidden rock.

Chapter One

ARCHER KANE PLUCKED a dangly gold nipple tassel off his cheek and sat up in the king-sized bed, scrubbing his face. Overturned furniture, empty shot glasses, and champagne flutes littered the hotel room while a red thong dangled from the flat screen. He inched his fingers to grab the Stetson resting atop the tangled comforter. The trick lay in not disturbing the two women snoring on either side of him. Vegas trips were about fillies and fun—mission accomplished.

Right?

"What the?" A dove dive-bombed him, swooped to his left, and perched on the room-service cart to peck at a peanut from what appeared to be the remnants of a large hot fudge sundae. Who knew how a bird got in here, but at least the ice cream explained why his chest hair was sticky and, farther below, chocolate-covered fingerprints framed his six-pack. Looked like he had one helluva night. Too bad he couldn't remember a damn thing. He should be high-fiving himself, but instead, he just felt dog-tired.

He emerged from beneath the covers and crawled to the bottom of the bed, head pounding like a bass drum. As he stood, the prior evening returned in splintered fragments. Blondie, on the right cuddling his empty pillow, was Crystal Balls aka the Stripping Magician. The marquee from her show advertised, "She has nothing up her sleeve." Dark-hair on the left had been the assistant . . . *Destiny? Dallas? Daisy?*

Something with a D.

How in Houdini they all ended up in bed together is where the facts got fuzzy.

A feather-trimmed sequined gown was crumpled by the mini bar and an old-man ventriloquist's dummy appeared to track his furtive movements from the corner. Archer stepped over a Jim Beam bottle and crept toward the bathroom. Next mission? A thorough shower followed by the strongest coffee on the strip.

Coffee. Yes. Soon. Plus a short stack of buttermilk pancakes, a Denver omelet, and enough bacon to require the sacrifice of a dozen hogs. Starving didn't come close to describing the hollow feeling in his gut, like he'd run a sub-four-hour marathon, scaled Everest, and then wrestled a two-ton longhorn. His reflection stared back from the bathroom mirror, circles under his green eyes and thick morning scruff. For the last year a discontented funk had risen within him. How many times had he insisted he was too young to be tied down to a serious committed relationship, job . . . or anything? Well, at twenty-seven he might not be geriatric, but he was getting too old for this bed-hopping shit.

"What the hell are you doing?" he muttered to himself.

The facts were Mr. Brightwater wasn't looking his best. His second cousin, Kit, gave him that nickname after he graced the cover of a "Boys of Brightwater" town calendar last year to support the local Lions Club. He'd been February and posed holding a red cardboard heart over his johnson to avoid an X rating, although as his big brother Sawyer dryly noted, "Not like most women around here haven't already seen it."

In fairness, Brightwater, California, didn't host a large population. For a healthy man who liked the ladies, it didn't take long to make the rounds at The Dirty Shame, the local watering hole. Vegas getaways meant variety, a chance to spice things up, although a threesome with Crystal and Donna—*Deborah? Deena? Dazzle?*—was akin to swallowing a whole habanero.

He reached into the shower and flicked on the tap as a warm furry body hopped across his foot. "Shit!" He vaulted back, nearly going ass over teakettle, before bracing himself on the counter. A bewildered white rabbit peered up, nose twitching.

"You've got to be kidding me." He squinted into the steam with increased suspicion. Hopefully, Crystal's act didn't also involve a baby crocodile or, worse, a boa constrictor. He hated snakes.

The coast was clear so he stepped inside, the hot water

sending him halfway to human. There was a tiny bottle of hotel shampoo perched in the soap dish and he gave it a dubious sniff. It smelled like flowers but would do the job of rinsing away stale perfume and sex. He worked a dollop through his thick hair, shoulder muscles relaxing.

He'd always prided himself on being the kind of good-time guy who held no regrets, but lately it seemed like there was a difference between dwelling on past mistakes and reflecting in order to avoid future ones. Did he really want to live out these shallow morning-after scenarios forever like some warped version of *Groundhog Day*?

The hair on the back of his neck tingled with the unmistakable sensation of being watched. He swiped suds from his eyes and turned, nearly nose-to-nose with the blank stare of the old-man ventriloquist's dummy.

"Fuck," he barked, any better word lost in shock.

"Great Uncle Sam don't like it when menfolk cuss," the dummy responded in a deep, Southern drawl. Other than the puppet on her hand, Dixie-Dorothy-Darby wore nothing but a suggestive smile.

"Uh . . . morning, beautiful." Thank God for matching dimples, they'd charmed him out of enough bad situations.

"No one's ever made me come so hard." The puppet's mustache bobbed as he spoke and more of last night's drunken jigsaw puzzle snapped into place. Desdemona-Diana-Doris had gone on (and on) about her dream of becoming a professional ventriloquist. She'd brought out the puppet and made Great Uncle Sam talk dirty, which had been hilarious after Tequila Slammers, Snake Bites,

Buttery Nipples, and 5 Deadly Venoms, plus a few bottles of champagne.

It was a whole lot less funny now.

"Hey, D, would you mind giving me a sec here? I'm going to finish rinsing off." When in doubt, he always referred to a woman by her first initial, it made him sound affectionate instead of like an asshole.

"D?" rumbled Great Uncle Sam.

Damn. Apparently an initial wasn't going to cut it.

Okay think . . . Dinah? No. Two rocks glinted from her lobes—a possible namesake. "Diamond?"

Great Uncle Sam slowly shook his head. Maybe it was Archer's imagination, but the painted eyes narrowed fractionally. "Stormy."

And so was her expression.

Not even close.

"Stormy?" he repeated blankly. "Yeah, Stormy, of course. Gorgeous name. Makes me think of rain and . . . and . . . rainbows . . . and . . ."

"You called it out enough last night, the least you could do is be a gentleman and remember it the next morning!" Great Uncle Sam head-butted him.

Add splitting headache to his current list of troubles.

Archer scrambled from the shower before he got his bare ass taken down by a puppet. You don't fight back against a woman, even if she is trying to bash your brain in with Pinocchio's demented elderly uncle.

"Get the hell out." Stormy's real voice sounded a lot more Jersey Shore than genteel Georgian peach farmer. She wasn't half bad at the whole ventriloquist gig, but now wasn't the time to offer compliments.

He threw on his Levi's commando-style while Stormy eyed his package as if prepping to go Category Five hurricane on his junk. Scooping his red Western shirt off the floor, he made a break for the bedroom. His boots were by the door but his hat was still on the bed, specifically on Crystal's head. Her sleepy expression gave way to confusion as Stormy sprang from the bathroom, Great Uncle Sam leading the charge.

"What's going on?" Crystal asked as Stormy bellowed, "Prepare to have your manwhore ass kicked back into whatever cowpoke hole you crawled from."

Hat? Boots? Hat? Boots? Archer only had time to grab one. He slung his arms through the shirt, not bothering to snap the pearl clasps, and grabbed the hand-tooled boots while hurtling into the hall. Yeah, definitely getting too old for this shit.

"Pleasure to make your acquaintance," he called over one shoulder as the dove swooped.

He bypassed the elevator bay in favor of the stairwell. Once he'd descended three floors, he paused to tug on his boots and his phone rang. Pulling it out from his back pocket, he groaned at the screen. Grandma Kane.

He could let it go to voice mail. In fact, he was tempted to do just that, but the thing about Grandma was she called back until you picked up.

With a heavy sigh, and a prayer for two Tylenol, he hit "answer." "How's the best grandma in the world?" he boomed, propping the phone between his ear and shoulder and snapping together his shirt.

"Quit with your smooth talk, boy," Grandma barked. "Where are you?"

"Leaving church," he fibbed quickly.

"Better not be the Little Chapel of Love."

"What do you—"

"Don't feed me bullhickey. You're in Vegas again."

Sawyer must have squeaked. As Brightwater sheriff, he was into upright citizenship and moral standing, nobler than George Washington and his fucking cherry tree.

"Did you forget about our plans for this weekend?"

"Plans?" He wracked his brain but thinking hurt. So did walking down these stairs. Come to think of it, so did breathing. He needed that upcoming coffee and bacon like a nose needed picking.

Grandma made a rude noise. "To go over the accounts for Hidden Rock. You promised to set up the new purchase-order software on the computer."

Shit. His shoulders slumped. He had offered to help. Grandma ran a large, profitable cattle ranch, but the Hidden Rock's inventory management was archaic, and the accounting practically done by abacus. In his hurry to see if an impromptu Vegas road trip could overcome his funk, the meeting had slipped his mind. "Let me make it up to you—"

"Your charm has no currency here, boy." Grandpa Kane died before Archer was born and Grandma never remarried. Perhaps he should introduce her to Stormy's Great Uncle Sam. Those two were a match made in heaven, could spend their spare time busting his balls.

He closed his eyes and massaged his forehead. "I'm

sorry, I completely forgot, okay?" Not okay. Grandma counted on him and he let her down.

"Funny, guess you're probably too busy using women like disposable silverware." Her tone sounded anything but amused. "Even funnier will be when I forget to put you in my will."

Grandma's favorite threat was disinheriting him. Who cared? The guy voted Biggest Partier and Class Flirt his senior year at Brightwater High was also the least likely to run Hidden Rock Ranch.

The line went dead. At least she didn't ask why he couldn't be more like Sawyer anymore.

Whatever. Archer had it good, made great tips as a wrangler at a dude ranch. His middle brother took life seriously enough and he hadn't seen his oldest one in years. Wilder worked as a smoke jumper in Montana. Sometimes Archer wondered what would happen if he cruised to Big Sky Country and paid him a surprise visit—maybe he had multiple sister wives or was a secret war lord.

Growing up after their parents died in a freak house fire, they all slipped into roles. Wilder withdrew, brooding and angry, Sawyer became Mr. Nice Guy, always the teacher's pet or offering to do chores. Archer rounded things out by going for laughs and practical jokes and causing trouble because someone had to remind everyone else not to take life so seriously. None of them were getting out alive.

He kept marching down the flights of stairs, tucking in his shirt. Grandma's words played on a loop in his mind. "Using women like disposable silverware."

Lord knew—those women used him right back. It was fun, didn't mean anything.

Meaningless.

He ground his jaw so tight his teeth hurt. Casual sex on pool tables, washing machines, countertops, and lawn chairs filled his physical needs, but these random hook-ups were starting to make him feel more and more alone.

On the ground floor, he slammed open the stairwell door. There were two corridors ahead. He turned left for no reason other than that's the hand he favored. Seemed like he chose wisely because a side entrance gave him a quick exit. He walked out, wincing at the morning sun even as he gulped fresh air, fresh for the Vegas Strip, but a far cry from the Eastern Sierras's clean mountain breeze. His heart stirred. He'd have some breakfast and hit the road. As much as he liked leaving Brightwater, he always missed home.

Archer reached to adjust his hat and grabbed a hand-ful of wet hair instead. Twelve stories above, a stripping magician had found herself a mighty fine Stetson.

He stepped onto the street, jumping back on the curb when a city bus turned, the side plastered with a shoe ad sporting the slogan, "Can You Run Forever?"

Hell, he'd been running from accountability, stability, and boring routines his whole life.

Another thought crept in and sank its roots deep. Was he really running from those things, or was he letting his fears of commitment and responsibility run him instead?

RIGHT WRONG GUY

Chapter Two

EDEN BANKCROFT-KEW HAD a secret so dark, so terrible, that she never confessed it to anyone. It wasn't that she sang "Ob-La-Di, Ob-La-Da," when she showered or that her left boob was bigger than her right. Those facts were a little embarrassing but nothing to make anyone raise an eyebrow.

But who can admit to hating *Forrest Gump*? People might chase her with pitchforks.

First off, life was no box of chocolates. Boxes of chocolates came with helpful identification charts that allowed you to choose the chocolate-covered cherries and ignore the nougat. Secondly, the film suggested that if a man kept after you, eventually you'd love him.

Eden hit mute on the hotel television as jogging Forrest, beard to his belly button, wiped his face on a bystander's towel, leaving a cheesy '70s-era smiley face behind. With a sigh, she reached across the bed and plucked up her veil, cut to land stylishly at the end of her chin, like a bride from a bygone era. She crossed her legs, thank goodness her dress was a comfortable 1940s tea-length style, and gave herself a pat on the victory rolls—focusing on her complicated hairdo rather than her impending fate.

Within a few short hours, she'd become Mrs. Reginald Winter, uniting two long-friendly families.

Such a thought shouldn't freeze the blood in her veins, but nerves—*please just be nerves*—had been growing since Reggie's proposal a few months ago. This morning they'd reached King Kong dimensions.

Here's the truth, Forrest: If a man keeps after you, you'll never love him, but you might eventually say yes.

Especially when your dying mother made it clear this marriage was her single most cherished dream for your future. Reggie, or Reginald George Bartholomew Winter the IV's bloodline made up a Who's Who from the *Mayflower* if that sort of thing turned you on. Personally, Eden wasn't hot for Puritan genes, especially when her own relatives were on the same ship.

Throughout her childhood, Reggie had always been kind when their paths crossed at society functions, or at least not actively mean, unlike the classmates at her elite all-girls school who had dubbed her "Eden the Ew," snapped secret locker room pictures of her late-blooming body, and emailed them to their "brother" school. These days, she flat-ironed her bushy hair into subservience and Mother had paid a king's ransom to straighten her teeth. Being bullied might have made her stronger, but there was no denying that interacting with others rendered her cautious and a little weary. A perfectly normal reaction after having her A cups rated as D's and F's by cute guys across MySpace.

When Reggie proposed the evening of the funeral, repeatedly reassuring Eden it's what her mother wanted, what made sense for both their families, she said yes because she loved what he represented: security. Daddy died in a freak ski accident fifteen years ago and losing Mother meant she was an orphan at twenty-seven. Not as if she would clutch a bowl of gruel à la Dickens or be beaten at a reform school like Jane Eyre, but she craved a family. Children. Laughter. Home-cooked holiday meals that weren't silent catered affairs but full of squeals and spilled food. And a man seated across the table.

Perhaps strangely, she never pictured anyone's specific face, just a vague sense of "rightness," a kindhearted nature and booming, infectious laugh.

Mother's agoraphobia had grown in conjunction with her terminal diagnosis until she could barely cope if Eden popped away from the penthouse for an hour to volunteer at a no-kill rescue shelter, take a cooking class, or go for a run. Committing to any sort of professional work schedule had been out of the question. Taking care of Mother had been her life. Now, Reggie would take care of her. And maybe she'd figure out her life's purpose at last.

In the outer living room, beyond the bedroom, the suite's door opened. "We're meeting at half past ten in front of the chapel." Reggie's cultured New England drawl rang out.

Eden froze, ears pricking. What was he doing back at the room? She'd cancelled her hair appointment to mope in private after he announced his intention to spend the morning camped out in the hotel's complimentary workspace.

"Relax, babe. Everything is going exactly to plan." Reggie used an unfamiliar cajoling tone. "Not a single mention of a prenup."

Eden balled her fists on her lap. Who the hell was this "babe" and why was her fiancé talking prenups?

"How about we spend the weekend at that little place in the Hamptons as soon as the honeymoon is over?" A pause. "Babe, stop, don't be like that. This is all for you— us. Getting Eden to marry me saved our asses." Another long pause. "Fine, yes, you saved my ass, Suki. It was a stroke of genius working through the mother. Rolling that crazy old bat was almost too easy."

Suki? Reggie's PA, Suki? Suki who had attended the philharmonic with them last week? Eden crushed the veil between her hands. This couldn't be happening. Impossible. A bad dream. But maybe most surprising is that she was surprised at all.

Did Eden the Ew get the guy? The happy ending? She punched her fists against her thighs as her throat grew thick.

No.

Nothing had changed in all these years. She was still the butt of the joke. But why? There'd never been a clear reason why she'd been bullied. Most teenagers went through an awkward phase. It was as if there had been an invisible sign hanging over her head reading "Easy Target."

Her private dream for a sweet, stable family life drowned under the nightmarishly wet kissing noises Reggie made into his phone. Guess she hadn't experienced enough embarrassment and shame. There was always room for a little more.

"Hey, I've got to change into my suit and suck down at least three drinks to survive the ceremony," he continued after still more nauseating lip smacks. Was he actually tonguing the speaker? Disgusting. "I'll call again soon. Love you too, babe."

Oh no. Reggie was about to discover her frozen on the bed, hulk smashing her veil, and would realize in a flash that his dirty little secret was out of the bag. She jumped up and eyed the closet. No, not there, that's where his suit hung. She ran to the bathroom, relieved her bare feet provided a noiseless retreat, and slid into the tub, inching behind the curtain, back pressed against the tiles. Could she win an award for the most cliché hiding spot?

Please don't let him have to pee . . . or worse.

A small bit of luck. Reggie changed without entering the bathroom. *"Forrest Gump,"* he said, giving his obnoxious chuckle on his way back to the living room. "What a great movie."

EDEN DIDN'T BUDGE for ten minutes. Ten minutes that felt like ten ice ages grinding away with glacial slowness. Betrayal and anger left her insides scoured. Reggie had lobbied for a no-fuss Vegas elopement and now it made sense. She dropped the veil into the tub and trudged, dazed, back into the bedroom. He planned to marry her for money. What had he done to squander his own sizeable trust fund?

She bit the inside of her cheek, drawing blood. Not her problem. She and Reggie had known each other since they were infants. True, she hadn't loved him, not in a heady romantic way, but she assumed they'd build a life fostered by mutual affection and respect. That he wanted what she did, loving children and stability.

Turned out she didn't know Reggie. She didn't know anything.

What was that old saying? *When you assume, you make an ass out of you and me.*

Well, she wouldn't sit here and allow her two-timing fiancé to play her for an ass a moment longer. Her tennis shoes perched next to the dresser and a single word blasted through her mind.

Run.

She slid her feet in and tied up the laces. No socks, but they felt otherwise fine.

Yes, run away. She grabbed her purse and bolted from the lavish suite without a backward glance.

The hall was empty but the elevators were risky. It would be her luck if Reggie lingered in the lobby. A fresh surge of rage increased her pace. How dare he think to manipulate Mother in her fragile final months? And the nerve of Suki, putting through Eden's calls at his office with an air of friendly professionalism. That two-face must have laughed off her Jimmy Choos.

A door flew open and a scantily clad black-haired woman tumbled from her room, brandishing a wooden ventriloquist's puppet.

"Where is he?" she screamed.

"Who?" Eden leapt back.

"That fucking cowboy."

"Sorry," Eden said, creeping away. The woman looked ready to commit bodily harm. "No cowboys out here."

The woman rubbed her nose, amped, clearly on something. "He's not with you?"

"Me?" Eden pointed at herself, breaking into an incredulous smile despite the morning's insanity. "Cowboys aren't my type." Western music put her teeth on edge and the only plaid she preferred was on the kilt of a fictional Scottish lord.

"Well, la-di-da." The woman snorted, marching back into her own suite. "Lucky you."

"I wouldn't say I'm lucky," Eden muttered as the door slammed behind her. There was a stairwell at the far end of the hall. At least this exit gave her a better chance at avoiding unwelcome detection. Throwing open the door, she nearly collided with a tuxedo-clad waiter bearing a silver room-service tray.

"Oh! Sorry about that! Sorry," Eden said, windmilling her arms.

"Congratulations." He executed a neat sidestep with a glance to her wedding dress.

"Thanks." She forced a grin. "I'll be sure to pass them along to my fiancé and his mistress."

He gave her a double-take, probably wondering if he

heard her right, and then she was alone. This was the top floor so nowhere to go but down.

When she reached the bottom of the stairwell she peered through the door. This wasn't the lobby but a service area. Two hallways split before her. Which would be the best route to follow?

Seeing how her previous life-decision-making methods had totally failed, perhaps she needed to return to a more time-tested approach. She pointed between the two, mumbling "Eenie, Meenie, Miny, Mo."

Left it was.

As she jogged down the hall, an exit door appeared. She pushed through and stood outside. People walked past without a second look. Obviously there were stranger sights in this town than a wild-eyed, panting bride on the sidewalk in tennis shoes. She smoothed her skirt as if one less wrinkle would improve her out-of-control situation.

What now? She crossed the street and aimlessly walked up the block. The idea of returning to Manhattan raised the hair on the back of her neck. Her few acquaintances were better friends with Reggie—they'd side with him, that is, if they didn't already know about his duplicity. The penthouse would always be Mother's, the dark, antique-stuffed castle she'd used to keep the world at bay.

With no real friends, no family, and no job, there was simply no compelling reason to go back to New York. It didn't feel like home, it never had.

Up ahead, Reggie's gelled hair came into view. He faced the opposite direction, up at the crosswalk waiting for the light to change, on the phone yet again.

Please, please, please don't turn around.

She couldn't afford a confrontation before having some semblance of a plan, and certainly not while wearing this wedding dress like a little fool. The smell of coffee and hash browns wafted past. She glanced at the overhead sign: "Sal's Diner." Perfect. Her shoulders dropped from below her ears. Maple syrup could drown her sorrows and the sugar buzz would help fuel her next steps.

She needed an escape plan and fast.

Chapter Three

VEGAS AND HANGOVERS went together like Tabasco
and eggs. Archer drained his first cup of coffee, waiting
for the waitress to circle back and take his order. *Hurry
it up, sweetheart.* In another two minutes, he'd resort
to pounding back a few of these nondairy creamers. A
woman slid into the vacant stool beside him, the only
one still available at the counter this crowded Sunday
morning. He didn't have to glance over to know it was
a woman—the air changed, faintly infused with warm
vanilla sugar, sensual yet comforting, like lingering in a
kitchen with a baking cake.

The inside of his mouth, on the other hand, tasted like
he'd gargled with a dead possum. He tugged the Lifesavers from his hip pocket and unwrapped the foil. First
choice was cherry, his favorite.

"May I have one of those?" The husky sweetness in his
neighbor's voice caused a tight knot to form in his chest.

The tone was ambiguously cultured. Not from around here.

He turned, extending the pack and met a pair of sparkling grey-silver eyes, the same shade as the meteorite Sawyer displayed on his mantel. Forget trying not to stare. Something inside him twisted then righted. "Yeah sure."

All. Those. Freckles.

If he had one weakness, it was for a woman's freckles, and the powers that be had seen fit to allocate this stunner with more than her fair share.

"Thank you." She popped off the cherry and hesitantly placed it onto the end of her tongue. "My dad used to eat these." Her expression grew wistful as she lost herself in memory. "I haven't had one in forever."

He absently took the next in the roll, barely noticing the pineapple flavor.

"Ready, Freddy?" The waitress slammed her order pad on the Formica, drumming chipped red-painted nails.

"Ladies first." Archer gestured toward Freckles, unable to remember his planned breakfast order, let alone his name. Lust at first sight was nothing new to him, but this was something entirely different, like an invisible undertow had caught him in its grip and he didn't mind the receding shore.

Freckles scanned the menu, chewing her distractingly adorable lower lip. "You have cinnamon-swirl bread?"

"Sure do." The waitress snapped her gum.

"I'd like two slices of that, please," she said quietly.

The waitress nodded before glancing to Archer. "What about you, Cowboy?"

"Excuse me?" Freckles leaned forward with an apologetic smile. "I wasn't quite finished. I'd like the cinnamon-swirl bread, but as French toast."

The waitress's eyes narrowed. "That's not on the menu."

"Yes, I see that, but French toast is. Perhaps the chef would be amenable to making a slight substitution?"

"Chef?" The waitress smirked. "Gary," she called over one shoulder to the cook line. "Someone here just called you a chef."

"And so they should." The yell from the kitchen rose over the sound of sizzling grease. "This place deserves a Michelin star." Raucous laughter followed.

"If Gary could sprinkle some chopped nuts on top, and include a dollop of whip cream, that would be wonderful. Oh, and are the spiced apples homemade?"

The waitress propped a hand on her ample hip. "Nope."

Freckles gave a soft sigh. "Okay."

"Okay you want 'em or okay you don't?"

"Yes, I'd like them, please. And a nonfat cappuccino."

"We have caff or decaf here."

"Caff, then. I mean, caffeinated would be fine." She frowned at the nondairy creamers. "And real milk, if you don't mind."

"As you wish, Highness." The waitress didn't bother controlling her eye roll. The look she leveled at Archer said, "You going to be a pain in the ass too, sunshine?"

"I'll have what she's having," Archer said quickly. "But with a side of bacon—wait, make that two sides." He grinned at Freckles. "Everything is better with bacon, am I right or am I right?"

"Sorry." She unfolded her napkin and placed it over her lap. "I don't eat red meat."

His smile faltered. Guess no one was perfect. Freckles didn't have a flirty fun look either. In fact, this was a type he normally avoided like the plague. Prim. Proper. Prudish. The three P's of doom. Still, he was curious what she'd look like farther down the alphabet. Sexy. Seductive. Sultry.

After the waitress left, an awkward moment passed while "Rock Around the Clock" blared from the tinny sound system. Besides those eyes and freckles, her hair was red, not carrot-orange but with the same threads of tawny gold, amber, and rose as in a mountain sunset. Her mouth formed a perfect bow, the kind normally seen on actresses in the late-night black-and-white movies he watched when unable to sleep.

But for all his gawking, he'd missed a key detail, a vital fucking piece of information. Freckles wore a wedding dress. His heart dropped a few inches. A stupid reaction because he'd head home in an hour, and Vegas was the last place a man should fall head over heels.

"Excuse me." He coughed into his fist. "Looks like congratulations are in order."

"Why?" She reached out to take the white mug and plastic glass of milk the waitress slid forward.

"Where I'm from that's what people normally say on a wedding day."

"Of course." She mumbled, as if in afterthought, "Thank you." Her hollow-eyed gaze didn't sit right. Something was off.

"Where's the lucky guy?" He glanced around, as if a dude in a tuxedo was suddenly going to materialize.

"Otherwise occupied." She checked her thin gold wristwatch. "He'll be at the chapel down the street in thirty minutes."

Otherwise occupied with what? Unless her fella was an A-grade asshat, no business could be more important than being right here.

"Tell me something," Archer said, casually fiddling with his fork, wanting to press, but in a way that didn't arouse her suspicion. "How does it feel? Knowing you're about to take the plunge?"

"I . . ." She threw up her hands with a rueful smile. "There are no words. Guess I'm speechless."

He swallowed back the unexpected lump of jealousy. "Sounds like the real deal then." Nothing was wrong with the situation. She had nerves and he was being an idiot.

"What about you?" Freckles asked.

"What about me?"

"Do you have a girlfriend?"

"Nah." He gave a sheepish smile. "Never been that kind of guy."

"Oh, I'm terribly sorry." She ducked her head and tore a corner off her napkin. "I should never have made such a supposition. How heteronormative of me."

"Heteronorma-what?" Sounded like a medical condition.

She smoothed a finger over her eyebrow. "I assumed you were straight."

"Oh I'm not gay, sweetheart." He threw back his head, laughing. "But I'm not the settling down type either."

What type of guy are you? Eden thought her cowboy looked like he'd been thrown from a bull and ridden over by a horse. Correction. Not her cowboy. He was so not her cowboy. In fact, she never understood the national fixation with them. Sure they had nice butts or whatever, but give her a man in French cuffs any day of the week.

Although the idea of a jacket and tie only made her think of Reggie, and she couldn't picture her about-to-be jilted fiancé if she wanted a prayer of keeping down breakfast. And truth be told, that cinnamon bread French toast looked amazing, even if those were canned apples and bottled whipped cream swirls.

Cowboy turned and waved a strip of burned bacon in her direction. "Sure I can't tempt you?" That teasing mouth and carved jawline could tempt a nun, but the bacon left her stone cold.

"I'm perfectly fine, thank you."

"Your loss." He crammed the end into his mouth.

Bacon was quite possibly her biggest food dislike, yet here she sat, practically breathless, watching his square jaw bunch and flex. She cut her own bite but it was impossible to swallow with such a dry mouth. Did her pulse accelerate? The waitress returned to top up the coffee and Eden placed a hand over her mug.

"May I switch to decaf, please?" Clearly they brewed their coffee to the consistency of jet fuel in this joint. Jitters coursed through her body and her hands trembled.

Breathe. Focus.

She had more pressing matters to attend to, like what on earth was she going to do? She had her purse, and a wallet full of cash and credit cards, but the idea of booking a return flight to her nonexistent life in New York didn't sound comforting. What she needed was a fresh start in a place where people didn't remember her as Eden the Ew or dismiss her as another vapid, snooty blue blood. Her blood was as red as the next person's, darn it, and somewhere real life waited, far from the Upper East Side.

But where?

"Looking forward to the big honeymoon?" Cowboy asked.

"Honeymoon?" Eden feigned a sip of coffee.

Twisting his body slightly, he faced her dead-on. "Your man better be taking you on one," he replied firmly. "Otherwise I'm following you to the chapel to kick his dumb ass."

Hey, there's a most excellent thought. Cowboy did seem to have more than his fair share of muscles and Reggie deserved a thorough beat down.

"Wait, let me guess." He held up a big hand, studying her face with intent. "A woman like you? Where would you like to travel?"

Hint one: not to Mexico to wander the beach alone while my cheating new husband goes deep sea tuna fishing.

"Let's see." He traced a musing thumb over the dark scruff roughing his broad cheek.

Ridiculous she noticed such a detail, or the way thick cords of forearm muscles disappeared beneath his rolled-up shirtsleeves.

"You're the type to do it up fancy." His voice was deep, vibrantly so. "Go to Paris. Stay in a big, luxury hotel and eat overpriced snails."

"Nope." Even more ridiculous was this disappointment creeping through her stomach that a random cowboy hadn't guessed the secrets in her heart. She smoothed her hands over her lap, the fine lace from her dress itching her skin. The reminder of what she wore did little to improve her composure. What was the matter with her? She couldn't have sexy feelings for a stranger on her wedding day, even if it was going to be a not-wedding-day.

"You're right." He swiped a drop of syrup from the corner of his mouth and sucked it off the pad of his finger.

Sweat broke out across her palms.

Vibrant was the perfect word to describe him, that or *magnetic*. Those mischievous green eyes had some sort of pull, drawing out the most startling tingles along her spine, up her thighs. She slammed her knees together.

"Hmmmm. That's what someone would assume a woman like you might prefer," he continued. "In fact, know what I think? You'd look damn fine on a horse."

"Excuse me?" The unexpected statement startled a giggle from her.

"Sure. A pretty thing like you?" He leaned in, close

enough she felt, actually felt, heat emanate from his body. "With wind mussing up that gorgeous hair and mountains rising behind you?"

"You . . . you think I'm pretty?" Her poise must have run off with her luck. But no one had ever called her that before.

"You? Pretty? Come on, a blind man would agree." He shrugged. "Anyway, you must get that all the time."

She subtly rolled her shoulders, fighting to relax. "No, not really." *Or ever.*

His brows rose fractionally. "Your husband better tell you how beautiful you are every morning you wake up beside him. And every night that should be the last thing you hear before falling asleep."

The last thing she ever heard falling asleep with Reggie was him barking into his phone in halting Mandarin, making deals on the Asian markets.

"Be sure you tell your man I said that. And make him take you to a ranch."

She attempted a smile. "Is that what you do?"

"Yep."

She blinked. "Wait, you're a real cowboy?" A lot of guys on the strip seemed to dress the part, but she assumed it was a fashion statement. "I didn't know those jobs even existed anymore."

"A few of us still roam the West."

"Are you from Montana?" The idea was oddly appealing. Big Sky Country. Untamed wilderness.

"Nah, though my oldest brother lives there. I'm born and raised in California."

"There are cowboys in California?"

His mouth quirked. "We can't all be movie stars or tofu eaters."

"I guess I never thought about it that way." Her ears grew warm.

"My town was founded during the western expansion in the mid-nineteenth century. The buildings are old, and so are most of the families. Mine have been there since the first wagon train."

She wanted to listen, she did. But when he maintained such intense eye contact it was hard to focus. She glanced to her plate. Poked at the remnants of her toast. When he touched the side of her arm, she nearly jumped.

"Close your eyes," he ordered softly.

"My eyes?" she echoed.

His gaze dared her. "Go on, unless you're chicken."

She was sick of being a chicken, so she complied, feeling three kinds of silly, not to mention vulnerable. With her eyes tightly shut, his spicy, woodsy scent intensified. *Don't sniff. Don't sniff.* Too late, she breathed in deep and someone gave a stifled whimper. And worse, that someone was her.

"Picture a valley with a wide, lazy river meandering through the center, flanked by peaks, some as high as fourteen thousand feet, snow nestled on the high points." He spoke in her ear, each word a hot breath against her sensitive skin. "Imagine taking a breath that cleans you inside and out. And when you quit talking all you hear is wind."

"Lovely." It was a lame response, but all she could

muster while worrying her hardened nipples might pop through the dress.

"That's Brightwater. My home."

"Brightwater?" She straightened . . . could it be Vegas luck existed for her after all? "You mean . . . Brightwater, California?"

"You've heard of it?" He gave a deprecating laugh. "Not surprised. It got famous after that movie was shot there. *Tumbleweeds*."

"*Tumbleweeds?* Oh, yes. That's the one that won an Academy Award last year, isn't it?" she murmured vaguely.

If her nerves had been on edge before, now they were in free fall. She hadn't seen the film, not being a fan of Westerns, but Brightwater, California, is where her cousin, Quincy Bankcroft, recently purchased a home. She and Quincy weren't particularly close, the entire Bankcroft family, her mother's side, worked in media, but they were friendly enough to trade the occasional text. Unfortunately, Mother hated to fly so they only ever saw each other infrequently. Last month, he shared photos online of the gold-rush-era mountain lodge he'd purchased as a rural getaway.

Quincy could help, or at least provide her with a place to stay while she figured out her next steps. But how could she tell all of this to a strange cowboy?

"Are you staying in town long?" she asked, refusing to meet his eyes in case something in her gaze reeked of desperation. If she casually asked him for a ride, wouldn't he think she was some sort of stalker?

Probably.

Worse, a woman with a cowboy fetish.

"Nah, I'm taking off after breakfast. Time to saddle Philomena and ride into the sunset."

"You came to Vegas on a horse?" Her hope sank into her running shoes.

He laughed quietly. "No, Philomena is my truck, a green vintage '54 Chevy and all-around finicky pain in my ass. But what can I say? I'm a sucker for high-maintenance as much as the next guy."

The waitress returned with checks and he grabbed hers.

"No," she protested, attempting to snatch it. "You don't have to do that."

"I insist." He dug out his wallet and tossed a few bills beside the empty plates. He reached out and took her hand, the rough calluses grazing her soft palm. His finger slid over her knuckle, circling Reggie's two-carat engagement ring as he paused, his eyes darkening. "Hey, listen. If your guy leaves you to have breakfast alone on your wedding day in a place like this, and then doesn't take you on the honeymoon of *your* dreams. He doesn't deserve you."

Her calm mask slipped as she flinched, only seconds from revealing the terrified mess underneath.

He shook his head, his face relaxing. "Never mind me. It's been a strange morning. And hey, it was nice to meet you. Go and have yourself a happy ever after now, you hear?"

He pulled away fast, so fast it was as if he'd never

touched her at all. Then he was gone, striding toward the front door without a backward look.

She swallowed a small gasp, her head fuzzy as if she drank something much stronger than coffee. Her phone vibrated. *Ugh, Reggie.*

"Darling, it's time, where are you?" His aggravating chortle did a poor attempt at masking his impatience.

"Don't you think of 'darling-ing' *me*, bucko." Her short-tempered tone was unrecognizable, not at all quiet or hesitant. There was a pause, a pause where the cogs almost audibly turned inside Reggie's slimy brain. He'd once been captain of his university debate team and often talked circles around her. But this wasn't the time or place to listen to him backpedal and try to smooth things over.

"Darl—"

"The wedding is off, Reggie," she snapped, storming out onto the sidewalk. "Why don't you take Suki to Cabo, that is, if you can afford the trip on your own?" People walking past swiveled their heads, leveling curious looks. She ducked her head and took a deep breath. It wouldn't do to make a scene. She hated scenes.

"Darl—"

She hit the red end-call button. It didn't have the same satisfaction of slamming down a landline phone, but felt incredible all the same. She shoved the cell in her purse and dug out one of her emergency Hershey's Kisses. Unwrapping the foil, she popped the dark chocolate into her mouth.

A minute later her phone buzzed with a text. Honestly,

Reggie had to realize a message wasn't going to change anything. She glanced down and her lungs constricted.

Fine. It's actually a relief as you bore me to fucking tears. But it's not over, sweetheart. Call me back ASAP or I will ruin you.

She glanced up, unable to see much through her tears. How was this happening? Was he threatening her? Who was he?

Yes, Reggie was short-tempered, narcissistic, and aggressive, but so were most stockbrokers. He certainly never resembled a mustache-twirling bad guy. This left her feeling like a sniffling victim on the television saying, "He seemed like such a nice man." She'd never known him at all, the man who had been in her life one way or another for twenty-seven years. The idea that she could have been so oblivious to the sleeping danger was almost as unsettling as his capacity for evil.

Almost but not quite.

Reggie believed she was weak, able to be manipulated in his games like a pawn. Cowboy was a block ahead, an unlikely knight in shining armor, but perhaps a stroke of luck. He'd take her to Brightwater, to Quincy where she could find refuge while coming up with a plan. It was time to gain control of the chessboard. She had to catch this guy.

Chapter Four

ARCHER SIDESTEPPED A dubious sidewalk splatter. Vegas lost its glitz and glamor in the harsh light of day. This morning, the strip drained him. He'd cut out of Sal's Diner fast, hating goodbyes. There was no point pining over red-haired strangers on their wedding day. Although Freckles' gorgeous face would stick with him for a long time, the memory tinged with an unfamiliar and melancholy regret.

Jesus. He rubbed a hand over his brow, kneading his temples. What was he doing with his life? Yeah, sure, wrangling had its good parts, hanging out with horses for one, plus spending the day outdoors. After that it mostly boiled down to keeping city slickers from spooking the animals. He often got lucky with an attractive tourist, but was this how he wanted to be living in ten years?

No.

He needed more—but what? His duffel bag was still in

the back of his cab. He'd wandered through a few casinos last night before hooking up with Crystal and Stormy. Another night like that wasn't in the cards, not with the memory of Freckles branded into his brain.

Soon she'd be married to some lucky bastard. Good for her. She's the kind of woman to fall in forever love with. That kind of idea normally sent him running in the opposite direction, but with the right girl, who knew? Maybe settling down could be fun. In fact, it didn't have to be settling at all, but the start of a bigger, lifelong adventure.

Amazing how a cup of strong coffee, French toast, bacon, and a silver-eyed woman could change a man's outlook.

A drop of rain splattered on the nape of his neck. Time to duck into the 7-Eleven on the corner—no point suffering the long drive home without a well-stocked supply of junk food—but he needed a hat if the ominous clouds overhead let loose. He walked to the open-air parking lot across the street, popped the truck's lock, and grabbed the John Deere cap from the passenger seat, before turning sharply to scan the half-crowded sidewalk. Strange. The hairs on the back of his neck tingled like he was being watched. He chuckled and shook his head. Unless Stormy and Great Uncle Sam hunted him down, the lack of sleep and leftover hangover were making him jumpy.

He jogged across the street, ducked inside the convenience store, and grabbed a pack of beef jerky, a sandwich, corn nuts, four king-sized candy bars, and a two-liter bottle of Coke. That should hold him over, for a few hours anyway. People always asked where he put it and his typical response was to raise an insinuating eyebrow. The truth was, he ate whatever the hell he wanted and his body kept the same rangy physique typical to all the Kane men. He wasn't as tall as his two big brothers, but at six feet, no complaints.

When he stepped back outside, the weather had turned well and truly foul. Rain in the desert? Now he'd really seen everything. The torrent pissed into gutters, splashing his jeans as he crossed the street. He leapt into the cab of his truck, tossed the plastic bag of goodies on the seat and started the engine.

The radio played Willie Nelson, "On the Road Again." Good ol' Willie, there's a guy who knew what's what. Archer put the truck in reverse as an unexpected pang struck. Freckles might be saying "I do" to her lucky bastard right now.

Maybe, someday, he'd be a lucky bastard too.

He glanced in the rearview mirror and started to reverse, slamming the brake when someone lightly tapped his window. A person stood beside the truck, in the pouring rain. And not just any person. Freckles, red curls plastered to the sides of her face, as white as the wedding dress she wore. What the hell was she doing out in this weather?

He threw the truck in park and jumped out, tearing off his jacket to hold it over her head like a poor man's umbrella.

"Hey there, C-c-cowboy." Freckles didn't stutter. Her teeth chattered. This wasn't the time to ask what was

going on. Her stare held enough surprisingly wild reck-
lessness to make his heart pound, even as it clenched.

"You can't stay out in this rain." He got her settled
into the passenger seat before jogging back to the driver's
side to start the engine and blast the heat.

She pushed the wet lock of hair from her face. "Bet
you're wondering what I'm doing here."

"The thought crossed my mind." He smiled in spite of
himself. "But first, are you okay?"

"The weather turned fast but I'm more or less f-fine,"
she said, as if testing out the words and seeming to realize
they were true. "This is going to sound crazy, but hear me
out, please. I need a ride."

His brows shot up even as his stomach sank. "To the
chapel?" Christ, what next? A request to walk her down
the aisle?

"No, Brightwater."

"Brightwater?" he repeated blankly. That set him back
a bit. "My town? Why?"

"I'm Eden." She held up her hand. "Eden Bankcroft-
Kew."

"Eden." He cocked his head. She certainly did look like
a piece of paradise. He almost added a habitual wink, but
something checked him. Freckles—Eden—didn't seem
to need or want the flirty version of himself. "Archer
Kane." His grip enclosed her small hand and he pressed
tight, as if able to infuse warmth into her skin. Her name
niggled in the back of his mind. "Bankcroft, huh?"

"Quincy Bankcroft is my first cousin on my mother's

side. He recently moved to Brightwater. Are you acquainted?"

Freckles had relations in the Brightwater Valley? The muscles in his stomach knotted as his chest warmed. "No, but everyone knows he bought the biggest house in the county."

"Yes! That's it. The Dales." She shot him a swift look before redirecting her gaze out the windshield. "He emailed me real-estate photos last month. A lovely old estate."

"It's practically a castle." He kept the truck idling in neutral and softened his voice. "You should have asked me for a ride at the diner."

"I could have, but discovering you were from Brightwater seemed too good to be true . . . and then the words didn't come fast enough. What you said, about how my fiancé should treat me . . ." She frowned, shaking her head. "Turns out he's not a good man."

"No wedding?" He kept his features outwardly calm, but inwardly, tension radiated through his back.

"No wedding."

She filled him in on the cheating fiancé situation in short, unadorned sentences that left his blood boiling. He gripped the steering wheel, imagining it was that sack of shit's neck.

"What a rat bastard," Archer said grimly. He'd like nothing more than to track this Reggie down and give him a hard lesson in how to treat a lady. It's not as if he was Captain Chivalry, but sleeping with one woman while marrying another was the lowest sort of low. Instead, he tucked a strand of wet hair behind her ear, wanting to move his hand to her brow and erase the worry lines. "I'll take you to Brightwater, and promise to do whatever is in my power to help you succeed."

She closed her eyes briefly, but when she turned back, her gaze was bright and earnest. "I'm glad we crossed paths. You're the right guy at the wrong time."

"Usually I'm the wrong guy at the right time." His laugh contained more than a hint of unease as he ground the clutch, something he hadn't done in years.

Traffic was light due to the storm and it didn't take long to leave the Vegas city limits. Freckles withdrew into the corner, making herself as small as possible. After a few long hours, quiet beyond the country music station's warbling, Archer stopped for gas. "Can I grab you a snack?" he asked, not liking her pale cheeks.

"No thank you." She shook her head, hard to do when half her forehead pressed against the window.

She needed something to eat, but what? An old hot dog from the roller grill wasn't an option after she'd nicely refused the beef jerky and candy bars. *Shit*. He filled up and headed into the station, decked out for St. Patrick's Day, shamrock streamers crisscrossing the ceiling. The guy behind the counter wore a t-shirt that read "Let's get ready to stumble" with a picture of two drunken leprechauns toasting beer steins.

"Comin' from Vegas?" the cashier asked with a knowing smile.

Archer chucked pretzels on the counter. "What's the giveaway?"

"Looks like you haven't slept in a while."

"Guilty as charged."

"Well, you must not be Irish, because you're flat outta luck today." The guy slipped a fat pinch of chew into his lower lip. "That big storm caused a landslide and a major accident. Highway patrol says the road ahead will be closed for hours."

That meant more hours alone with Freckles, with her warm vanilla smells, sweet smiles, and serious gazes that made him wish he were a better man with more to offer. He squinted at the overcast sky while exiting the station, truth clobbering him over the head. Here was a woman who made him want to dig deep for his best self—she surprised and fascinated him, and made him smile, one of those grins that makes you get warm down deep. Since he was a kid, he'd been the one trying to get others to take life less seriously, but the joke was on him. If he ever wanted a prayer of deserving a woman like this, he had to get his ass in gear.

Freckles stood behind Philomena, bracing her hand on the bumper and wiping her mouth.

"Are you okay?" He scanned her face with concern.

"Just a minute." She held up a hand, taking a deep, shuddering breath. "I need a little more fresh air."

"Is it the flu? Or—"

"Car sickness." She grimaced. "I've had it since I was a child."

"Why didn't you say anything? Ask me to pull over?"

Her shoulders slumped. "I—I was afraid if I tried to talk, I'd throw up."

He reached into the truck and grabbed her a water bottle. "And here I thought you were just . . . quiet."

Her lips crooked into a ghost of a smile before she took a sip. "I can be that too."

What now? Archer rubbed his unshaven jaw. He couldn't load her back in the truck to risk getting sick all over again, especially not if they could be stuck for hours. His own head pounded and she looked ready to topple over. A motel sat across the street, small, plain, and cheap, the same dull brown as the surrounding Nevada desert. "Big Dick's Inn: No Meth Heads Allowed." Seriously? Well, beggars can't be choosers. He waited until she climbed in the passenger seat and then steered into the adjacent parking lot, cutting the engine.

"Wait here."

Her eyes widened at the sign. "Why are we stopping?"

"The guy in the gas station said there's an accident ahead. The road closure could last hours and you look like you need a proper rest. Don't worry, I'll get separate rooms."

"Please don't put yourself to extra trouble," she muttered, dropping her gaze. "I hate being a nuisance."

"You've made yourself my business," he responded firmly. "And a nap will do you a world of good." Damn, he sounded as bossy as Grandma.

"Very well." She reached in her purse with a sigh and withdrew a crisp bill. "Take this."

He traded a bemused stare with Benjamin Franklin.

"For the rooms," she pressed.

He waved her off. "I don't need your money."

"Please take it anyway. I know you're only stopping because of me."

"Leave it alone." His voice took on an uncharacteristically testy edge. Did she think he couldn't afford this dump? He slammed out and stalked into the office before she could say another word.

Inside, a big man sat in an undershirt and red suspenders, watching *Days of Our Lives*. This, presumably, was Big Dick.

"Hi there, I need to book two rooms."

Big Dick dug a hand into his bag of pork rinds, eyes fixed on the small screen. "Can't do that."

"This is a motel, right? You book rooms here."

Big Dick burped into his fist. "If I got 'em, I can book 'em."

"You're full?" This place was smack dab in the middle of nowhere.

"Big landslide before Beatty. Road is closed, might be all night. People've been stopping for the last hour."

Archer dug out his Lifesavers, took one without looking at the flavor and bit down. Pineapple. *Figures.* "You don't have any rooms?"

Big Dick gave a slow blink. "No."

"So you do?"

"No."

Archer took a deep breath and crushed the candy between him molars. "Are you messing with me?"

"I've got a room. Single." Big Dick held up a thick finger. "Uno."

Would Freckles go for that? Sharing a room with a

stranger? The other option was a long detour to the 373, take the 190 through Death Valley and then cut north. But she'd already called off her wedding and vomited. It was time to call it a day.

"I'll take it," he said, digging out his wallet.

When he came back out to the truck, Freckles stared at the sole room key.

"There's only one available," he said. "It looks like other people had the same idea about stopping rather than being stuck in their cars. Don't worry, if you're uncomfortable, I can crash in the truck."

"That won't be necessary," she said, even as she clutched her purse. "I'm hardly worried you'll rob me, seeing as I can't even force cash on you."

"Where I come from, a gentleman does the paying," he said, helping her out.

"Where I come from, men and women have equal rights and it's called the twenty-first century."

"If I ever venture to your part of the country, you can take me out, how's that for a deal?"

She gave a faint smile. "Acceptable."

"You sure you don't want to keep me in the truck? I don't mind. I've slept in worse places."

She paused, cocking her head. "I've made the decision to trust you. I can, can't I?"

"Yeah, because I'm not some sort of serial killer scouting victims on the strip."

She wrinkled her nose. "You couldn't be—you're too nice."

"First rule about serial killers is that they always seem

nice. That's how they lure you in." An unfamiliar instinct rose inside him. He needed her safe and protected. "Promise you won't jump in the truck of the next man who's friendly to you at a diner."

"This isn't my normal routine," she whispered. "Just so you know."

He didn't think so but was damn curious about how she lived her day-to-day. He unlocked the front door. The room was cramped, with dingy Hawaiian-print drapes, but relatively clean. The '80s-era bedspread featured leopards and tigers lounging against a lush jungle backdrop.

"Classy joint. Now, let's get you into a hot shower. I mean—" He cleared his throat. "You'll get yourself in the shower. I can scrounge us a late lunch." *And try not to picture you under the steaming spray.* Ah, hell, who was he trying to kid? Freckles might rival Jules Verne for being out of his league, but it would be impossible not to imagine her naked and soapy. "I'll be back in a few minutes. There's a roadhouse next door, I'll humble myself and check if there is anything meatless on the menu."

"Grilled cheese would be fabulous," she answered. "That's hard to mess up. But would you please request that they use real cheese, none of that plastic kind? Also if they have sliced pickles, see if they could be included."

"In the sandwich?"

She looked at him like he was an idiot. "A pickle is an essential grilled cheese sandwich ingredient."

"I am going to have to disagree."

"What could be better?"

"Uh . . . bacon?" he answered, holding up a finger. "No wait, more bacon."

"You and your bacon." She gave a faint laugh. "That's all nitrates and sodium, linked to cancers and heart disease."

"We all have to go sometime, sweetheart," he said with a grin. "Have yourself a nice shower."

Her expressive eye roll made him chuckle as he left the motel room. Ah, last words could be so perfect. He went into the roadhouse and it turned out they could make grilled cheese Freckle's way so he placed an additional order for himself, plus two sides of fries, and root beer. He popped one of the lids as he walked back to the motel and took a bite. Aw, man, was that ever good. Note to self: Let Freckles order forever.

He tripped in a parking lot pothole. Not that he'd have a forever with Freckles. She was no doubt nursing a broken heart behind that reserved exterior while he had to knuckle down and figure out his life. But—he paused, halfway into the room—it was impossible not to let his imagination wander when she stood there almost naked. At least wonderfully exposed from mid-thigh down, and yep, that was definitely cleavage poking above the towel.

"I didn't bring a change of clothes," she said, shifting her weight in the bathroom doorway, her ear tips a dark shade of red.

He could look away, but he'd never pretended to be a priest. Any all-American, red-blooded male was honor bound to bear witness to Freckles with wet, mussed hair, and in a too-small towel hinting at sexy-as-sin curves beneath.

Except her gaze didn't appear alluring, instead her eyes looked tired and more than a little embarrassed.

Well, shit. He might not be a priest but he could act like a gentleman, at least once in a blue moon. "Hey now, I've got to have something that you can borrow." He set down the cardboard lunch boxes on the bed and unzipped his duffel bag.

Her eyes widened. "I'm not sure if you've noticed, but we have a significant size difference."

He tossed her a t-shirt. "As much as I'd like you to wear nothing but that towel for the rest of the evening, you'll be more comfortable in this."

"I'm not sure if I should be offended or flattered," she said, balling the cotton in her fist.

He kicked off his boots and sat on the edge of the bed. "I have that effect on people." He opened his sandwich box and shoved a fry into his mouth.

She retreated to the bathroom. "I suppose you think this is funny," she called out.

"What can I say? I like a laugh," he responded.

"Hardy har har." She reemerged. The white t-shirt hung to her knees and read "Save a Horse, Ride a Cowboy" in a bold red font. Beneath were bare legs. Nice legs. Fantastic actually.

Damn.

"Got to say, that's a good look on you, Freckles," he said, his throat thickening.

"I'm well aware you can play connect the dots on my face."

He caught the hurt in her eyes and hated that he'd put it there. "Hey now, I didn't mean any disrespect. I like your freckles. They are sexy as hell, in a purely platonic way of course." He hustled to change the subject. "So, Eden Bankcroft-Kew, your name is long."

Long? He resisted the urge to face palm. Looked like his game had packed up and left town.

At least the uncharacteristic fumble earned him a tight smile. "You'll never guess my middle name."

He cleared his throat, trying to make a recovery. "What is it, Victoria?"

"No, but not far off. It begins with a V."

"Vanessa? Vanna? Vivienne?"

"Valentina."

"How did you remember to spell that as a kid?"

"Slowly," she quipped, and he laughed good and loud.

"I like you, even if you are a little crazy." Yeah, she might be an Eden to the world, but inside there was a hidden sense of humor, definitely more of an Edie. Although in his arms, she'd be Freckles. He cleared his throat, raking a hand through his hair. "All right, Eden Valentina Whatchamacallit Bankcroft-Kew. Sit down and eat your sandwich and tell me more about yourself."

She perched on the opposite side of the bed, crossed her legs and opened the food box with a muted groan of appreciation. "Oh, you got French fries too. For that, I'll agree to anything."

He'd have the rest of the afternoon with Edie, and how

great would it be to wake up and see her in the morning? The idea should scare him half to death. He'd never had anything like this happen to him, feelings that were complicated, layered, and so fast he had whiplash. He had a simple road to follow, get her safe and sound to Brightwater, but his heart seemed eager to travel in a new direction for the first time.

Chapter Five

DESPITE THE DAY'S miserable circumstances Eden found herself with a suddenly ravenous appetite. The carsickness abated and the fact she wasn't married to Reggie made her feel more alive than in recent memory. Soon she'd be safe with Quincy and he would help her figure out how to deal with Reggie's vague but sinister threat. It would be nice to reconnect with her cousin. Some good had to come from this awful situation. When a door slammed, a window always opened. At least that was life according to *The Sound of Music*, and far be it from her to criticize the wisdom of her favorite movie.

For too long she'd lived a half-life in Manhattan, and that chapter was finished. Tomorrow she'd turn a fresh page, travel an unknown road to a new destination. Turned out change was mysterious and yet a little exhilarating—who knew? She took a big bite of sandwich. The sourdough bread and cheddar cheese undercut with a hint of sourness tasted better than anything in recent memory. "You know," she dabbed her mouth with a paper napkin, "pickles might be my favorite food."

"That a fact?" Archer sounded amused, wiping his palms on faded-denim-clad knees. "Back at the diner, you seemed like a woman who had more . . . how do I put this . . . gourmet tastes."

How did his jeans fit like a second sexy skin? "Well, I do adore tiramisu," she croaked, trying to distract herself, and beginning to ramble. "Or . . . oh, I know, breaking the top of a perfect crème brûlée! Ooh and what about a nice brioche with raspberry jam? Pure heaven. Cooking is my favorite hobby after all, baking in particular." She gave a self-conscious laugh. "That's why my next favorite hobby is running. Bake. Eat. Run. Repeat. My life motto."

His right eye twitched. "You run for fun?"

"It releases endorphins—the body's feel-good chemical."

He pulled a face. "I can think of plenty of other ways to make a body feel good that don't require pounding the pavement for miles."

"Oh yeah? And what is it you do for exercise?" Those hard, lean muscles certainly required a vigorous regime.

His eyebrow raised an imperceptible fraction and, oh, that crooked smile had the devil in it.

Vigorous indeed.

"Never mind." She shot out her hand, covering his mouth. "I've got the picture loud and clear, Cowboy." The gesture was meant as a joke, but his lips, warm against her skin, weren't funny, nor were the intensely hot shivers shooting through her thighs. That wasn't a blush heating her cheeks. It was a raging wildfire.

She leapt back and automatically moved to wipe her hand on one of the bedspread's reclining tigers. Instead, she balled her hand into a fist, as if to hold his touch closer, a silly impulse. *What are you doing, Eden?*

Frown lines etched across his broad forehead. "You okay there, Freckles? Eat too fast? Ketchup poisoning?"

Pressure built inside her body as if she were strapped to a centrifuge and subjected to an inhuman amount of G-force. If she tried to speak it might come out all distorted and slow motion. Instead, she sneezed, a reflex whenever anxiety struck. At least it cleared her head. "I'm not sure what came over me, probably stress." She made a show of pressing her fingers to her temples and rubbing in a gingerly fashion.

What kind of head case was . . . was . . . aroused by a stranger the day she absconded from her own wedding? Mother's former psychotherapist could have a field day with her neuroses. Hey, maybe she didn't love Reggie, and accepted his proposal with her head rather than her heart. But never again. If she ever considered another relationship, and that was a big if—*huge!*—then it would be to the right man, for the right reasons.

"Riddle me this," he said gently. "What's the plan after getting to Brightwater?"

"What do you mean?" she mumbled, blinking at the chilled-out lions and then back to him.

"Your next steps."

Figure out how to be happy? She smoothed back her

hair and searched for the right words. "I've been running from myself for a long time. It's always been easier to try and fly under the radar, that keeps everyone who matters pleased and let's everyone else forget about me. But it's time to figure out what I want."

"And what is it that you . . . want?" His gaze dropped to her mouth and she fought the urge to lick her lips, or move, even a fraction of an inch. She almost succeeded, except there could be no hiding the rapid rise and fall of her rib cage.

"I'm not sure," she whispered. "I've always liked baking and am pretty good at it."

"A nice hobby," her mother used to say with a tone of dismissal. After all, heiresses host dinner parties, they don't hang out in the kitchen kneading bread with the staff.

But deep inside, maybe some of her genes still carried that pilgrim spirit, a pioneer's innate love of working with their hands. Plus she had this instinctive, almost primal need to nourish, and not always with healthy food because, let's face it, red velvet cake can be just as vital to the body as zucchini. But how could she say all this to him, what if he laughed? Opening up meant trusting, sharing.

No easy feat given the day she'd had, or the life she'd lead up to this point. Being vulnerable was terrifying— she'd learned early how awful people could be if given the opportunity.

But then again, she was already alone in a rural Nevada motel room with a stranger she'd met in Las Vegas. The idea she could consider putting faith in anyone after today was remarkable. But Archer didn't seem to take himself so seriously and that meant he was less likely to judge others. His ready willingness to accept her at face value gave her a jolt of courage at a time when she could have been rendered weaker than ever before. Some hesitancy still existed, she'd be mad not to retain it, but at least her faith in humanity more or less remained.

"I've often dreamt of opening a bakery." She smiled to hear her secret hope spoken out loud. "After all, what other work can I do where I get to eat my mistakes?"

He laughed at that, in that deep, booming way that made her toes curl even as she joined in. Archer was all raw testosterone, clearly confident about his effect on the opposite sex, but so far he'd behaved more or less like a gentleman. But there was only one bed. A bone-splitting yawn tore through her chest as she arched in a subtle stretch wondering what to do. This whole experience ventured so far from her normal world she felt no better than Dorothy in Oz.

"It's high time you get some sleep. How about a nap?" Archer leapt to his feet, cleaning off the food boxes, and turning down the blanket. "Climb under the covers and I'll tuck you in."

She pressed her lips together as something warm flickered in her belly. "It's been twenty years since anyone's tucked me in."

"Well"—he ran his fingers through his thick hair— "I've never tucked anyone in, so there's that."

She scooted backward across the mattress, conscious

of the t-shirt riding up on her bare thighs, but Archer kept his gaze trained on her face. Again the inexplicable trusting sensation welled within her. Once she lay down, he carefully arranged the blankets over her chest, keeping a more than appropriate distance from her breasts.

Too appropriate.

Eden Valentina!

What did she want? A mauling? Honestly. But there was no doubt he'd make an excellent cuddler. Those strong arms were made to hold a woman close, make her feel safe and secure.

"How was that for my first time?" he asked gruffly.

"Fabulous effort." She burrowed into the pillow, rubbing her eyes as if the gesture could scour away the bewildering physical impulses firing inside her. "I'm so grateful for everything. You've earned a perpetual place in karma's good books."

"Hah," he chuckled. "I don't believe in any of that."

"What goes around, comes around?"

"Nah. I've always thought that each day is its own—a clean slate."

"That's a different outlook," she conceded.

"Well, there's probably a whole hell of a lot about you that is different from me."

"Yeah, what else?" She rolled on her side and pushed a lock of hair from her face.

"Well, you are a city girl for starters."

"You say that like it's a bad thing."

"My apologies." He appeared genuinely contrite. "I only meant that you've got style and class in spades."

Again with the compliments. She didn't have the first idea how to handle them.

"Seeing you again in that parking lot was the last thing I ever expected. But hey, not all surprises are bad. Sometimes life's great moments are in the unexpected."

"That's rather profound." The next yawn was a monster, she covered her mouth but the sound filled the room.

"Profound if you're a minute from sleeping." His mouth tipped in a lopsided grin. That full bottom lip would make angels weep. "Before you nod off, tell me, is there anything else you need?"

"Need?" A curl of heat licked through her.

This is your wedding day. Even though she'd taken irreparable steps to ensure it wouldn't be, the least she could do is show a modicum of respect for the institution, even if she didn't respect the man. Actually. No scratch that. That was Old Eden's way of thinking, the woman crushed under the weight of tradition, rules, and expectations.

But new Eden crashed in Nevada motels with cowboys, wore suggestive t-shirts, ate grilled cheese from a paper box, fries without a fork, and that felt more like herself than she had in months. Maybe ever.

"Earth to Freckles." Archer waved a hand.

She gave a slow, warning blink.

"What can I say?" He shrugged with a wicked grin, this time letting his gaze linger across her body, as if she was covered in lace and silk, and not a tacky jungle cat bedspread. "The nickname suits you."

He clearly did whatever he damn well pleased. She'd be annoyed if she wasn't so captivated.

She shook her head. "Would you please get my phone from my purse?"

He crossed to the dresser, opened her handbag and grabbed it, handing it over wordlessly.

"Thank you." She quickly checked her messages. Nothing. At least Reggie hadn't followed through on any additional threats yet. No point watching, waiting, and fearing. She powered down her phone and set it on the nightstand next to an ancient clock radio. She didn't know much about what would happen next, but one thing was certain. Reggie would never see a single dime from her. If he'd been in real trouble and come to her, she would have listened, and depending on the situation, might have been happy to help.

But not like this. No, never like this.

Archer grabbed a spare pillow from the closet and moved to the floor.

"What are you doing?"

"I know it's not all that late, but I'm beat too. Late night. Naps all around."

She peered off the edge of the bed to the discolored carpet with dismay. "But I can't let you sleep on *that* floor."

"It's nothing," he said simply. "I want you to rest, and I'm a big strange guy. Plus, I'm a cover hog."

She let out a quiet breath. He was willing to inconvenience himself and put up with a little discomfort to make her feel protected. How could some men be rotten and others so kind? Humans were a mysterious species indeed.

"Seriously, don't worry about me. I've had plenty of nights sleeping outside with a rock for a pillow. This is luxury." He extended a hand. "Sweet dreams, Eden Valentina Bankcroft-Kew."

What would it feel like to have these big rough hands moving across her skin? She squeezed his fingers, the warmth and strength in his grasp stalling her breath even as her heart raced. "Thank you, Archer Kane."

ARCHER WOKE TO a blood-curdling scream that liquefied his insides. Fuck. Who was getting murdered? Where was Freckles? Before he could react, a warm body crashed on top of him, the vanilla scent snapping the situation back into crystal clear focus. Until five seconds ago, he had been sleeping soundly on a motel room floor. Turns out the scream wasn't a helpless victim, but the alarm clock radio blasting Guns N' Roses' "Paradise City."

Disorientation faded fast because those were breasts pressed against his chest, soft, perfectly formed ones. The light seeping beneath the brown curtains hinted at dawn, and he had one hell of a case of morning wood.

Edie's face was inches from his, her pupils dilated and the freckles clustered around her parted lips begged to be kissed. He couldn't breathe let alone move.

"Sorry! I'm so sorry. The radio woke me up. I reached to turn it off and . . . fell." Edie scrambled to a straddling position over his waist. He'd stripped out of his jeans to sleep. She wasn't improving the situation and would realize what she sat on in three . . . two . . . one . . .

"Oh. Oh dear." She rocked backward and that certainly didn't help a fucking thing.

"There's a new one," he said, affecting a lazy smile, even as his pulse pounded through his ears.

"New what?" She froze, that grey-eyed gaze locked on his bare chest.

Did she like what she saw? "I've gotten quite a few oh gods in my time, but never an oh dear."

Her eyes widened a fraction, even as her lips quirked. "You seem to have quite an opinion of it."

"I try not to let compliments go to its head."

She clapped a hand over her mouth but it did nothing to mask her snickers.

"Now see here," Archer said in mock outrage. "You're going to hurt its feelings."

"Your . . . your . . . penis has feelings?"

"He's a sensitive soul."

She slid off and the place where her thighs had bracketed him held lingering warmth. Almost good enough to make him forget the painful spasms taking hold at the base of his spine. *Shit.* A night on the floor followed by the crash of her body hadn't done his bad back any favors.

"What's the matter?" she asked.

"Nothing."

"Something's wrong, the way your jaw is clenched, and your eyes are—"

"It's nothing, a stupid injury is all. I got thrown off a horse last year. I'll be fine after an ibuprofen." *Or three.*

"Okay, let's see you sit up."

He scowled. "Don't want to." What a shitty situation.

Impossible to impress while splayed on the ground like a damn starfish.

"How about you go see if the coffee from the gas station across the road is any good?" he ground out. That might provide him enough time to crawl to his feet and hobble into the shower. Hot water worked miracles.

"I can't." She yanked down the t-shirt she wore. "This is all I've got, unless I run around in my wedding dress."

"Didn't stop you yesterday." He didn't mean to snap, but his back pain was kicking into gear, and this beautiful calm, collected woman was the last person he wanted watching him fall apart.

"It's your back. That's what's hurting you?"

He gave a single nod, closing his eyes.

She stood and walked to the nightstand behind his head.

He hurt so bad he could barely remain quiet, but he'd have to be unconscious not to look at what she wore under his shirt.

Pink silk, and legs for miles.

She glanced down. "Are you checking me out?"

"No, ma'am."

"Here I am, fetching you a pain reliever from my bag, and you're sneaking a peek. I'll get you a glass of water, but remember, I'm not your dirty nurse." She returned, sinking to her knees, handing him two pills, and bracing his neck as he swallowed. "Did I hurt you when I fell?"

"Nah, a stallion bucked me off last summer. Flares now and again."

"Like when a woman jumps out of bed on you." She

glanced down at his hips, a flush creeping between her freckles. "The way I landed, ahem, down there, I was afraid I might have broken something else."

"Hah, will take more than a buck-twenty of woman to hurt me there."

She arched a brow. "Roll over."

"Excuse me?"

"I can help you." She slipped her fingers under his side and started to push him over.

He pressed back firm against the ground. "What are you going to do?"

"Give you a massage."

"Nah, that's fine. I'm okay."

"I used to have back problems when I was younger and regular massage worked wonders. Trust me, I know what to do." She must have felt him tense. "Big brave man like you? You probably aren't afraid of diddly squat."

"Diddly squat?" The pain twisted his laughter into a groan.

"It's something our housekeeper used to say." She had a determined look on her face and he didn't want to go up against her in this state. Gritting his teeth, he rolled over with a ragged moan, hating his weakness. Edie rummaged through her purse again. *What now?* There was the sound of a lid uncapping and then a squeeze. "What are you—"

"Lotion." She slicked small, surprisingly strong hands over his tight muscles.

Oh fuck. That smell, sweet vanilla sugar. Despite the pain, his morning wood became a damn drill. He'd be punching a hole through the floor any minute. Edie's fingers felt around until she hit the place where he twitched.

"Right there?"

"Yeah."

She worked him like a ball of dough, kneading his lower back in a way that hurt and felt incredible.

"Where'd you learn how to do this?" he choked out.

"I'm going by instinct," she murmured. "Also, not to brag but I'm an excellent bread baker. Someday you'll have to try my focaccia."

She leaned into him and her hair fell across his spine, tickling his skin.

Yeah, he was definitely leaving a hole in this floor. He'd never been so hard when clothed, if being in boxer briefs counted as clothing. Normally, commando was his style, but he'd thrown a pair in his duffel and thank God for that. If Miss Eden Valentina Bankcroft-Kew had landed on him bareback she'd have bucked off and galloped to the hills. But the way she rocked her palms on either side of his lower spine, relaxing him on a deep level, maybe she was . . . how'd she phrase it, going by instinct. That's how he operated between the sheets, went by feel, what seemed to work in the moment. He had his tried and tested moves, same as any guy. Even a few big moves. But improvisation was key.

"Okay. The knot is almost gone. Why don't you try moving now?"

He rocked back and forth, teeth clenched but he released them slowly as he realized there was no pain. Shit. She'd done it.

"Don't twist, sit up and see if you can do it without pain."

It felt good to lie here pain-free, but if he didn't move, she'd keep touching him, and God knew, he wasn't famous for self-control. *Take it easy.* This woman meant to say "I do" yesterday. He promised to usher her safely to Brightwater, not see if she could have multiple orgasms.

The idea of Freckles face flushed with pleasure, her delicate neck arching as she moved against him . . .

Quit it.

"Here goes nothing." He sat slowly. "Yeah. I'm good, you cured me." Incredible.

Her gaze swung below his waist before traveling back across his abs and bare chest. Archer kept free weights in Kit's garage and they'd lift a few nights a week, but under her inscrutable stare, he felt something he could barely name.

Uncertainty—huh, that's a new one.

"Well," she stood and finger combed her hair. Her scent infused the air, made her seem edible.

God, he'd love to coat her with frosting and lick her clean.

"You should take a shower. That combined with the massage and pain relievers will make it better for now. Sorry again for that wake-up call."

"Best one I've had in a while." He hauled to his feet and shrugged. No point trying to hide what was happening downstairs. There wasn't a need to flaunt it, but hell if he'd hold a sheet to his waist like a twelve-year-old popping his first stiffy. They were all adults here.

"Well, at least I didn't break it." Her gaze dipped and held a fraction too long. Was it his imagination or were her pupils dilating?

"Nope." He made a show of glancing down. "Looks like it's open for business."

She blinked three times fast and pointed at the open bathroom door. "You. Shower. Now," she ordered.

He saluted and sauntered past. Before he got the door closed she squeaked, "And better make it a cold one."

Chapter Six

"ARCHER?" EDEN STARED in the motel bathroom mirror, her reflection a study in horror. "Please tell me this is a practical joke."

"We're in the middle of Nevada, sweetheart. There's no Madison Avenue swank in these parts." Archer didn't bother to keep amusement from his answering yell through the closed door. "The gas station only sold a few things. Trust me, those clothes were the best of the bunch."

After he got out of the shower, a very long shower that afforded Eden far too much time for contemplating him in a cloud of thick steam, running a bar of soap over cut v-lines, he announced that he would find her something suitable to wear. She couldn't cross state lines wearing nothing but his old t-shirt, and while the wedding dress worked in a pinch, it was still damp. Besides, her stomach lurched at the idea of sliding back into satin and lace.

She'd never be able to don a wedding dress and not think of the Reggie debacle. She couldn't even entirely blame him, her subconscious had been sending out warning flares for months. She'd once been considered a smart woman, graduated from NYU with a 4.0 in Art History. So how could she have been so dumb?

Truth be told, it wasn't even her mother's dying wish that led her to accepting him, although that certainly bore some influence. No, it was the idea of being alone. The notion didn't feel liberating or "I am woman, hear me roar." More like terrified house mouse squeaking alone in a dark cellar.

She clenched her jaw, shooing away the mouse. What was the big deal with being alone? She might wish for more friends, or a love affair, but she'd also never minded her own company. This unexpected turn of events was an opportunity, a time for self-growth, getting to know herself, and figuring out exactly what she wanted. Yes, she'd get empowered all right, roar so loud those California mountains would tremble.

Right after they finished laughing at this outfit.

Seriously, did Archer have to select pink terrycloth booty shorts with a Q and a T in rhinestones, one letter on each butt cheek? And the low-cut top scooped so even her small rack sported serious cleavage. "Get Lucky" was emblazoned across the chest, the tank top an XS so the letters stretched to the point of embarrassment. If she raised her hands over her head, her belly button winked out.

As soon as she arrived in Brightwater, she'd invest in proper clothes and send for her belongings back home.

Until then . . . time to face the music. She stepped from the bathroom, chewing the corner of her lip. Archer didn't burst into snickers. All he did was stare. His playful gaze vanished, replaced by a startling intensity.

"Well, go on then. Get it over with and make fun of me." She gathered her hair into a messy bun, securing it with a hair elastic she found in her purse.

"Laughing's not the first thing that jumps to mind, sweetheart."

Her stomach sank. "Horror then?"

"Stop." He rubbed the back of his neck, that wicked sensual mouth curving into a bold smile. "You're hot as hell."

Reggie had never remarked on her appearance. She sucked in a ragged breath at the memory of his text. *Bore me to fucking tears.*

"Hey, Freckles," he said softly. "You okay?"

She snapped back, unsure what her face revealed. "Tiny shorts and boob shirts do it for you?" She fought for an airy tone, waving her hand over the hot pink "QT" abomination and praying he wouldn't notice her tremble.

He gave a one-shouldered shrug. "Short shorts do it for all warm-blooded men."

"I'll keep that in mind," she said, thumbing her ear. He probably wasn't checking *her* out, just her as the closest female specimen in the immediate vicinity.

He wiggled out of his tan Carhartt jacket and held it out. "You'll want this. Temperatures are going to top out in the mid-forties today. I've stuck a wool blanket on the passenger seat and will keep the heat cranking."

Strange. He might be a natural flirt, but for all his easy confidence, there was an uncertainty in how he regarded her. A hesitation that on anyone else could be described as vulnerability, the type of look that caused her to volunteer at no-kill rescue shelters and cry during cheesy life insurance commercials. A guy like this, what did he know about insecurity or self-doubt? But that expression went straight to her heart. "Archer . . ."

He startled at the sound of his real name, instead of the Cowboy moniker she'd used the last twenty-four hours.

His jacket slipped, baring her shoulders as she reached to take one of his big hands in hers. "Thank you." Impulsively, she rose on tiptoe to kiss his cheek, but he jerked with surprise and she grazed the appealing no-man's land between his dimple and lips.

This was meant to be a polite gesture, an acknowledgment he'd been a nice guy, stepped up and helped her out—a stranger—when she'd barreled in and given him no choice.

He smelled good. Too good. Felt good too. She should move—now—but his free hand, the one she wasn't clutching, skimmed her lower back. Was this a kiss?

No.

Well . . . almost.

Never had an actual kiss sent goose bumps prickling down her spine even as her stomach heated, the cold and hot reaction as confused as her thoughts. Imagine what the real thing would do.

He stepped away first, an easy grin affixed on his features as if the almost kiss hadn't happened, and it hadn't, not really. Almost isn't actually. Even though she instinctively licked her lips as if his taste lingered on her mouth. He stared at her tongue and she felt distilled to that single body part. What was she doing? This guy couldn't be farther from her type. Wranglers? A belt buckle the size of her hand? A Western shirt with pearl-covered clasps?

Those should all be counted as strikes.

But those intelligent, light green eyes were something else. So was the thick hair perfect for sinking fingers into. Throw in his rock-hard body, and wow.

Imagine it hard in the wrong places? The naughty thought slammed her back to reality. Sure, if she was the sort that flirted, she'd flirt with Archer Kane. Handsome was handsome after all.

But she wasn't that sort of carefree woman.

Plus, she was a runaway bride who needed to stand tall and be her own person without hiding behind her family's wealth and privilege. Or a man. She'd reached out to Reggie in a moment of weakness, longing for children and security, and what did it get her? Nothing good. It was time to take an indefinite hiatus from men—a depressing notion as she'd only ever been with one.

Archer Kane of the good smells and better body, had a lot of things going right, but for a woman in her situation, he was all kinds of wrong.

But did she want to give up a chance at getting her hands on all those muscles, waking up to his sexy smile, and seeing the depth this man hinted at in those green eyes? She'd never seen anything close to that kind of raw emotion and conviction in Reggie's gaze. Could this guy, so far from her type, be right for her?

You're crazy, Eden.

Yeah, a little cowboy crazy.

ARCHER TURNED DOWN the radio; they'd driven in near silence the final few hours. Freckles didn't seem interested in talking much and for once in twenty-seven years, he didn't know what to say. Back in the motel, when she stepped shyly from the bathroom, her sweet curves shown off to maximum benefit by that small, silly, gas station outfit, he'd been a goner. Brain obliterated. He'd leaned in for the kiss before grasping she'd pecked him on the cheek, not like a man but a friend, or worse, a relative. He'd frozen, mouth half on her soft lips and half not, realizing that what he wanted and what she wanted were on two opposite sides of the coin.

The last few hundred miles were an opportunity to try to make peace with the fact she wasn't interested. *Try* being the optimum word.

But Grandma always said, "If at first you don't succeed, try, try again. Then quit, there's no use being a damn fool."

He made sure to pull over every half hour and let her get some air. That seemed to help. She wasn't nearly as pale as yesterday. Her gaze covertly skimmed in his direction and he glanced over only to catching her hurriedly turning her attention to the view outside. His blue balls made road bumps sweet agony. Most women seemed to like a bad boy, but Edie wasn't most women. Not by a long shot. Why? And what was it precisely about her that drove him nuts? Because it wasn't just those freckles, that killer body, and her long red waves. There was an innate goodness hidden behind her reserve, but he sensed a bad girl there too, a woman who could get into a whole lot of rowdy mischief. She might not even know it yet, but no one hitchhiked hundreds of miles with a stranger unless they were batshit or a little wild.

And Edie sure as hell wasn't batshit. He'd left batshit behind at the Vegas hotel yesterday morning—hopefully for good. He felt a little nervous, but also zinging with anticipation. He was finally ready to tackle responsibility. All he needed was the right plan.

"Here we are." He pointed out the green and white wooden sign on the right-hand side of the road.

Welcome to Brightwater
America's Biggest Little Town.
Home of 750 Nice Families and 1 Old Grouch.
Est. 1865

"Home sweet home," he said, rolling down the window and taking in a deep gulp of pine-scented air. "It can take forty-five seconds to walk down Main Street, but forty-five minutes if I stop and talk to everyone I know." He slowed to fifteen miles per hour and checked his rear-view mirror for any sheriff's vehicles. It wouldn't do to get pulled over by his big brother while Edie wore little more than his work jacket and pink hot pants.

Not that Sawyer would be surprised, but damned if Archer could bear causing Edie even the slightest embarrassment.

"This place is charming, a real Main Street from a movie. Look at all the old brick storefronts and filigree balcony railings. I'll bet most of these are registered historical landmarks. And that firehouse," she said, pointing out his window. "That's a fantastic representation of neoclassical Greek revival–style architecture. And there's a bookshop here? And wine bar too?" She eyed A Novel Idea and Bottom of the Barrel, the two newest shops to open since last Christmas, with avid interest.

"Yeah, the town is changing all right." His mouth tugged down in the corner. "For a long time things stayed the same, then came that movie *Tumbleweeds*—add a few magazine features and next thing you know every Johnny Someday wants to buy a vacation home in this valley."

"You say that like it's a bad thing."

Archer gave a one-shouldered shrug. "Property values quadrupled in two years. For those born without a silver spoon in their mouths, which is all of us raised here, it's become damn near impossible to buy a place to live and that's not right. Seems like it's a revolving door, old timers moving on as newcomers pour in."

"Wow," she said softly. "That sounds really hard."

He shrugged, wanting to find an easy brush off, a way to dismiss the painful subject, but he couldn't lie, not to her. "It is. Anyway, there's the local Save-U-More." He nodded at the small grocery store. "If a Whole Foods replaces it, that's when I'll worry. Anyway, I'm starving.

What do you say we stop to get a bite before heading to The Dales?"

"Stop?" She glanced at the bare expanse of her upper thighs with open alarm. "But I can't go in any place dressed like this. They'll think I'm soliciting."

"The Baker's Dozen is next door to a clothing shop that's also new, and female."

"Female?" Her brows knotted.

"Sells skirts and shit."

"You should consider a career in advertising," she said with a giggle as her nose practically touched the windshield. "Tell me, do you ever get used to the view?" The Eastern Sierras rose up in a dramatic wall, thrusting straight from the valley floor. Clouds skimmed the highest peaks, providing tantalizing glimpses of snow and glacier-carved rock.

"I haven't yet," he said, and that was God's truth. He liked to get out of the valley for the odd adventure, but if he didn't see these mountains for long, he felt himself getting twitchy. This was home and he knew deep in his heart he'd never live anywhere else. "We call it The Granite Curtain, keeps the rest of the state at bay, or at least it used to."

"I haven't been in the mountains for a long time."

"Let me guess, the last time was the Alps?"

"I'm not a stereotype," she muttered.

His lazy gaze drifted over. He wasn't sorry for pushing her buttons. In fact, he sort of enjoyed it. "I'm right though, aren't I?"

"Maybe—ah!" She broke into a muddled yelp as

Archer grabbed the back of her head and forced her face down on his lap.

She twisted back and forth against his denim-clad thigh. "What are you doing?" she hissed. "Let me go this instant."

"Hang on, hang on," he muttered. *Shit. Do not get hard. Do not get hard.* "It's my Grandma. Remember how the welcome sign said 'one grouch'?" Of all the bad luck, he'd pulled up at the single traffic light in Brightwater and the pickup beside him just so happened to be Grandma Kane's. He didn't want her bifocaled gaze resting on Freckles. Grandma judged any woman badly who kept his company. His reputation wasn't going to recommend him for character medals anytime soon. That never bothered him much before, but for the first time, worry cooled his gut.

If Edie stuck around, what gossip would she hear?

Grandma cranked down her window. "Didn't expect to see you back so soon."

"What can I say, Grams, I missed you." He gave his best grin but as always Grandma proved genetically immune to his charm.

Her eyes narrowed. "My house, dinner tonight."

"I might have plans." The warmth from Edie's cheek radiated into his leg. He glanced down and the sight of her red hair splayed over his lap sent blood rushing to the last place he wanted while talking to Grandma.

The light turned green and a horn beeped, likely a newcomer, here to spend time in their second or third home, who'd not yet felt Grandma's wrath.

"Cancel them," she said. "We need to have a serious talk about the ranch."

"Hidden Rock?"

"No, the other four-thousand-acre ranch I own."

He flexed his grip on the steering wheel with a prayer for calm. "What's happening?"

"You'll find out tonight," she snapped. The horn sounded again and she stuck her hand out the window, flipping the luxury SUV the bird.

Archer waited until Grandma hit the gas before shifting into first. "Sorry about that," he said, releasing Edie with no small regret. It wasn't even the thrill of having her face nearly between his legs that sent his heart into a caterwaul, but the idea of holding her.

His pulse beat like a ticking time bomb.

He was so fucked for this woman, so why did the idea make him do nothing but grin?

Edie sat, smoothing her hair with a frown. "What was that all about?"

He swallowed hard, tricky to do with a dry mouth. "My grandma was next to us."

"Okay?" Her brow wrinkled. "Why did you act like you were people smuggling?"

"I didn't want her getting the wrong idea."

"Which would be?"

"Grandma doesn't think a lot of most people." He paused, looking at her. "And less about women who go around with me."

"Do you have a reputation?" she asked, absorbing his words.

76 LIA RILEY

You could say that. "It's a small town. People talk."

She tipped her head, struggling to understand. "And what is it that people say?"

He maneuvered his truck right in front of Bab's Boutique. Saved by the perfect parking spot. "Let's get you some new clothes." He hopped out before she could ask a follow-up question. Edie was too sharp for her own good, and he seemed compelled to tell her the truth. What was he going to say? He was the most infamous manwhore in three counties?

No thank you.

Besides it was nice spending time with someone who was interested in more than what hung between his legs. He had a brain too. He opened her door and extended a hand.

She took it hesitantly and stared at the place where her cool, porcelain skin pressed to his tanned palm. "I can't wait to change. I feel like pre-makeover *Pretty Woman*."

He glanced at the clothing shop. Hmmm. He knew Babs in the biblical sense. It was doubtful that she'd take kindly to him escorting a half-dressed woman inside.

"Tell you what, I'll go into the bakery next door and order. You meet me there after you're finished."

"How will you know what I like?" she said.

He gave her a long look. "Don't think that'll be a problem, sweetheart."

That lovely blush made her freckles more frecklish.

"S-sounds good," she stammered. "I shouldn't be long."

Clutching his Carhartt jacket around her slim frame, she hunched and dashed through Bab's front door.

She appeared in the bakery fifteen minutes later, just as the owner, Marigold Flint, was getting around to bringing out the coffee. Goldie flashed a coy smile, but Archer pretended to be busy unfolding his silverware.

He glanced up and there she was, Edie, stepping through the front door and glancing shyly around the mostly empty room. He'd seen her in a wedding dress, his t-shirt and a pair of pink booty shorts, but never like this.

"So . . . what do you think?" She slid into the booth. Her black leggings hugged every curve exactly right and her off-the-shoulder shirt, a deep emerald, set off her hair and the silver tones in her irises.

He opened his mouth but no words came.

She fidgeted in her seat. "I've never dressed like this before."

"You're joking."

"I'm more of a Banana Republic gal."

The idea of the shimmying Chiquita banana woman flashed through his head, a pleasant thought, but he didn't think that's what she referred to.

"You know the store, right?" Her forehead furrowed as if he'd announced himself to be a visiting alien conducting research for his home planet. "Oxford shirts and khakis?"

He shrugged, unwilling to be pegged a dumbass, and knocked back the rest of his coffee—ugh, tasted like it had sat burning in the pot for hours. "I'll just say this look, it's . . . whoa."

The set of her mouth told him she didn't get compliments often. That wasn't a blush of pleasure, but open distrust. "These flower arrangements are really pretty," she said, as if to change the subject. Every table sported a small vase with a cheerful sprig of daisies, the one part of the café that Marigold seemed to take real pride in.

"Edie, I meant what I said." He leaned in on his elbows. "You look great."

"I thought you might be making fun of me," she mumbled.

He gaped at her. Had she never owned a mirror? "How don't you see that you're gorgeous?" he blurted. Jesus, what was going on? He never blurted. Blurting was for suckers.

She made a noncommittal sound and picked up her mug with a touch of desperation before coughing into her hand. "Is the kitchen connected to an oil-change shop? This isn't coffee, it's engine grease."

"I made that pot an hour ago." Marigold Flint arrived to take their order. The annoyed way her high-set ponytail bobbed indicated she'd heard Edie's disparaging remark.

It wasn't that Edie was wrong, Marigold's place was known to have gone downhill, but it was the only lunch spot in town so you took what you got. Plus, Goldie had a temper, one he didn't feel like going up against.

"Hey there, having a good day?" Archer sought his smoothest tone. Goldie was pretty enough, but most men in town kept their distance due to her even prettier temper, which is why no one ever sent back the undercooked eggs or stale toast. Marigold's mother ran The

Baker's Dozen until her death a few years back. He'd never got the impression Goldie was particularly happy taking up the mantle, but hard to say as sucking lemons seemed to be her usual expression.

"You planning on ordering or complaining?" Marigold addressed Edie, the look in her eye enough to send most people ducking for cover.

Strangely, Edie seemed unaffected. Instead, she narrowed her eyes right back, even as she shredded a sliver of paper napkin, rolling it into a tight ball. "What do you recommend?"

Marigold pointed to the wall. "Blue plate specials are listed on the board. The usual. Meatloaf. Chicken fried steak. Baked mac and cheese."

"Is the vegetable soup homemade?"

"No."

"I'll stick with the coffee thanks."

Marigold's smile was scarier than most people's frowns. Archer remembered her giving him that face on the playground once, right before kicking him in the balls.

"Think we'll take the check, Goldie." He'd lost his appetite for once. If he didn't get Edie out soon, Marigold would grind her through a sausage maker.

"You're not from around here." Marigold didn't phrase it as a question.

"I'm not." That's all Edie offered in reply.

Archer looked back and forth, trapped between two generals on the cusp of battle.

"In fact, who needs a check? It's coffee. Keep the

change." He slapped a ten on the table and slid from the booth, grabbing Edie's hand. The over-seventy bridge group glanced from their game at the corner table. "Let's get you to The Dales."

"The Dales?" Marigold glowered at Edie with open suspicion. "That's a pretty hotsy-totsy address."

"Mmmm." Edie replied in a noncommittal tone, but Archer felt her shaking.

"Word to the wise," he said once they reached his truck. "If you're planning on sticking around Brightwater, don't get on Marigold Flint's bad side."

Edie shook her head. "She's a bully who doesn't care about service or the quality of her food. Is that really the only bakery in town?"

"There's one at the Save-U-More but that's about it. Brightwater's not big."

"But people here deserve nice things."

"I guess we're all . . . used to the way things are."

"Well, I'm not." Edie slammed back in her seat, her stare lingering on the "For Rent" sign across the street— the cozy, old red-bricked building was where the old five-and-dime used to be.

"You look like you're getting an idea," he said.

She glanced over with a private smile. "It's strange, but once I start to look, it's as if the possibilities are everywhere."

A sharp ache spread through his chest.

Funny, he had the exact same feeling.

Chapter Seven

"QUINCY!" EDEN FLUNG herself against her older cousin the moment he opened The Dales' ornately carved front door. She wasn't a hugger by nature, but seeing a familiar face after the last bewildering day threatened to overwhelm her. She'd sent him a tongue in cheek text after leaving the bakery. *Heat the kettle. I'm popping around for a cup of Earl Grey.*

Are you in Brightwater? Quincy's response hadn't come until Archer steered through the elaborate gates and drove up the winding hedge-trimmed drive.

"Oh, okay, that's the way. Good-oh." Quincy gave her an awkward shoulder pat. None of the formal Bankcrofts were big on body contact or emotional displays. Mother's idea of affection had been an air kiss. "It's been a long time," he said. He'd grown up bouncing between North America and England and his soft, ambiguous accent reflected a man who'd lived many places.

"Over five years." She pulled back with a rueful expression. "I'm sorry to appear unannounced like this."

"Pish posh." Quincy adjusted his fitted sleeve. Apparently, her cousin used his time in Brightwater to kick back and relax, there was no other explanation for why he'd be dressed in a black cotton Onesies in the middle of the day . . . or ever. But then Quincy always had had a daring fashion streak. He never minded wearing contrasting prints, or black with brown, and there was that one Easter brunch when he arrived in a monochromatic pink suit.

"Come inside and I'll have Giles fix you a cup of tea—oh . . . why hello there, Mr. Rugged Handsome." Her cousin perked up, noticing Archer standing at a discrete distance, his hands thrust into the pockets of well-worn jeans that did an exceptional job of emphasizing all the right places. It was impossible not to draw your eyes toward his zipper, the way the denim cupped the bulge—

Stop! Warning! Danger—restricted area.

"Quincy, let me introduce you to my friend, Archer Cock. I mean Kane, definitely Kane . . . not . . . what I just said." Eden faltered, trying and desperately failing to ignore Cowboy's sudden boyish grin.

Was he a friend? Maybe, yes. But she'd never had a friend cause invisible sparks to heat her skin while raking a lingering stare down her legs.

"A pleasure." Quincy skimmed over her mortifying faux pas as if it had never happened. God love the man. "There are quite a few Kanes in this valley, are there not?"

Archer set his hat back. "About a hundred, give or take who is coming in or checking out."

Quincy gestured to the open door. "Any friend of Eden's is welcome here. Are you a tea drinker perchance?"

Archer's gaze traveled over the three-story mansion, four-car garage, and the Italianate fountain. A former summer home of a gold baron, the ostentation contrasted with the stark landscape.

"Thanks, but I should be getting on. Hey, before I go, Freckles, I've got something you need." Archer turned and jogged toward his truck.

A corner of Quincy's mouth twitched upward. "Freckles?" he murmured. The amused glint in his eyes revealed he hadn't missed her Cock-Kane tongue slip. His shoulders shook with restrained laughter. "I'll bet he has what you need."

"We met in Vegas," she replied shakily. "It's a long story."

"Give me all the gory details," he whispered back. "I've seen this one around town. He's got a face you don't soon forget."

No. But right now she had enough to figure out without mooning around about a hunky, shiver-inducing cowboy.

Archer loped back across the circular driveway, her wedding dress flung over one shoulder. "You don't want to forget this."

She did actually. She wanted to forget all about her failed wedding. If it weren't for Reggie's big mouth and utter lack of tact, she'd be en route to Cabo San Lucas for a weeklong honeymoon at an exclusive Mexican spa, and being played for the biggest fool in the hemisphere.

The fact she was Eden Bankcroft-Kew in Brightwater, California, felt much better, but still not quite right.

Who was she really?

But she didn't say any of that. Instead, she murmured, "Thank you," cradling the gown as if it were an unwelcome corpse.

Archer clapped his hands together, rocking on his heels. "Well, guess I better get moving."

"Yes, you have dinner plans." She'd be sorry to see him go. It had been reassuring to know he was close these last twenty-four hours. They couldn't have less in common, but she felt safe in his presence, comfortable in a way she never had before.

He issued a matter-of-fact shrug. "Grandma will sharpen the carving knife if I'm late."

"Then I won't keep you." She hefted the dress to one arm and stuck out her hand. "Goodbye for now."

He took it carefully, as if he didn't want to let go, but maybe that's because she gripped him back, suddenly unable to release him. Brightwater wasn't big. She'd see him around, even from a distance. As dangerous as he was to her sanity, there was no denying he had a friendly face, and she'd need one during the uncertain days ahead.

"You take care now, Freckles." Despite his insistence on using that aggravating nickname, there was no denying his smile was beautiful, if she could call it that, which she never would, at least to his face. But privately, he sported the best, most perfect, most beautiful mouth she'd ever seen on a man.

"I will." Her own smile faded as slowly, centimeter by

centimeter, she allowed his strong hand to release from her own. Little jolts of electricity shot between them. She was halfway surprised her hair didn't stand on end.

Was that hesitation? No. He probably wondered why her eyelid twitched.

God.

"Quincy, good meeting you, man. Take care of this little troublemaker." The broad planes of his handsome face relaxed, the opposite of the clenching occurring in her stomach. And when his mouth tipped in a slight curve? Yeah, there was more clenching, this time of the between-the-legs variety.

Stop. She begged her body. *Please. I'll feed you peanut butter chocolate ice cream for a year. I'll throw in bags of Doritos and hot Cheetos. Just settle down and play nice.*

"Do come by anytime. A friend of, ahem, Edie's"— Quincy gave her a look that said we're discussing this the moment his truck is out of sight—"is a friend of mine."

"Sounds like a plan."

"You might want to see this." Quincy handed over his smart phone once Archer started the engine. "It came in over the wire moments before I received your text."

"Runaway Bride? Heiress Eden Bankcroft-Kew jilts long-time family friend."

"Already?" Eden slumped her shoulders at the sight of the tabloid article. So Reggie wanted to play hardball. He knew how she valued her privacy and must relish stripping it from her. "We need to have a serious talk."

"For what it's worth, Reggie has no idea where you are," Quincy said gently. As the head of Bankcroft Media, one of the most powerful media companies in the nation, he'd no doubt have sound advice on maintaining a low profile.

"He rang me last night," her cousin continued. "Claimed you got cold feet and left him high and dry. He wanted to know if I'd heard from you. I said no but must admit, I had people start looking. You did an excellent job covering your tracks."

"I got lucky finding help." She gave Archer's departing truck a grateful look.

"Well, you've got more help now. That's what family's for, is it not?" In his Onesies, Quincy didn't appear like an Arthurian knight, but he was a hero in his own way, like the cowboy driving off.

What a fool she'd been. Marrying Reggie because she was afraid of being alone. She did have extended family, and now, in Archer, a friend, at least of sorts.

She sniffled, frustration threatening to spill over. *Don't cry. Not yet, there's too much to be done. Keep a stiff upper lip.* "I'm not going to hide," she said, wiping her eyes. "I've done nothing wrong. But I want—I want a fresh start, and without the expectation of being a Bankcroft-Kew. In fact, I'd . . . I'd like to change my name." How sweet it felt, saying the idea. The same way it did when she announced wanting to open a bakery. Who knew saying what you wanted could taste so delicious?

"Change your name? To what?" Her cousin frowned. For all his open-mindedness, the Bankcrofts had a firm sense of tradition.

"I'm not sure yet. I'll have to think on it."

"What about your life back in Manhattan?" he pressed.

"What life?" Eden didn't mean the words to sound as harsh as they did. "Sorry," she tempered, placing a hand over her forehead. "It's been a long twenty-four hours. But honestly, my life was simple. I volunteered at a well-staffed animal shelter, baked, ran, and supported a few charitable organizations. Since college, the majority of my time has been devoted to caring for my mother. I think it's long past time to do something entirely for myself."

"As long as you don't make any rash decisions," Quincy said.

She met his look of consternation with a small smile. That's exactly what she wanted to do.

"Archer calls you Edie?" With Quincy's accent it sounded more like *needy*. Which she wasn't, even if she rubbed her thighs together.

"Yes. I kind of like it, at least it's better than his other nickname for me, Freckles." Did he dole out pet names to all the women?

"You like him."

A horn honked in the distance. Archer must be leaving the property, turning onto the road.

"He was the right guy at the wrong time." She tilted her head back and let the mountain wind caress her face. "Not to change the subject, but to change the subject, how do you like the sound of Edie Banks?"

"For what?"

"'That's what I'll go by while here in Brightwater. A new name. A new me."

Chapter Eight

ARCHER PARKED BY the barn at Hidden Rock Ranch and gazed up at the clouds moseying across the sky. Freckles planned to stick around Brightwater and he couldn't wipe the resulting grin from his face. The thought "that's not a woman you say goodbye to" popped in his head as clearly as if he'd spoken the words out loud. Maybe it was the voice of reason, the one that for too long had been drowned out by a louder one that said, "Shut up and let's get people laughing."

"What are you over there smirking about?" Grandma closed her garden gate, clutching a trowel and leveling a suspicious look. She was never one to beat around the bush.

"Can't a man be happy?" Archer jumped from his truck and slammed the door. Hold on, that wasn't suspicion on her face, but anger. His good mood ran for cover. What had he screwed up now?

"I've got no problem with a man being happy, but I draw the line at perverts." She dragged her turquoise bifocals to the end of her pointed nose, a sure sign she bordered on ballistic.

Archer pulled up short, his neck muscles tensing. "Who're you calling a pervert?" Yeah, sure, he enjoyed a full-range of extra-curricular bedroom-related activities, but his eighty-year-old grandmother didn't know about any of that, did she?

Jesus, did she?

Hopefully not, otherwise, he might need to figure out how to invent a memory-erasing serum and slip it into the Lipton tea she sipped religiously before bed, the one laced liberally with brandy even though everyone pretended not to notice.

"Archer James Kane, I should be on the phone with your older brother right now, ordering him to arrest you for indecent acts and public exposure." She raised her garden trowel in a threatening manner. Leave it to Grandma to figure out how to make a tiny shovel look as threatening as the axe Michael Meyers lugged around in *Halloween*.

"Hey now," he said in the same slow, easy tones he'd use with an angry bull, "I don't know what you're talking about. I'm innocent."

"Methinks the cowboy doth protest too much. That's to paraphrase Shakespeare. Ever heard of him?"

"Hold up. I'm literate, more or less, never skip the sports page." Here's hoping his grin masked the annoyance burning through his chest. He didn't read much, only an occasional spy or adventure paperback, but who was Grandma to judge? He and Sawyer discovered her stash of naughty books last December in a box innocuously labeled "Christmas Decorations." Turned out she had a thing for Fabio, and he could never unsee that.

"There are stories in this town about you that make my hair curl, but to engage in fellatio on Main Street, I'm shocked. Shocked to the core."

An innate sense of self-preservation choked down his nervous laugh. This was about earlier today, in the truck, with Edie. "Grandma, settle down before you give yourself a turn. Now, I'm not sure what you think you saw but . . ."

"A red-haired woman's head in your lap at the traffic light."

Jesus Christ and a bag of chips. Grandma had glimpsed Freckles. With her recognizably molten hair, Grandma would never forget.

Not unless he tried something totally uncharacteristic. He needed to tell the truth, no bullshit, just the facts, straight up. "I can explain."

"All right." She folded her arms, mouth set in a disapproving line. "Let's hear you talk yourself out of this one."

"I met somebody."

"A woman who by all accounts is as depraved as yourself. Congratulations. "

"No, she's nice, Grandma. Smart, funny, and pretty—"

"Where's she from?" The question sounded deceptively simple but was as dangerous as a cornered rattler. Grandma didn't take kindly to newcomers moving into the valley.

"She's from back east," he said after a long moment. "But—"

"A city?"

This wasn't going to go down well. "New York, I think."

"You think?" Grandma shook her head. "If the head on the top of your neck received half as much the attention as the one between your legs, you'd win a Nobel Prize."

Archer closed his eyes and prayed for strength. Please let Grandma talking about what was between his legs be a bad dream, a nightmare that he'd wake from as soon as—

"Are you listening to a word I said?"

I'm trying my damndest not to. "Listen, what you think you saw, is just that, what you think you saw. But the eyes can play tricks and you need to believe me, I wasn't doing anything that I shouldn't be doing."

"Trust you? Ha, says the boy who tells me he's at church when he's really in Vegas. Francine Higsby cashiers over at the pharmacy and told me all about the condoms you purchased before leaving town. Your whoopee-making makes me sick."

Damn Francine, damn Grandma, and, truth be told, damn himself for being the kind of guy that Edie wasn't going to trust an inch, let alone a mile, once she got wind of his reputation. A good girl like her would run screaming in the opposite direction.

"The reason I pushed her into my lap was to hide her from you," he snapped, pushed to the brink.

"Hide her?"

"She's funny, sassy, smart, sophisticated, beautiful, and I didn't want you seeing her with me and jumping to conclusions. I know I have a history, but that's for me to overcome. It's time for me to wise up and get more serious about things."

Grandma gave him a long searching look. Had he struck a chord at last?

She broke into slow, exaggerated clapping. Looked like the answer was a strong negative.

"Say what you like about me, but I'm not going to stand here and let you tear into her."

"You like this woman?" she said.

"I have only just met her, but yeah, I do. A lot."

"Then do her a favor and leave her alone. What do you have to offer? A steady job? No, you show off for city folk who want to live out their cowboy fantasies for a few days. Do you have a house? No, you sleep in the spare room above the barn like an animal."

"I fixed it up," he protested. And he'd been saving, socking away money for a down payment on a property of his own.

"I'm not in the mood for you and your excuses tonight. Dinner's cancelled."

"Fine." Archer ground the toe of his boot trying to tamper his temper. It took a lot to get him going, but once he was set off? Hoo boy.

Grandma paused, coughing. "Here's what I brought you here to say. I'm not getting any younger and it's time I decide on an heir to the ranch. There's a short list and, Archer Kane, so help me God, you're on it."

"Me?" His jaw dropped. "What about Sawyer? Or even Wilder?"

"I haven't seen Wilder in years. By all accounts, which haven't been many, mind you, it seems he's content with his life in Montana. As for Sawyer, well, that boy's happy as sheriff. It's a role that suits his nature."

Grandma's voice betrayed a fondness that set Archer's teeth on edge. She'd always favored Sawyer, never made it a secret. Even though Archer looked up to his middle brother something fierce, knew Sawyer was a good man and friend, a secret jealousy roiled inside him. It made him feel a little like Jan's "Marcia, Marcia, Marcia" from *The Brady Bunch*.

Sawyer was the star pitcher in high school.

Sawyer never caused trouble with teachers.

Sawyer always helped others.

Sawyer had clear focus and exhibited a dedication to his career.

Sawyer bought property from Grandma and then built his own cabin.

Sawyer. Sawyer. Sawyer.

How did a guy like Archer compete with that?

Short answer? He couldn't. But his whole idea of living like you might die tomorrow had one big error. At some point, he quit challenging himself, and responsibility avoidance became the safe road. What if embracing the moment didn't mean anything goes, but jumping at the right chance when opportunity presented itself?

Grandma wanted an heir apparent to the ranch. Hidden Rock was a large and profitable landholding.

The man, or woman, who owned it would become one of the most prosperous residents in the county, the kind of person who made something of themselves.

The type who could provide for a woman like Eden Valentina Bankcroft-Kew.

"Here's what I'm thinking," Grandma's eyes hardened. "You've got what it takes to run this ranch in every way but the one that matters most. Do you understand how an operation like this works? Yes. Are you good with people, able to motivate them to work hard? Yes. Most importantly, this land is in your blood. Never forget, I came here as a twenty-year-old newlywed, scared to death, not knowing a tallyman from a tail rider. Five years later, I was a mother and a widow, with an extended family ready to snap this place from my clutches at the first sign of weakness. But I had the thing you lack—gumption. The sheer determination to stick it out, and that's what I've done.

"The years haven't been easy, life isn't always a big party, but if you put your head down and focus, obstacles have a funny habit of falling away. I intended for this place to go to your father, but that fire took him from us far too soon. It doesn't have to go to one of you three boys, but I'd like it to. I'd like it to go to you, if you can show you have the guts to knuckle down."

Archer stared over the ranch, the animals grazing in the backfields, the mountains in the distance, and his blood stirred. This was home. He knew the property inside and out, had lived here since he was a four-year-old orphan.

Grandma appeared to measure his emotions. "Prove to me you've got the heart, and all this is yours."

He passed a hand over his prickly stubble. If he became the heir apparent to Hidden Rock Ranch it wouldn't be due to any act of benevolence. She'd own him and would no doubt ride his ass hard, but maybe the reward was worth the risk. High time to stop running away from responsibility and see what he was made of.

Instead of living up to his reputation, he'd create a new one.

For years he'd noticed simple ways to improve efficiencies, and what else could be better than working outside in God's country? An image flashed through his head, of a fire-haired woman on the ranch house's front porch, near the roses, a child clutched in each hand.

His children.

His woman.

"You have the summer to convince me." Grandma snapped, glaring with an expression that said, *Get your head out of the clouds.*

Archer blinked. "What do I need to do?"

"Show me you can be an adult. Give notice at the dead-end dude-ranch job. No more trail rides for tips. No more running wild with tourist women. No more late nights at the bar. You will stay here, work hard, and learn the accounts. You don't sneak off to Vegas and you sure as heck don't engage in lewd sexual acts on Main Street."

"Grandma, I told you—"

"Until the end of summer." She held up her hands. "Part of me doesn't know if you'll last three days."

"I can do it," he said firmly.

"We'll see." Grandma narrowed her eyes. "We shall see if you're the sort of man who puts up or gives up."

"Oh, I'm putting up."

"As long as you aren't putting out. If I hear you're wasting time with random women, that's it . . ." She mimicked cutting with finger scissors. "Chance over."

"No random women." He didn't care about women, only one woman, but no point splitting hairs when Grandma inadvertently left him a big gaping loophole. "Deal."

He stuck out his hand.

Grandma stared at it.

"Go on, or do you want to spit shake?"

"Not on your life." She shook it.

Damn, she had a firm grip for an eighty-year-old woman.

Despite the weight of responsibility descending on his shoulders, a lightness filled him. He had a purpose. Get the ranch. Get the girl. Life appeared to be a series of choices. Merely wishing for dreams to come true wasn't good enough. To unlock what life has to offer, he had to be willing to admit he was the key.

Chapter Nine

IT DIDN'T TAKE long living in Brightwater before Edie
realized two facts: (1) She was going to open up a coffee
shop, she'd even thought of the perfect name, *Haute
Coffee*. It would have a small, ever-changing menu and
offer only the highest quality caffeinated beverages.
(2) Archer Kane had a reputation that would make a
drunken sailor blush.

If she casually dropped his name into a conversation
with a local, she'd immediately be met by a knowing
smile and a "Did you hear about the time . . . ?"

*Did you hear about the time Archer Kane got caught
bare-assed in the back of a Buick at the rodeo grounds?*

*Did you hear about the time Archer Kane helped the lost
French tourist find more than directions to Lake Tahoe?*

*Did you hear about the time Archer Kane hooked up at
the radio station and accidentally live broadcast it to the
entire town?*

I heard that was a threesome . . . No, a foursome . . . Uh-huh, a bona fide orgy.

Did you hear about . . . ?

She'd hoped the discovery would make it easy to put that ruggedly handsome cowboy out of her mind. But the man everyone described wasn't the man she met. It was hard to reconcile the two sides. But then, hadn't she gotten everything wrong with Reggie? Her ex-fiancé had pulled the wool over her eyes and anyway, she didn't need to get distracted.

This was a time for looking forward.

She signed a lease on the old five-and-dime, delighted to discover it came with a one-bedroom apartment upstairs. The plaster on the walls was cracked and the floors were crooked in subtle but noticeable ways. It was a place that would horrify Mother but she wasn't Eden Bankcroft-Kew anymore. Her family fortune was safely out of Reggie's sticky fingers, and she spared no time assembling a team to retrofit the old store into the coffee shop of her dreams. What should take months could be accomplished in half the time, for the right price.

Edie had waited her whole life for something to happen. She didn't mind paying extra to make that something start as soon as humanly possible.

Despite her wealth, she didn't want to be viewed around Brightwater as a Bankcroft first, connected to her cousin's vast riches, which rivaled her own. Quincy argued this point until he was blue in the face but she didn't budge. She needed a fresh start, and Edie Banks was a reboot of her old self. The alter ego she'd always imagined while suffocating in her sumptuous Upper East Side penthouse. Her trust was helpful, but she wanted to work, she wanted to be simple, she wanted to be normal.

Edie Banks could live in a dingy apartment while creating her own thriving business.

Edie Banks was independent.

A warm sensation spread through her chest like a ray of sunshine. She bent and slipped into her running shoes, lacing them up. Happiness, yes that was the feeling coursing through her. Happiness to be living beneath these beautiful mountains. Happiness to be taking control of her life. Her past was just that, and all she wanted to do now was race toward the future. Edie Banks would also compete in the Sierras's half-marathon at summer's end, a perfect way to burn off the confections she'd been sampling in her kitchen, plus serve as a tangible reminder she remained tough, in body and spirit.

She fled the back door and took off down The Dales' long driveway. This was her last night at Quincy's. Tomorrow she'd be moving to the new apartment, becoming Edie in earnest. Reggie hadn't contacted her again, but unease lingered that he'd disappear so easily. He was a Wall Street shark, clearly saw her as an investment, and played not only to win, but also to obliterate the competition.

She increased her pace, breathing hard. Moving to Brightwater was an unexpected opportunity. As much as she hated the impetus, there was no denying her new home felt . . . well . . . homey. She loved shopping at the Save-U-More, greeting the cashiers on a first name basis.

There was a bench in the town square beneath a maple tree that always received the perfect amount of dappled afternoon sun. The fresh air zapped stress and there was a security in being surrounded not by concrete and advertisements, but jagged peaks and forest, a scene that inspired child-like wonder. Life in New York was no picnic—sure it had more than its fair share of glitz and excitement, but amid the bustle and relentless pace she often felt utterly alone.

The country road was quiet, and cool morning air filled her lungs. God, she loved this, really loved this. Running early in the morning when the rolling fields were blanketed in light fog, the sun hovering but not quite breaching the peaks. These were mornings to believe in dreams. Not dreams of a stale, safe life with a man who didn't truly love her but one where she could someday have that dinner table surrounded by family, messes, and children's laughter. But instead of Reggie sitting beside her, there could be another man, a good man, with the laugh and easy smile.

If thoughts of a certain cowboy entered, wondering where he was, what he was doing, she pushed herself harder. Soon, sweat slicked her back and she reached a long driveway right as her watch beeped the four-mile mark, her halfway point for today. She'd been going farther every week, getting stronger and faster. Bracing her hands on her hips she peered through the trees, caught sight of a run-down white farmhouse up the hill, the roof canting to one side and covered in a thick sheath of moss. A sign near the mailbox hung on one hook, squeaking in the breeze—"Five Diamonds Farm." "Diamond in the Rough" would have been a better choice. She paused to do a series of quad and calf stretches as a cloud of dust kicked up farther down the gravel road. A truck approached, not Archer's green Philomena. She couldn't help checking any truck she saw these last few weeks. In ranch country this meant having a perpetual swivel neck. Stupid, but she wasn't able to stop. Since leaving her at The Dales, Archer had made himself scarce. He'd called to check on her once and she was polite, distant even, as the phone shook in her hands. His deep, friendly voice affected her whole body, imagine what seeing him again would do?

The truck geared down abruptly, slowing to a crawl. Edie waved cautiously, aware she was alone on a back-country road. Relief sank through her to see an elderly woman behind the wheel, peering through turquoise bifocals and leveling a stern scowl. If looks could kill Edie'd be on the ground with a kill shot blasted through her forehead. Then, just like that, the older woman hit the accelerator and tore off.

Edie coughed in the ensuing dust cloud. Who knew what had gotten into that woman. Make a mental note to avoid her at all costs in the future.

Add that bullet point right after the one about no messing around with a cowboy flirt. This was the time to be disciplined. Focused.

But Quincy kept the "Boys of Brightwater" calendar in his kitchen, tucked in a junk drawer. She'd found it while searching for a teaspoon, snuck a peek, and there on the cover was Archer. All those delicious muscles keeping her up at night were on display for her own personal ogling. And despite what she heard around town, she kept creeping back to drool over that dang calendar. It's okay to look if you never touched, right? It was clear Archer had made conquests all over town. Did he want her to be another? Her mind raced at the possibilities, even as it felt dangerous, like accelerating toward a cliff. Safer never to find out.

ARCHER STEPPED THROUGH the doorway into the Brightwater sheriff's office. Straight ahead sat the deputy, his second cousin, Kit, sleeves rolled to reveal half of the *Semper Fidelis* tattoo inked across his forearm, black boots perched on his desktop. The radio was turned to full volume. Over the speakers, someone shared their opinion, loudly. Another person chimed in, talking over them. He knew those sorts of talk shows made Sawyer's skin crawl. Everyone had the right to vent, but who needed to hear it? The only reason his brother tolerated the noise was because Kit couldn't deal with the alternative, silence.

"What crawled up your ass?" Kit called. "You look as down as a lone kid on a seesaw."

"Good day to you too." Archer wandered to Sawyer's big center desk, and took a bite out of the peanut butter and strawberry jam sandwich sitting on a square of wax paper. His brother had been eating the exact same lunch for nearly twenty-nine years. Steady, predictable—that was Sawyer. Archer moved to set the sandwich back down when his brother seized his wrist, not looking up from the report he was reading.

"Touch my food again and you're a dead man."

"Don't think executions fall under your jurisdiction."

"Where've you been hiding?" Kit raked a hand through his ginger hair. "Your bar stool is getting cold over at The Dirty Shame. I was wondering if we'd have to order a search party."

"Take Sawyer along. He could use a drink." *Or five.*

"That guy?" Kit cocked a chin at Sawyer with a grin. "Nah, he's a long beard and a few mumbles away from being a hermit."

"That guy," Sawyer muttered, turning the page on his report, "is your boss. He has the authority to fire your ass."

"Ah, you'd miss me too much," Kit said good-naturedly. "But seriously, where've you been, man?"

Archer shrugged. The Hidden Rock deal was between him and Grandma. No one else's business. "Just tired from working." That part was the gospel truth. Up at five a.m., he wasn't hitting the pillow until eleven at night.

"Do I need to get you an AARP card?" His cousin chuckled low and long. Kit liked serving up shit, which would be fine, if he'd take his own medicine. He tapped a deck of cards on the table. "How about some Texas Hold 'Em, boys?"

"I'm up to my neck in paperwork," Sawyer said tersely.

Archer knew he didn't like to gamble. That's fine. Some men made their own luck, and his brother was one. But it was time to stop being jealous of Sawyer. His brother worked damn hard and Archer was learning sustained drive and dedication were traits to admire in a man.

"It's not goin' anywhere," Kit wheedled. "Come on, man, one quick game. Stop being the boss for once."

Sawyer whistled for his dog Maverick to come over and he gave it an affectionate scratch behind the ears. "Lucky bastard. No one questions your choices." He glanced between Archer and Kit with his customary stoic expression. "I want to finish up and take this guy out for a run."

Archer rocked on his boot heels, in possession of a bit of information that would certainly fluster his unflappable brother. "Hey, Sawyer, guess who I saw parking outside the Save-U-More this morning?"

"No idea."

"That's why they call it a guess."

Sawyer folded his arms behind his head. "I never guess."

"Guess not."

"Wise guy." The phone on his desk rang, and Sawyer picked it up.

Wait until his big brother found out Annie Carson, his first love, was back in town after ten years. She'd grown up on the farm next to the Hidden Rock Ranch, the younger daughter of Kooky Carson, a local artist who might be a world-famous photographer, but was locally famous for staging the first and only hug-in at the Brightwater Town Square, and often espoused theories that airplane contrails were actual poison from the government or that aliens from Area 51 were relocated to the valley for integration.

Annie didn't seem to have any screws loose, but he couldn't wait to see his brother's reaction when he discovered she was home. He for one, looked forward to seeing his collected brother get a little rattled. But if Sawyer wanted to shoot him down, he could discover this information the hard way, by himself.

Besides, he wasn't here for Annie.

Sawyer hung up while Kit muttered under his breath. Brightwater wasn't a hotbed of law enforcement. Did the small-town beat get boring for his cousin, especially after two tours in Afghanistan? Kit never said. He'd ramble like a smartass all day, but never about himself.

Well, too bad, Archer wasn't here for a card game either. He'd heard whispers about Edie's new shop buzzing around town, and not the good kind. He might not be a genius, but it didn't take too many brain cells to determine the source of the ugly rumors. Marigold Flint had been working overtime to make sure Freckles' dream was dead on arrival.

"Tomorrow, I need you to do me a favor."

Both men looked up. It wasn't like him, or any of them to ask for help.

"The new coffee shop in town—"

"I heard it has a rat problem," Kit said with a shudder. For a big guy, he hated rodents.

"I heard the owner's under investigation from the FBI." Sawyer shook his head. "But the source was suspect."

"Marigold Flint?" Archer asked tightly.

They both nodded.

"No offense, but Goldie is full of it," he said, directing the "no offense" part to Kit who used to date her before he enlisted in the marines. There was no love lost between those two, but still, you don't insult a man's woman, even if she's a former woman and town gossip. "People respect you guys. Tomorrow can you invite a few friends, or escort a couple of sweet little old biddies to the opening?"

"Why do you care?" Sawyer asked with a frown.

"Because I do."

"Are you hitting that?" Kit slammed his fist into his palm.

"That's enough." Archer had talked crudely with his cousin about women in the past, but the idea of treating Edie that way made his stomach do a sick flip-flop.

Sawyer studied him. There was a guy who never kissed and told, or participated in dirty-talk conversations. Archer used to think it meant his brother was a wet blanket, but now, fuck, he found himself respecting him even more.

This turning-a-new-leaf business was disorienting.

"We'll do it," Sawyer said. He didn't ask any questions. It seemed enough that Archer had asked.

"Thanks, man. It means a lot." He left before Kit tried to worm out any more details. Outside, he allowed himself a smile. If Haute Coffee succeeded that meant Freckles would stick around. He glanced in the direction of the coffee shop, a block up on the corner. The windows were covered with newspaper. A few locals stood in front, reading the opening hours on the door.

He'd given Eden space since she arrived in town. Patience wasn't a virtue he held much stock in, but if he wanted to make a play, common sense said not to circle the wagons on a woman who'd been about to get married, especially since her ex-fiancé turned out to be such an asshole. There was no point pulling a cake from the oven before it had time to bake. If he rushed things, he wouldn't get the right result.

But the dust had had time to settle. Haute Coffee's grand opening was tomorrow, and if he had his way, the coffee wouldn't be the only thing getting hot.

Chapter Ten

EDIE GAVE THE plate glass a final, flourishing wipe. The retro hand-painted lettering spelled out *Haute Coffee* in black script. According to locals, the old five-and-dime had sold cheap personal goods, greeting cards, and household items. It cost a pretty penny to retrofit the space into a simple but high-quality kitchen and inviting dining space. But it was money well spent. Once the dingy, stained plaster had been stripped, original red-bricked walls were revealed in all their former glory, and underneath the green linoleum hid weathered wood polished to gleam with a homey radiance.

Two chalkboards hung over the counter. The coffee menu would stay the same . . . a simple and straightforward espresso menu featuring the best roasts from the Bay Area. The drinks weren't anything over fancy—cappuccino, espresso, café latte, Americano, hot chocolate, or a pot of tea—but the quality was of the absolute highest. The other board offered bakery treats intended to change daily. For the grand opening, she'd carefully chosen four specials. First, strawberry rhubarb pie, the fruit locally sourced from the Carson Valley. Next, buttermilk scones lashed with Manzanita honey butter. Then, chocolate chunk cookies, the dark chocolate hand-chopped and sprinkled with a pinch of coarse sea salt straight from the oven. And finally, hazelnut cupcakes smothered in Nutella frosting.

She took out her iPad and hit go on the compilation playlist. Mellow acoustic music filled the space as sun flooded the front window highlighting the intimate booths and tables while the copper ceiling overhead gleamed with a rich burnished shine.

She smoothed back her hair and reset her paisley headband. This was it, the moment of truth. Time to see if the many cooking classes she'd taken over the years as a hobby to beat away boredom were finally of use. Could she make a fresh start and go from Eden Bankcroft-Kew Heiress Homebody to become Edie Banks Coffee Shop Proprietor?

She squared her shoulders and marched to the door. Taking a deep breath, she turned the lock to open and flicked the sign from "Closed" to "Come on in!"

Then she walked back behind the counter and crossed her arms. There wasn't much time to wait. Her heart pounded as the first customer approached the front door but her stomach sank at the sight of the high ponytail.

Marigold Flint stepped in and looked around the space, wrinkling her pert nose. "Well, la di dah. Isn't this place fancied up?"

"May I help you?" Edie curled her toes in her shoes. *Don't back down. Don't be cowed.* When facing a bully better to be assertive than aggressive.

Marigold set a hand on her hip. "You think you're something, don't you? Waltzing in here, from who knows where with your fancy espresso drinks and your..."—her eyes raked the chalkboard for inspiration—"... Nutella. But Brightwater is my home turf. I was born here, and I'll be here long after you've moved on."

"I'm fully intending to make this my home too."

"Oh, please." Marigold snorted. "These days, I walk down the street and half the time don't know who's passing me. Strangers are filling up the place fast, but don't forget this land isn't easy. Everyone thinks they are going to come live in a perfect postcard. It's not all mountains and pretty pictures."

"Why do you do what you do?" Edie wiped an invisible speck of dust from the counter.

Marigold pursed her lips. "What's that supposed to mean?"

"The Baker's Dozen. Why do you run that place?" Edie asked. Marigold seemed to dislike her work, and maybe that unhappiness bled into all aspects of her life. Or maybe her unhappiness blended into her work. It was hard to say if the situation was the chicken or the egg.

Marigold arched a thinly plucked eyebrow. "It was my mother's."

"But is it what *you* want to do? What's *your* dream?"

A blend of emotions danced across Marigold's delicate features. Surprise, suspicion, and shame all took their turn. Then she smiled, or at least bared her teeth. "Now that's exactly the sort of question I'd expect from someone like you."

Now it was Edie's turn to be confused.

Marigold blew out an annoyed breath. "What I want doesn't factor into things. This is the kind of town where we locals have a job, and we get on with doing it. We don't go to therapy or mess around with yoga or talk to our inner children. We make do, because that's real life. But you wouldn't know how to hack that."

"You don't know anything about me or what I can or cannot hack." Edie slapped her hands on the counter.

Marigold snickered. A nasty, ugly noise. "You know, you do have one thing in common with most women in this town." Wickedness glinted from her eyes. "You've slept with Archer Kane."

Edie's head jerked as if she'd been struck. "I have done no such thing."

"Oh, honey." Marigold waved her hand. "It's practically an initiation. You don't get to live here and not sleep with a Kane."

Did Marigold and Archer ever—oh, Lord, she was such a fool.

"No, not me," Marigold read her thoughts. "At least not Archer. Let me say, you're better off keeping a safe distance from most Kane men. They're all heartbreakers. I don't consider you any sort of a friend, but that's one piece of honest advice."

"Won't you take a cupcake for the road?"

Marigold frowned at the glass case. "I have my own at

my shop. And what's with having only four things on the menu? Who is going to like that?"

"The menu will change every day."

"People here like the same. Stability," her over sweet tone contained a sprinkling of snark.

Edie kept her face carefully deadpan—a reaction would only weaken her. "People everywhere like quality and service better."

"Well, may the best woman win then. This town isn't big enough for the both of us."

A shiver ran through her. "My intention isn't to drive you out. We can both succeed."

Marigold's eyes narrowed. "It must be nice to live in a fantasy. But the reality is kill or be killed."

"Is that a threat?" Edie refused to look away, or back down, no matter how uncomfortable this made her, no matter that behind Marigold stood the ghosts of all those who used to laugh behind her back, trip her in the halls, or exclude her from tables during lunchtime.

"It's a fact." Marigold stalked to the door, slamming it behind her.

"We'll see about that," Edie said to the ghosts before turning her back. The past wouldn't haunt her, not anymore.

A COW WAS missing. Archer swore as he drove his truck through the field to the ranch's furthest corner. Today Edie opened Haute Coffee. He watched the shop take shape from a distance, waiting, even though his patience was unused and rusty. Never had he met someone like Edie, a woman he wanted to savor. She wasn't a shot of tequila but a slow sipping whisky.

He could pretend he was playing it cool, that whatever happened would happen and all that *c'est la vie* bullshit, but there was no denying that the thought of seeing that quiet, refined redhead left him equal parts excited and shaking in his boots. For all his noble "give her space" self-talk, the fact was that in part, he'd put off seeing her because what if she realized the obvious—that he wanted her but she could do far better?

Well, no point navel gazing. It was time to sack up and see, scared or not, but first he had to find the missing cow. Hidden Rock was a large ranch and he couldn't go anywhere until the case of the mystery cow was solved, not because Grandma would otherwise fry his balls alongside her habitual hash browns for breakfast, but because it was the right thing to do.

The right thing to do.

Archer Kane, doing the right thing. What a novel notion.

He got out and walked the bluff, the last area he hadn't explored. No bovine in sight. What's left to do? Yell "hey, cow"?

Hell no.

The wind picked up, carrying a low moo from the west. He cocked his head, ears straining and there it came again, once more, and faint. He tore off in the direction and spotted her through a dense thicket. *Shit*. The cow stood in the middle of the bog, it was likely she could move, but had gone and gotten herself good and spooked. He jogged back to Philomena, grabbed a length of rope out of the bed and fashioned a simple lariat. Then, heading back down, he swung the rope easy, like he used to do showing off for tourists at the dude ranch, and landed it square around her thick neck.

"Come on, big girl. Let's do this nice and easy." He pulled and she stared with baleful brown eyes. His stomach rumbled. It was past lunch. Damn it. He still needed to clean up and drive into town if he wanted to make it in time for Edie's opening day. "I said, hustle that bustle, girl." He pulled again and this time she grunted in annoyance, taking a step back.

So she could move, just wanted to play hard to get.

So like a woman.

"Fine," he said through gritted teeth. "You want to be wooed? Time to dance, sweetheart." He dropped the rope and kicked off his work boots, stripping from his Carhartt pants and denim shirt in quick efficient movements. He strode bare ass into the bog, sinking past his ankles in the slimy silt. "Goddamn it's cold," he muttered, nuts crawling inside. He got all the way to the cow and gripped the neck loop firmly. "Move," he commanded, and magically she took one step forward, and then another.

That's all she needed? He was here buck naked and cold and not in the mood. "Stupid cow," he muttered and she tossed her big head. He hadn't anticipated the sudden movement and the gradient of the bog changed, deepening. There wasn't time to think as he lost his balance, only to squeeze his eyes shut. The water wasn't deep, around three feet, but now he reeked like swamp water and was officially freezing. He stood and groaned. Leeches dotted his legs.

"Happy now?" He snarled.

She mooed, as if to say, "That's what you get for forgetting your manners, mister."

"Yeah, you're happy all right." He had a few more choice words but apparently this cow suffered from delusions about being treated like a lady.

He plucked the leeches off and blood trickled down his knees. Great. Just great. They stumbled from the bog, and he checked his legs one more time, before slipping on his jeans, throwing on his shirt, and getting Her Majesty into the truck. Mentally, he promised her a one-way ticket to Burger King. They didn't name animals on the ranch, but if they did, this one would be Double Whopper.

The cow stared and guilt bubbled in Archer's belly. Who was he to begrudge it wanting a little taste of adventure? Still, he barely had enough time to get back, rejoin the cow to the herd, and shower. He opened up the truck to step inside and his cock twinged, and not the good kind of twinge either. What was up with his junk? Tearing down the zipper, he ripped his jeans open.

"Fucking asshole." A swollen leech gorged on the vein running up his shaft. Jesus H. Christ, if that wasn't a sight to inspire terror in a man's heart then he didn't know what was. Gritting his teeth, he pulled and the damn thing stretched. "Let go," he growled, because who the hell in his right mind would hold a lighted match to that region?

Finally the little bastard gave way, and damn did it ever sting. He threw its slimy body into the tall grass, sorted out his pants and hopped in the truck, adjusting the mirror. He caught a glimpse of his reflection, expression uncharacteristically frazzled.

This is what happens when you try to be responsible?

He scratched the side of his neck and his fingers passed over yet another slimy blob. "Oh, shit." Another leech. This one came off in one quick grab. He tossed it out the window and threw the truck in reverse.

His brief regret about thinking ill thoughts about the cow vanished. For this little stunt, Burger King was the kindest fate he'd wish for that damn animal.

Chapter Eleven

ARCHER PARKED ON Main Street, breathing hard because he'd hauled ass with two hands. The coffee shop was due to close at four. He hadn't walked by the front door every other day and not noticed the stenciled hours of operation. During these recons, he'd never run into Freckles, but every time he peered through the newspaper sheets covering the windows, the coffee shop had changed. Who'd have ever imagined that old run-down shop could turn out so inviting?

Edie clearly possessed more magic in her little finger than most people had in their whole body. She went by that name now too. Around town people referred to her as Edie Banks. A fresh start—he understood the appeal.

He checked the town clock. Five minutes to close. He caught his reflection in the glass before yanking the door open. His shirt was tucked in and hat straight. Good enough. Fuck, he was more nervous than the time he asked Angela Woods to the senior prom. What did he want? Just to see her. No, that was a lie. He wanted her to see him not for the man he'd been, but the man he was trying to be—the guy who might be worth a chance.

No pressure.

"We're almost clo—" Edie appeared around the corner, wiping her hands on a dish towel. Her hair was tied in a messy bun and flour dusted the tip of her snub nose. She looked exhausted and happier then he'd ever seen. "Archer!"

"Successful first day?" Good, his tone stayed light and casual.

"Yes, I sold out of the baked goods by two o'clock." she said proudly. "So many people came. Quincy, of course. Oh, and your brother stopped in too with a friend. That was nice of him."

Archer made a mental note to owe his brother one.

She gestured at her flour-dusted face. "I decided to bake a couple extra pies for tomorrow. The strawberry rhubarb was a huge hit."

"Who doesn't love pie?"

"They sold like hot cakes. I'm adding a plum and a bourbon pecan." She gave him a considered look. "Wait right here, I have something for you." She stepped from around the corner, her intoxicating scent wafting as she passed. Her shirt was almost backless, but the white eyelet fabric kept the look classy. Then there was her small but sexy ass clad in dark denim. Not much there, only a handful, but perfectly shaped. Damn, she looked as edible as she smelled. She reached out and flipped the sign from "Come on in!" to "Closed."

His heart thudded. What did she have planned? He flexed his palms, aching to trace all those small curves, commit her body to memory. What if she asked him to step into the back and pit her plum?

Jesus, cool your jets. That's the old way of doing things. He wanted her more than air, but he needed to go slower.

It took him a second to realize she'd disappeared into the kitchen, another to note he was a goner, and a third to find he'd grown rock hard. "Down boy," he ordered. "Think about leeches."

That did the trick. His cock damn near ran off for an extended visit in the foothills.

"Who're you talking to?" She returned and glanced around the empty room with a puzzled expression. The pie on the plate in her hand must have come straight from the oven because the generous scoop of vanilla ice cream was already melting down the sides. His stomach growled, a reminder he hadn't eaten since breakfast.

"Nobody," he answered quickly, pulling out a chair and taking a hasty seat. "Is all that for me?"

"Yes." Her cheeks turned a pretty pink. She blushed so easily and it was adorable. "As a thank you. I wondered when our paths would cross again. I thought I saw you peek into the shop once but you were gone by the time I came outside."

"I like what you've done with the place," he said. The fact he didn't confirm or deny his presence deepened her light flush to crimson.

Her long look was a little uncertain and a lot of something, something that caused his blood to heat. Maybe he had a chance here. *Please don't let me fuck this up.* "I want you to know that pie and coffee are on the house for you in perpetuity." She set the plate on a table and they both stared at each other. "As a thank you," she added, absently chewing the corner of her lip. "Let me pour you some coffee. How do you take it? Black?"

"With sugar."

She stood with a small smile. "Of course you do."

"How you liking Brightwater?" he asked as she returned, carrying the mug. She sat opposite him and when her foot bumped his boot, she quickly drew it away.

"I'm happy." She glanced out to Main Street. "This town has so much potential."

"Potential?" Archer sat back, folding his arms. "What's the matter with how it is now?"

"Oh, nothing." She responding quickly, wiping an invisible crumb from the table. "Nothing at all. But it's changing, and I feel like I can help in a small way. People here deserve nice things, and if they want to go out for a coffee and a cupcake, they shouldn't have to put up with what Marigold serves."

"It doesn't sound like you made a friend for life in Goldie." Deep down he knew Marigold wasn't a bad person, but who knew what crawled up her ass the last few years.

Edie gave a one-shouldered shrug. "Not so much. But"—she forced a brighter smile—"that's no matter. Everyone else in town has been perfectly friendly and kind."

"Present company included?" He cast the fishing line but from the way she frowned, it looked like he wasn't getting a bite.

"Actually, I should say that I . . . I . . . well, I've heard quite a bit about you." Her eyes fluttered down to his neck and held, her cheeks deepening from pink to crimson. "You and women in Brightwater. And others towns within a fifty-mile radius."

Shit. She'd struck the iceberg of his reputation, and the situation was fast taking on water. "All good things?" He affected a lazy grin despite the fact a flurry of nerves made his stomach protest her delicious pie. He'd set the course, had to see it through, even though his desired destination now seemed like an impossible fantasy. The captain always went down with the ship.

"Apparently you leave lots of satisfied customers."

"Goddamn," he said with a forced laugh. "That makes me sound like Brightwater's version of McDonald's." Who had he been kidding? She'd never see beyond his reputation.

Now what? He couldn't exactly deny the truth. Instead, he clamped a hand around his fork and shoveled in another big bite, giving an inadvertent groan. Now that was the best pie ever made. The ice cream sweetened the buttery flaky crust, and the berries popped with sweetness. Even Freckles' disapproving expression couldn't detract from the flavor

She braced her elbows and leaned forward. "Like I said before, coffee and pie are yours for the taking, whenever you want. I am grateful for how you helped me get out of Vegas. But I don't want to be another notch on your belt."

"Good," he said hotly, "because I'm not here for any . . . notching." But at this point he couldn't give his real reason without it looking like a cheap pickup line. The manwhore of Brightwater wanted to go a-courting? What a joke. Edie had probably been in town for all of a few hours before getting regaled with stories that would make a nun run straight to confession.

He pushed away the pie. Delicious as it was, he'd lost his appetite.

"Wait," she said, raising her voice to be heard over the violent slide of his chair. "I—I don't mean to come off strong. I am still getting used to speaking up for myself so I might have overcompensated."

"Don't feel like you owe me any apologies." Damn it, his voice was gruff, hurt. He was a guy who didn't do this, get tongue-tied or feel lost. His job was to make a girl comfortable and have all the big moves.

"I truly didn't mean to hurt your feelings," she said softly. "I owe you so much. After all, you are the reason I got here in the first place. You were my knight in shining armor when I needed one most."

He'd wanted to play the nice guy, and hell, he was a nice guy, at least, not actively a bad one. But Edie made it clear he had nothing to lose. Time to say what was on his mind and then get the hell out. Brooding in secret wasn't his style.

He took his time standing and ambled around the

table, setting a hand down on either arm of Edie's chair. He leaned down slow. As he drew closer, her eyes opened a fraction wider. When he was almost touching her mouth, a mouth that was suddenly parting, he changed course, dipping to her ear, allowing his own lips to hover, touching, but only barely, her soft skin. "I won't deny whatever rumors you've heard about me. I'm not perfect, Edie, but I am a man, and where I come from that means saying what you mean, and meaning what you say. Do I want you? Yes. I want you like nothing I've ever needed. But I'm not going to chase you. I'm going to prove that I'm the guy who's willing to wait."

She let out a sigh somewhere between a moan and a whimper.

"I know we'd be good." He moved a free hand and let his knuckles caress the arch in her neck. "You got to know we could be good. Every time I look at you"—he drew back—"at your mouth, all I can wonder is how good you'd taste."

"Archer . . . I . . . you . . . I want . . . ." She swallowed, blinking rapidly.

Someone tried the shop door. *Perfect timing.* He glared over his shoulder to see a couple frowning at the closed sign before walking away. When he turned back around, Edie stared at his neck.

"I nearly fell for it." Her mouth twisted into a sad smile as she stood. "Waiting, you've been waiting for me? How long? Since lunchtime? Or should I be extra flattered that you held off since breakfast?"

Her words threw him. Here he was, again on defensive, even after his big move. His jaw clenched. "What are you talking about?"

"Hickeys weren't cool in high school. They are much less so now."

"Hickey? I don't have a hickey."

She laughed at that, a real laugh as if she was completely unaffected. As if she wasn't trembling against his words a few seconds ago. "You don't know, do you? I almost feel sorry busting you, but really, you walked right into it."

"Busted me? Walked into what?"

"You don't have any idea you have a hickey the size of a fifty-cent piece on your neck?"

"What—how—that's impossible!"

She pointed at a brass-framed mirror on the wall and he crossed the room. He hadn't been with anyone since that ill-fated Vegas trip. He glanced in the mirror, nothing. Was she messing with him?

"Right at the collar line," she called.

He tilted his head and there it was, a bruise from the damn leech above his clavicle. "That's nothing," he said, giving it a rub.

"Oh, I'm sure it was."

"No seriously." He rubbed his thumb and index finger over his eyes. "I had an accident this morning."

"Bedroom mishaps must be an occupational hazard. Or are you going to say you ran into a vacuum cleaner?"

"I mean it. There was a cow stuck in a bog and—"

"Is this a convoluted metaphor?" She wrinkled her brow. "Because I don't need to hear—"

"Never mind." He'd blown this shot so hard that it vaporized itself. There weren't even pieces to pick up. "Forget it. There's no point explaining anything. You already think you have it all figured out, that you know all about me. But so help me, I know one thing. I want to know you better. And that's the part that makes you different to any other woman I've ever known." It hurt to look at her, see the little silver speckles in her eyes. It was agony to watch the slight outline of her breasts hitch with her inhaled breath.

She held up a hand as if to ward him off, averting her gaze.

He lifted his hat and scrubbed his forehead. Freckles didn't want to hear the whole truth, only the parts that pertained to his past, not his future. Outside, across the street, his cousin, Kit, walked through the saloon doors into The Dirty Shame. When in doubt, run—a drinking buddy was always there for you. If Sawyer worked late, maybe he could con a ride home after a couple of heart-deadening bourbons.

"Sorry to bother you." No point sticking around and making an even bigger fool of himself.

Edie reached out. "I'd like to be friends. Please . . ."

He stared at her hand. "I made myself clear. I don't want to just be your friend."

"Please." A raw twinge of desperation crept into her voice and, shit, those were actual tears gathering in the corner of her eyes. "I really could use a few."

He rocked on his boots. His resolve melting into a mushy puddle. This was a bad idea. He wanted her and despite the fact she gave him the boot, there was no denying her reaction when he leaned in close. Men and women who were attracted to each other couldn't be friends.

Apparently everyone knew this except Edie Banks.

But hell, she looked so hopeful.

And he knew, before he even opened his mouth that he was going to agree to the impossible idea.

EDIE LOCKED THE door behind Archer and yanked the blind cord closed. Well, mostly closed. There was just enough gap remaining for a peek. Archer crossed the street with his unhurried swagger. Why was that loose-limbed gait so appealing? Maybe because it was so different than what she was used to. In the city, men walked fast, with purpose, head down and rushing. There was something undeniably attractive about a man being confident about going a little slower, at a pace he set. If she teleported Archer to Times Square he'd no doubt navigate through the crowd with the same gait he maintained in Brightwater.

You could take the man out of the place, but the place didn't leave the man.

He turned as if sensing her secret ogling and glanced back. She dove behind the blind so fast the canvas swung from the action. Would he know she watched?

She pressed a hand over her eyes, attempting to take a deep diaphragmatic breath.

All her fine big talk had come straight out of her backside. Today had been a success. The shop had been full all day, and as soon as there was a lull, she had barely enough time to wipe off tables before a new person came through. For a quiet town, this was a more than promising start. And yet, every time the door opened, her eyes searched for a face where the jaw was a little too square, the mouth the perfect type of wide, the eyes a hypnotic green.

Wanting wasn't going to help her become independent. Neither was becoming jealous of the many women in Archer's life.

She needed to focus. This coffee shop was her big shot. And if she got quivery in her lady parts when Archer leaned in and set his lips on her ear, making her stomach flip, she had to ignore it.

Fantasies were dangerous and distracted from real life. She didn't even own a vibrator. The Big O existed only in memory. She picked up Archer's pie plate and mug and walked to the kitchen and dropped them in the sink. On the counter rested a block of baking chocolate. She broke off a corner and shoved a piece in her mouth, grimacing as the bitterness of the cacao spread over her taste buds. Talk about a bad idea. She grabbed a spoonful of sugar and shoved in a mouthful. Much better.

What was she doing?

Trying to prove chocolate was better than sex.

And it was, at least better than any sex she'd had.

But that leanly muscular, 100 percent male-grade body Archer pressed against hers promised something that even *mousse au chocolat* couldn't hope to deliver. She flicked on the stove, grabbed milk from the fridge, and poured a cup into a saucepan, adding more chocolate, sugar, and cinnamon and whisking furiously. Hot chocolate was a poor substitute for sexy times, but it would have to do.

She stared in the pan, watching the swirls undulate. She didn't need to rely on anyone except herself. Pouring herself a small mug, she started to cut herself a piece of cherry pie. Oh, who was she kidding? She grabbed a fork, slid to the floor, propped her back against the cupboard, and hoed in. If she didn't cut it, it counted as one piece. She hadn't eaten all day and ran five miles in the pre-dawn. It was a wonder she was still going.

"Oh yum," she groaned to herself. The pie was delicious if she said so herself. She took a sip of hot chocolate, reveling in the cinnamon. Sometimes all it took was a dash of the unexpected to zap the flavor into full force.

She slammed her knees together, ignoring her internal clenching, the want that still went hungry. More pie. She took a bigger bite but no matter how delicious the flavors were, nothing could drive away the memory of Archer Kane's perfect ass, lovingly hugged by faded denim, walking in the opposite direction.

Chapter Twelve

ARCHER SIPPED HIS top-shelf whisky or as top-shelf as it got at The Dirty Shame, which wasn't saying a hell of a lot.

"Incoming," Kit muttered beside him.

"Barely," he retorted, staring straight ahead.

The woman in question had tottered by twice before, weaving suggestively on her three-inch heels. "I'm not interested." He wasn't here for a one-night stand—unusual but the gospel truth. And besides, even in his heyday, he never took home anyone too drunk to walk.

He took another slow sip.

"What crawled up your ass and died?" Kit had a way with words.

"Tired, that's all."

"Sawyer mentioned you've been around Hidden Rock more. What's the angle?"

"I need an angle to help our eighty-year-old grandma?" Archer asked with exaggerated outrage.

"Something's up. Spit it out." Kit wasn't just a deputy sheriff. He'd been an interrogator/debriefer who screened and interrogated enemy POWs held on overseas bases. What went down during his military service was a mystery because Kit steadfastly refused to discuss his experiences. He laughed louder than anyone at Archer's antics, but when no one watched, his gaze would drift to empty space, his mouth drawing down on the edges.

"She asked me to help more." Archer shrugged.

"Grandma doesn't ask for help. She's up to something." Kit peeled at the corner of his IPA label. "Think you're tapped for Hidden Rock?"

Archer slugged more whisky in lieu of a reply.

"I don't know, man." Kit took his own swig. "You're full of mystery these days."

"Me?"

"There's been talk about you and a certain redhead who's new to town. You been holding out on me?"

"There's nothing to say," Archer muttered.

Kit looked thoughtful. "She's cute. Got to love a woman with that head of hair. Never seen anything quite like it."

Archer's throat tightened. He couldn't stake a claim. Edie made it clear that not only did she want to reinvent herself, she also didn't want anything to do with him, except for that blow off about the lifetime supply of pie and them being friends. Wasn't that the line women gave guys to let them down easy?

"Are you into her?"

"She's not interested," Archer mumbled.

"Come again?"

"She's not interested in me," Archer said louder, through gritted teeth.

Kit leaned in close, and for an unsettling second Archer got a sense of what it would be like to be grilled by his cousin. This guy didn't miss a trick.

"And you are?"

"More than that." Might as well tell Kit as much of the truth as he could. "Something about her has gotten under my skin. I've never had anything like this happen before."

"Sure it's not poison oak?" Kit cocked a brow. "An itch you can't scratch?"

"Fuck off," Archer grumbled. Forget it. He wasn't going to sit here and bare his heart like a chump only to have Kit bait him.

"Look." Kit's face grew serious. "If you really want this woman you're going to have to shoot straight."

"And you're one to give me advice?" If Archer was the manwhore of Brightwater, Kit was the monk. A wise-cracking, hard-drinking monk who always went home alone.

"Guess I am, and you better take it because if I have to spend the summer on this bar stool watching your ugly face look like it's about to burst into tears, I'm going to kick your ass."

"Burst into tears? Why I ought to—"

"I've known you since forever and I've never seen this." He waved his hand. "You. Torn up about a woman."

"I don't even know her. Not really." Just enough to understand Freckles was the single most fascinating person he'd ever encountered.

"Then get to know her, and keep being yourself . . . except without the whole sleeping with whoever comes your way part."

Archer shook his head. "I don't know."

"You're blushing like a school girl, so don't pretend you're not going to give it a shot."

And the shit of it was, Kit was right.

Archer stood. "I got to go take a leak, man. Back in a minute." The men's room was in an alcove near the front—he turned back to see Kit chatting with Bruce, The Dirty Shame bartender, and then walked out the door.

No matter what she said in the coffee shop, her eyes told a different story. It was time to get Edie out of his head and into his arms.

A CAT IN heat yowled in the alley. Edie turned up the iTunes volume on her laptop, but the whimsical *Amélie* soundtrack did little to mask its god-awful screams and moans. Probably the same bedraggled white cat that perched on the small balcony off her bedroom this morning. At this rate she should invite the poor thing in for a bowl of milk. Tell it to bring its friends. Might as well embrace being a crazy cat lady and buy tuna in bulk.

Someone pounded on the door and she jumped, glancing down at her bathrobe, her hair still wet from the shower. Who could that be? Quincy had flown to LA this afternoon for a meeting and no one else had cause to visit.

Tiptoeing across the room, she peered into the peephole.

A green eye stared back and she yelped, covering her mouth. "You came back."

"I forgot to tell you something," came the deep rumble.

Her next breath was nonexistent.

Archer.

She glanced down. Her red and green flannel robe might be comfy on cool mountain nights, but wasn't exactly alluring. Not that alluring was a good idea. No, alluring was a bad, bad idea. Her stomach flipped as heat spread through her body. Her hand migrated to the doorknob, opening it slow, hoping he couldn't hear her swallow. Hard.

"You scared me half to death. What are you—"

"I want to be a hell of a lot more than your friend. All I can think about is lighting that secret fire you've got kindling inside."

She couldn't say anything in response, not when she was too busy reaching for his shoulders and dragging his hot, hungry mouth over hers. Archer groaned, sinking his big hands into her hair. This wasn't slow but dear God was it thorough. His lips alone were absolutely lethal. What on earth would happen when his tongue tangled with hers? It didn't look like she'd have long to wait. Her inner muscles coiled as one of his hands slid to the nape of her neck, angling her head back to deepen their kiss. Every way he moved, from the crushing pressure of his mouth to the way he grazed his teeth on her skin was so explicit. Half teasing, half devouring.

He smelled woodsy, like nature and hard work, with traces of laundry soap and man. She throbbed, as if her pulse suddenly originated from her clit.

Raw heat emanated from him, yet she shivered, her nipples hard against the robe's rough cotton. She was all ragged edges even as her bones transformed to warm maple syrup.

And she wanted more, the rough and tender.

His tongue thrust, her back arched, and they both moaned.

"You taste like cherries and chocolate," he murmured, his voice ragged and husky with need.

She did this to him.

His own faint taste of whisky wasn't half bad either. Was it enough to get her drunk, because her legs didn't seem to have a prayer of supporting her. Luckily it didn't matter because his hands braced her ass, she didn't even know he'd moved, and then she was rising, feet leaving the floor. Her legs automatically wrapped around his waist as he pushed her against the open door. But she'd been in the shower five minutes ago and wasn't wearing panties. Her robe parted and he was there, his hard length rocking against her sensitive skin, the denim providing just enough friction to make her ache a dull pain.

Yes, oh yes, this was a need that hurt.

How long had it been since she'd come? Too long. It didn't seem worth it to count back that far. Not when she could be bucking against him instead, messy, urgent, and perfect. Her need came from a deep place, roaring awake, a forge that had been simmering. All she needed was more stoking.

And a little more stroking.

"Touch me." That was her voice. She said the words, and not just once. Over and over. "Touch me. Touch me."

Not even saying. Begging. Breathless. So breathless maybe he couldn't understand except he did because they were moving. He kicked her front door shut and then she was on the love seat. Well, technically, he was on the love seat and she was on him, her robe open, bracketing her exposed breasts and framing her sex. He stared over her exposed body with an expression that reflected the feeling surging inside her.

Consumed.

His gaze rose, locking with hers as he reached up and slid away the robe, let it fall down her back, crumple beneath her ass.

"Beautiful," he said, caressing the slope of her shoulders.

"I know why you're here," she said.

"No, you don't."

"Guys like you want one thing." And while that was true, God, she was going to give it. Regret could wait until tomorrow.

"Let's get something straight, Freckles." His hands slid oh-so-slowly down, grazing the sides of her breasts, outlining her curves. "I'm not here for one thing, I'm here for everything."

Before the words could even finish registering, he dipped forward. That mouth that had done wicked things to hers latched on to her breast. He took his time licking, tasting, alternating between both as if time didn't exist. He fluttered his tongue over the tip of one, and then sucking it in, slow and gentle, he gently squeezed the other. Back and forth he went, until she felt impossibly full, aching.

His hand dragged down leaving her breast. His mouth remained, sucking harder now and then, and then, oh God, and then, a finger teased between her folds. She didn't realize how wet she'd gotten. He slid straight over her clit and the twin action of his touch coupled with the pressure on her nipple nearly sent her backward.

His fingers moved against her and she had no choice, she had to move in response. It was slow what they did, as slow as a dance but a million times more intimate. She was fresh from the shower, but even still, could smell her need, sharp and clean. There was no hiding that this was everything she wanted, everything that she had fantasized about for night after lonely night.

When he pulled back from her breast she moaned in protest, but moaned louder for the lazy circles he kept on her center.

"Want to watch?" he muttered.

Her gaze drew downward. His long tanned fingers stood in sharp contrast to her red curls and pale thighs. He slid one finger into her heat but it wasn't enough. She needed more. She needed him. Her hands moved to his belt buckle, skimming the hard bulge.

"No," he ground out.

"No what?"

"Not tonight."

She paused. "I don't understand. I thought we were going to . . ."

"You're going to. Tonight is for you."

Despite the building pressure, deep in her pelvis, she was shocked to stillness. What guy offered up a woman pleasure while forgoing his own? Especially a guy with Archer's reputation.

"Stop thinking, feel," he ordered.

"But I—"

Two fingers joined the first and her eyes rolled back into her head.

"I said feel," he rumbled.

And there was nothing else to do but what he commanded. Archer filled her on the inside, while his thumb kept its insistent pulse. "Good, God, so good. You are so good."

She was getting close. And as much as she wanted to be there, she didn't want this to end. Because once it was over, logic would gather up her senses and remind her that this was one big fat terrible—

"Kiss me," he growled. "Kiss me and come."

And really, how do you turn down a request like that?

Oh, his taste, that faint smoky whisky and trace of spearmint. His tongue thrust a rhythm slightly different from his fingers, enough to keep her off-kilter, to produce sensations laden upon sensations until she was positive she couldn't take another second.

Then, he yanked back her hair, not enough to hurt, just to feel amazing, the same amount of roughness that his scruff had when skimming her neck. And that was it. She was flying. Or a pounding wave. Who cared, this was the single most powerful orgasm of her life, and Archer stayed there every step of the way, not backing off, not slowing down until she collapsed against him, ragged and spent.

Her pulse thundered in her ears. Did he feel the same pulse against the fingers still slipped inside her? After a moment, he slowly pulled his hand away.

"I've never seen anything as fucking gorgeous as you getting off, Freckles."

She giggled, slow and sleepy. This is probably a line he fed all the girls but right now she was as smug as a cat that got into the cream. If that's what it felt like to be used by Archer Kane, well, maybe she needed to rethink her priorities.

But he did something next that she never expected.

He hugged her.

His arms encircled her waist as he rested his forehead between her shoulder and neck.

"Your smell, the vanilla, I can't be around anyone baking these days or I go nuts. The other day, someone was baking cookies and I got hard."

"Shut up, no you didn't."

His laughter vibrated into her skin. "Well, it could have been because I was standing beneath your apartment."

"You're serious?" Two nights ago she had baked cookies up here, almond sugar.

"As a heart attack, Freckles."

"I'm not sure whether to be flattered or freaked out."

He gave the tip of her nose a soft kiss. "Welcome to my world, that's how it's been since I met you."

"I don't understand. You haven't come around. I haven't even seen you since the day you brought me from Vegas. I assumed . . ."

His eyes narrowed and he reached forward gathering up her fallen robe and handing it to her. "Go on, get what you need to say off your chest."

She slid off his lap, moving to the far end of the love seat, which meant her thigh was still grazing his. She'd ridden him like a bronco. She'd gone crazy from vitamin O deficiency.

"Are there any women in this town you haven't slept with?"

"Yes."

"I'm serious."

"So am I."

She stood and paced. "Stop being so literal. What I mean is, are the stories I've heard true?"

"I don't know which stories you've heard."

"Just tell me the truth," she snapped. She didn't want to dance around the edge. "I haven't come this far to put up with . . . with . . . more guy bullshit."

Archer raised a brow at that. "I have a reputation. It's not entirely undeserved."

"You use women."

He cocked his head. "Use? Yes, I suppose. But I never pretend. It's clear from the beginning. I'm not a guy who promises flowers and romance. I keep it simple, cut and dried. The woman knows full well what she's consenting to . . . it's sex and sex only. That's what they agree to, and if they don't, I'm out of there." He stood, dragging his hand through his hair. "But that's not what this is between me and you." He stared out the window, his palm resting against the center of the glass.

"Oh come on."

He whirled around. "I know it sounds like a line, but you're different. I'm fascinated. Captivated. From the moment I saw you I haven't been able to see anyone else. You're what I want, and what I want with you, I've never wanted with anyone else. Never thought about it."

Archer stood there, ripping his heart out and holding it raw and beating for her examination. Never had a woman affected him this way. It wasn't that he simply had to have her, although make no mistake, he craved her touch, the same way he needed air. But it was more than that. And that more is what left him off-kilter, because what if he was alone in this?

What did she want?

And why did two tears stream down her cheeks?

She wiped them away.

"What are those for?" he said, crossing the room, gently framing her face. Lord, her skin was so soft, so perfect. He could see a slight redness along her neck where his beard had rubbed.

She stared into a far corner of the room, her lower lip quivering slightly, still swollen from his kisses. "Nothing like this has ever happened to me. Nothing like you, I mean. Growing up, I was . . . . awkward. My teeth stuck out. My hair was so red, so bushy. In school, kids used to pick on me. It was bad. They'd write terrible things inside my textbooks. But I couldn't tell Mother. Daddy had died and she was devastated. She was so pretty, so elegant and refined—I was humiliated by what was happening to me.

"Eventually, I got braces and discovered a flat-iron. By the time I got to college, I fit in, more or less. But on the inside, I always expected the tables to turn. To do something or appear in some way that would send people after me again, like a pack of hyenas. It was easier to fade into the background, not draw attention to myself. I got so good at acting like a ghost that I became one. Reggie is the only man who ever paid me attention, and it was for all the wrong reasons. Until you."

Archer ground his teeth so his jaw didn't slam onto her floor. To stand here and listen to the most beautiful woman he'd ever set eyes on tell him that she was an ugly duckling didn't compute. She wasn't a ghost. She was a living flame. If men stayed away, it's probably because her looks intimidated them. Hell, they intimidated him too, but then he'd never had a problem playing with fire.

The imprint of her kiss burned into his body.

Tonight he came here to get her outside her head, to stop her thinking, to make her feel instinctively what they had here. This kind of chemistry just doesn't happen. He should know.

She set her hand on his chest and gave a little push. "I need you to leave."

"Eden—"

"Edie," she corrected. "I'm not sure what to think

about you, but earlier you said you weren't here for one thing."

"That's right. I'm not looking for a one-night stand with you."

"Then prove it and go home. Archer, please," her voice broke on his name.

He had her, even if she didn't realize it yet. She wanted him the same way he wanted her. If he pushed tonight, he could have her body.

But that would ruin everything, only serve to confirm her suspicions. This was a long game. He had to go slow if he wanted her heart in the bargain.

He leaned forward and she glanced up, lips parting. Damn it. He went for her forehead instead. His mouth smoothed away her worry wrinkles.

"I hate to leave you like this, but I'll go. Sweet dreams, Freckles."

And then he did the hardest thing he'd ever done in his life.

He went home to his empty bed.

Chapter Thirteen

EDIE FLOWED ALONG with the cheerful crowd pouring into the Brightwater Rodeo Grounds for the Fourth of July town celebration. The banner strung over the bandstand read "Welcome to California's Biggest Little Fireworks." A few pies were in the oven back at Haute Coffee, a little risky, but unthinkable to miss her first official small-town event. A half hour couldn't hurt when she was right down the block. She shifted the plate of cookies to one hand, and rolled her wrist, sore from kneading. If anything, the coffee shop's second day exceeded the first. She should be grinning ear to ear, heels clicking, and turning cartwheels, but instead unsettling images kept flitting through her mind.

The way Archer's lips worked across her breasts until she could barely see straight.

How his fingers pulsed and rolled against her sensitive skin in a rhythm that was gentle, wicked perfection.

Who needed fireworks when mere memories threatened to detonate her insides?

She squeezed her eyes shut, still feeling the slide of his tongue over hers as she came in a white-hot flash.

Stick a fork in me. I'm done.

But all those skillful moves had been honed somewhere. Still, Archer didn't hide his womanizing past. He wasn't a liar, except for when calling her stunning and gorgeous. No one had ever spoken such words to her and he made them sound convincing—too convincing. Who knew what he saw when looking at her, but it didn't appear to be untamed carrot-colored hair, a lack of sexy curves, or the surplus of freckles.

When his gaze locked with hers, she truly felt beautiful.

So why couldn't she believe it outside the moment?

The rodeo grounds were packed. People waved as she walked by, so many familiar faces. There was the electrician who did a fantastic job retrofitting the shop. His wife swore she'd never liked coffee until she'd tried Edie's brew. Then there was Old Fred, up on the stage, playing polka tunes on his ancient-looking accordion. This morning, he'd leaned across the counter and whispered that her pies tasted better than his wife's, making her pinky-promise never to repeat his confession.

Quincy was off on a business trip, probably for the best. If her cousin was here, they'd likely end up alone, sipping champagne from his gourmet hamper and ignoring curious stares as townsfolk covertly eyed the richest man in town.

Nicer to be plain old anonymous Edie Banks.

The potluck tables groaned under the weight of casseroles, salads, and desserts. She veered in that direction. Locals at the coffee shop made it clear the fireworks were synonymous with food and everyone contributed. She set her plate of peanut butter chocolate chip cookies down and surveyed the various goodies. There were a few questionable Jell-O salad molds, a yummy looking fruit salad, and some promising brownies. A cheesecake sat in an adorable daisy Pyrex dish. It looked tasty, but no one had cut so much as a piece. Strange. She leaned in and read the label printed on a small chalkboard label, "Avocado Lime Cheesecake."

She gave an inward wince. While the offering received points for creativity, avocado? In dessert? That seemed like an automatic no. Still, she bit her lip, considering— what made a cheesecake truly delicious was the creamy factor. What if the avocado amped that aspect?

Oh, no point dithering, be brave and give it a taste.

She cut herself a whisper-thin slice and people stared as she took a tentative bite. It was a little hard to chew under their direct stares, but everyone seemed genuinely interested in her reaction.

"How is it?" a woman muttered from across the table. "Kooky Carson's daughter made that."

Edie carefully swallowed. She didn't have a clue who Kooky Carson was, but she knew delicious when she tasted it. "The flavor is . . . wow, absolutely fantastic."

"Are you serious?" another woman asked. "Because the ingredients—"

"They might be unorthodox but trust me, this cheesecake is amazing." She gave a wicked smile. "I don't care if none of you believe me because that means more for my plate!" She cut herself a bigger piece.

A few other women crept in and cut small pieces. "If Edie says it's good, it must be," one said defensively to her skeptical friend.

A warmth spread through Edie's chest. It was a testament to a job well done if they thought she had good taste after Haute Coffee was open for only two days. "Who made this? I really need to get the recipe."

"Annie Carson." A woman pointed in the direction of a pretty petite blonde. The same woman who'd visited the coffee shop on opening day with Archer's brother, Sawyer. She was a blogger and had a cute style sense. The two of them sat together with her young son and Edie's heart warmed to see them all burst out laughing, clearly having good time. Maybe this woman could be a friend. She baked like a dream and shared similar taste in men. Sawyer possessed the same handsome features as his brother, although he always looked more serious, whereas Archer possessed those endearing dimples.

The memory of his hot kiss and clever hands . . . oh Lord. She shoved another bite of cheesecake in and, looking back, saw Annie's pan was empty. Better to walk it over and compliment the chef before melting into a pool of sexual frustration.

ARCHER CAME TO the fairgrounds with one intent—to find Edie. He'd spent the whole day feeling as if he could reach up and touch the big blue sky. He'd kissed her. Made her drop her elegant poise and ride him wild, eyes like quicksilver, hair like fire. She had to be here. No one in Brightwater missed the biggest night on the social calendar. Guess he had his internal GPS set to Freckles because there she was, chatting with Annie Carson and Sawyer.

Jesus. Imagine Edie and Annie becoming friends. He and Sawyer were on the slow-train to Screwed Town with these two beautiful women, but something told him they'd both arrive with great big grins.

He waited until she walked away and then approached. "Hey." His heart leapt at the flash in her gaze. *Hey? That's the best you've got, slick?* Her pale green tank top, jean skirt, and strappy sandals didn't allow his brain to articulate beyond a base level. *The beautifullest woman in the world*—it wasn't a word, but it should be . . . with her picture next to it in the dictionary.

There needed to be a whole new language to describe Freckles.

"Hi," she said, crossing her arms. The swell of her breasts rose above her tank top. He'd tasted every inch of them last night and his mouth watered at the memory.

"You know Annie Carson?" Archer asked. Looked like his big brother was losing no time in reeling back in the one who go away.

"She visited my shop on opening day and it turns out she's a pretty great baker. Her methods are quirky and yet she pulls it off. I like her. She seems sort of stressed . . . but funny."

"My brother's always carried a torch for her."

"I can see that," she said thoughtfully. "They seem so different and yet complement each other."

They stood in silent awkwardness as a country band began to set up the equipment on the grandstand.

"So—" he said, just as she went, "About yesterday."

They both laughed.

"Ladies first," he said, tipping his hat.

She brushed her hair out of her eyes and straightened. "I've done some thinking. It was initially a shock to discover you're the local bad boy, but maybe I was a little hasty to judge—"

"Hey, Archie!" A sultry voice piped behind him. Holly Higsby, a pretty black-haired woman sashayed close, wiggling her fingers in her customarily cutesy greeting. "Whatcha doin'? Wanna go repeat history?" She leaned in and set her lips against his ears. "We had a bang up time last Fourth, remember?"

He loosely remembered a twelve-pack, a party, and a warm body.

"Sorry." He stepped back and closer to Freckles. "I'm . . ." *Taken? Possessed? Locked up with the key thrown away?*

Before he could find the right words, Holly glanced to Freckles, taking her in with a rueful smile. "I see, your dance card's full for the night." She gave his hat a playful tip. "Well, call me next time you're free. Don't be a stranger."

He gritted his teeth and forced his gaze to Edie. "Sorry for the interruption. I really want to hear what you were saying."

"I . . ." She bit her lip. "I forget."

"Quit it." He set a hand on her shoulder. "I'm into you, okay? *You.* Only you. I'm all up to my ears with the idea of you."

Edie squared her shoulders. "But be realistic, *Archie*," she said. "What am I supposed to think about our situation? Our skill sets are totally unmatched. You play the field. I'm still in the dugout trying to figure out the rules."

"Don't kid yourself, sweetheart. You passed second base last night like one of the big leaguers."

She ducked her head, but not before shooting him a naughty smile that clenched his chest. "So what are you saying? You want to coach me to a home run?"

Archer coughed into his fist. "Jesus. What if I told you, you're the only one in the game, the only one I want to play with?"

She blinked. "I'm not sure what to do. That's the honest truth. When we first met, I thought you were a good guy."

His blood cooled a few degrees. "And now you don't?"

"You're the right guy for a little fun. But I'm not sure that's what I want. I'm not built that way. To hook up and move on."

"You aren't a hookup. I have nothing to say against any of those other woman . . . except for one thing."

She frowned. "What's that?"

"They aren't you."

Her posture relaxed. "Last night was amazing. I haven't"—her voice dropped to a whisper—"you know, had that happen in a long time."

"Really?" The idea hit him square in the chest. He gave

her pleasure, and he could do it again. And again. Every night, forever.

"Maybe that's my whole purpose in life," he said, realizing it was probably true.

She laughed at that, as if he was joking.

He could give her pleasure, that was easy, but he had a hell of a lot more inside to share. "Here's the thing, Freckles. I'd like to get you on my team, but the only game I want to play is one where I'm gunning for keeps."

Edie's eyes widened. If she could be candid, why not him? At least now there was no mistaking his intentions. Her gaze darted to the crowd, unable or unwilling to accept the truth. He'd have to convince her.

But, hell, what was he going to do? If he made a move now, after the Holly run in, she'd end up pigeonholing him. The same way Grandma did, and Sawyer, and hell, the whole damn town. He'd dug the hole damn deep, now he had to climb out, for her.

If he said he wasn't that guy anymore, she'd never believe him. No one would. Words don't mean squat without action. The band started playing a sweet country song.

"Come dance with me," he said impulsively.

She fiddled with her hair. "A few pies are still in the oven back at the shop. I have to set them to cool before the fireworks."

"Just one song." He needed time with her, time for her to see how right they could be.

"You don't take no for an answer, huh?"

He leveled her a straight look. "Sure, I do. But notice, Freckles, you haven't given me one." He leaned closer and whispered in her ear. "Relax, it's a dance in front of hundreds of people. What's the worst that can happen?"

"I . . . but . . . you . . . me . . . oh, what the heck. One dance." She reached out and took his hand. "But no funny business."

Nothing about this situation was funny, and yet, strangely he couldn't wipe the ear-to-ear smile off his face. He led her to the de facto dance floor, hard-packed earth where other couples swayed to the music as the summer sun sank, putting on a show of pale pinks and rich orange. It felt good doing this, gathering Edie up in his arms in front of the whole town.

"Anyone ever tell you that your hair matches the sunset?"

She dropped her head. "No."

Her body stiffened and he had that feeling again, the one that baffled him. How did this woman not know how lovely she was? Why hadn't a man snapped her up and treated her like a queen? Were the guys in New York that blind? He leaned in and her fingers tightened on his shoulders. "You want to know a secret?"

"Okay?"

He cupped her cheek. "You belong under the open skies, beneath these mountains, prettier than any wildflower." And the way she fit against him, he knew, sure as anything he'd ever felt, that they belonged together.

A hint of a shy smile danced across her lips, even as her earnest eyes darkened with yearning. "It feels strange to hear you talking about my looks."

"Well, you're a lot more than that gorgeous face,

Freckles. Anyone can compliment your features, but your beauty runs deeper. There is sweetness to you, but also fire . . ." He realized he'd been staring and for who knows how long. The sound he made was almost a groan. "I'm talking crazy."

"If that's true, then I like your brand of it." She rested her head oh so softly on his chest and damn she felt good. He wanted nothing more than to be able to hold her forever, to be able to make her feel more amazing and wanted. The sweet love song washed over them as they kept time with the gentle sway of their bodies.

All too soon, the song ended, changing to a wild honky-tonk beat. Edie didn't immediately step away. "My pies," she said uncertainly.

He understood what she was really saying. She needed space. Time to think, and he'd give it to her. "You go on." He adjusted his hat. "I'm going to head home myself." He didn't want her to think he'd be chasing skirt the minute she turned her back. "Go and take care of your pies and I'll see you soon." He flicked a piece of hair off her neck, smiling at her shiver when he ran his thumb over her skin. "Very soon."

Her answering blush crept down her neck, heading to all sorts of interesting places.

As he strode toward the exit, women called out soft hellos, asked what he was up to later. They were offers, and he'd once been a kid in a candy store with a heck of a sweet tooth. But now all he craved was something more satisfying, something that would be good for him.

He could be good for Eden too.

But how could he convince her that he was ready to be a one-woman man?

The thought plagued him the whole drive home. Back at Hidden Rock, Grandma's porch light glowed. She must be the only person in town not at the show. Better go check and make sure everything was okay.

Music poured through the open bay window, the record player going full volume, playing her favorite song, Margaret Whiting's "Guilty." Normally this kind of old-timey music cheesed him out, but tonight his heart melted faster than gouda on a hot day. Here was another tune he could imagine dancing to with Freckles.

He opened the screen door. Grandma sat in a parlor chair, tea in hand, watching the sun sink behind Mount Oh-Be-Joyful.

"Grandma?" he called softly.

She started, pressing a hand to her heart. "Glory be, you frightened the bejeezus out of me." Her previously dreamy expression faded as her thin eyebrows contracted. "What are you doing?"

"Came to ask you the same thing." Archer glanced around. This room hadn't changed since he was a kid. The only difference was the number of blue ribbons hanging from the mantel, victories won by Grandma's prize-winning tomatoes at the County Fair. "Why aren't you at the rodeo grounds?"

"Bah." Grandma swatted the empty air. "I haven't been to the fireworks in over a decade."

Was that true? Not that he kept track of Grandma's every movement, but hell, never to have noticed?

"When you get to my age, waking each new day is like its own firework." She paused and let out a rattling cough. "I don't need more excitement."

Archer sat on her plastic-covered couch and glanced to the side table illuminated by a candle. He'd seen Grandma's silver-framed wedding photo countless times, but this was the first he'd ever really looked at it. A much younger, black-and-white Grandma smiled in a way he'd never seen, her hair shiny, thick, and dark, half covered by a veil, her arms clasping a bouquet that spilled blossoms in all directions. A bearded man lovingly returned the adoring expression. His grandfather. A man who died when Archer's own father was a boy.

Then history went and repeated itself when Grandma's only son, his father, died in a house fire. Archer was too little to remember any details. Sawyer said he could only recall flashes. Wilder might know more, but his oldest brother was famously closed-lipped.

"You were pretty, Grandma," Archer said. "Not that you aren't still but—"

"I was, wasn't I?" Grandma said musingly. "Though I didn't know it at the time. Always thought my nose was too big, or that I was too tall. Like Olive Oyl. Beauty is wasted on the young."

The same way Freckles didn't see her beauty . . . but he did.

"How did you meet Grandpa Kane?" Archer asked.

She gave him a curious look. "None of you boys has ever asked."

Really? Grandma was part of his day-to-day life, but

come to think of it, he didn't know much about her, as a person, at all. "Did you know right away that he was the one?"

"Love at first sight is a bunch of baloney," Grandma said before grinning. "And yet, that's exactly how it went. My pa owned a service station in the Central Valley and your Grandpa pulled in for fuel. I was helping out behind the counter for some reason or another and our eyes met through his windshield. I knew at that moment my whole life would change." Her laugh was unfamiliar, soft and even tender. "Jack stuck around for the morning. His tire suddenly got a flat. It wasn't until much later that he confessed he stuck a nail in it. Then his engine wouldn't go. Again, he sabotaged it. Just to buy more time with me. I can remember thinking, *There is the handsomest man I've ever seen, and boy does he have bad luck with cars.*"

Archer joined in her chuckle. "So love at first sight can be real?" It seemed important to know this all of a sudden.

Grandma leveled a bone-cutting gaze, as if she lasered through his thick skull and read his mind. "It can be, but for most people, it's hormones. Nothing more."

Yeah, well, he knew all about hormones, and that's not what was happening here. "Hey, thanks for telling me that story."

"We danced to this song at our wedding, you know." She waved her finger back and forth as if conducting her own big band orchestra. "Today was our wedding anniversary."

"Oh, wow, Grandma. Congratulations."

The bright spark in her gaze dimmed. "We were only married for five years, but I've never been able to look at another man." She dabbed her eyes and blew her nose. "Oh, go on and get. Feel free to ignore the ramblings of a sentimental old woman."

Archer stood and held out his hand. "May I have this dance?" Here was yet another woman in his life that needed more cherishing and not being taken for granted.

Grandma stared at him. "Have you lost your ever-loving mind?"

"Maybe, but the offer is a firm one." He could do this, appreciate her, give her a moment to connect with her past.

"I haven't danced in fifty-five years."

"Well, no time like the present."

She rose and he drew her close as old-timey music filled the room.

"Grandma, you have moves," he said, surprised to find her so nimble.

She craned her neck at him. "You're a great deal like your grandfather. You both could charm the habit off a nun."

And for once, there was real affection in her tone.

Chapter Fourteen

AFTER HER FOURTH of July run-in with Archer, Eden poured all her energy into baking. Last night she catered an event for Quincy and her phone had rung off the hook with party requests all morning. Beating eggs and butter didn't ease sexual frustration per se, but it did give her an outlet that saved her from spontaneous sexual combustion. She stayed busy all day, but even while she juggled the million and twenty "to dos" in her mind, some part of her grey matter was focused on Archer at all times.

Rather than fighting her attraction, might as well admit she was totally gaga for a cowboy who had no idea what a Windsor knot was, let alone how to tie one. And that idea didn't bother her. Instead, all she wondered was why she dismissed cowboys for so long.

Maybe she should buy shares in Wrangler. There's a company to take to the bank, quality assured.

She stepped out the back door and locked up the shop.

The hairs on the back of her neck rose. She spun around, sensing someone behind her.

Archer stood there, holding a brown paper bag stamped "Save-U-More."

"You scared me," she gasped.

He leveled a lopsided smile. "I seem to have that effect on people lately."

"You've been grocery shopping?" She was making lame conversation, but only because her blood flow diverted to between her legs leaving her brain cells to die off in rapid numbers.

He shifted the bag in his arms. "Figured you baked all day. How about I make you dinner?"

She gaped at him. "You want to cook me dinner?"

"Well," he peered uncertainly into the bag. "Yeah. I thought you might like crepes with sautéed bananas and chocolate or is that too much sweetness for dinner?" He glanced up and grinned at her wide-eyed stare. "Grandma used to make a meal roster for me and my brother, and we each had to take shifts. I was the only one who took to it. I don't do it much on my own, but I can cook, if given the right inspiration."

Her smile threatened to split her cheeks. "I love crepes. Chocolate and bananas are my jam, unless we're talking about raspberry or blueberry preserves."

She led him up the narrow outdoor stairs to her apartment, very aware that her butt was shoved right in his face. She might have swayed her hips a little, but it was hard not to. He'd come and offered to make her a home-cooked meal? No one had ever willingly done that.

Mother hadn't even made her own toast.

When they entered her apartment, he glanced around. "Didn't see much besides you the other night," he said.

His gaze slowly scanned her walls and cobbled-together second-hand furnishings, an act almost as intimate as when it fell on her exposed body. Free to choose her own furnishings for the first time, she favored an eclectic vintage look. The old rocking chair from an estate sale was positioned to catch the early-morning light and the old tourism posters for Yosemite National Park and Mono Lake came from the library's gift shop. She'd ordered Mother's home in New York to be closed up, but requested a few precious knickknacks be sent.

Archer walked toward one now, running his hand over the engraved wooden box set on the side table. "I like this."

"It's a music box. Daddy gave it to me when I was a girl."

He opened it up and a song played. "I know this tune . . . but can't place it."

" 'Edelweiss,' " Edie said softly. "He used to sing to it before tucking me in at night." Her stomach gave a funny little flip-flop. Archer had tucked her in once at that Nevada motel, the first time she really glimpsed his innate tenderness. "It's been a long time. He died when I was in high school."

"You miss him."

"A lot." She was quiet a moment before walking over. "There used to be a ballerina inside that would spin to the music. I used to dance as a kid but was never anything approaching talented. Two left feet. But he knew I loved it. He'd take me to the New York City Ballet a few times every year, *Swan Lake, Nutcracker*, all the classics."

Archer brushed his thumb over the small hole. "That's where the ballerina fit?"

"Yes. While I was at NYU, Mother went out of town to spend the spring in France. It was the last time she ever willingly left the apartment. Reggie convinced me to have a party. I had never hosted one, didn't have many friends, even at my university, but he made it sound easy. And I trusted him. Should have learned my lesson then." She gave a rueful smile. "People came I didn't know. Many of them children of rich, famous, powerful people. Things got out of control.

"I never found the ballerina. The box was left on the floor, open, the jewelry inside stolen. But I didn't care about any of that. I cared about the ballerina. It was a part of my connection to my father that is forever lost." She shut the lid again and rubbed the hairline crack over the lid.

He reached out and rubbed the back of her neck with a strong hand, working out the deep aches.

"That's nice." She relaxed into him and he kept it up, and soon she felt looser, more comfortable, rolling her neck back and forth. "Thank you. I feel wonderful."

"Glad to help," he said. "Making you feel wonderful is a job well done in my book. Now let me get those groceries unpacked."

She followed him to the kitchen. He lifted out an old recipe box from the bag.

"Where'd you get this?" she asked, running her finger over the yellow tin lid. Images of fruits and vegetables were stamped on the side in a cross-stitch sample pattern.

Archer shuffled his feet. "Grandma gave it to me back when I was a kid. I copied down old family recipes as I learned to cook them."

Edie's smile grew. "May I have a look inside? I'm wildly curious."

" 'Course." He rubbed the back of his neck. "You don't . . . think a guy cooking is unmanly, do you? I used to really like it, but people gave me shit about it once I got to high school so I sort of quit."

"Are you kidding? I can't think of anything hotter," she said honestly. "In fact, did you know that humans are basically hardwired to equate food with love? The digestive system produces hormones that act on the hippocampus, a part of the brain that plays a key role in memory."

He didn't look at her like she was crazy. Instead something in his gaze flickered. "That's exactly what I liked about it. Made me remember happy times or even feel as if I was creating a new memory."

She opened the lid and pulled out the first card, sighing inwardly at the earnest childish script. "Bacon Potato Salad, okay, sorry, but that one wouldn't be my favorite."

Archer grinned, his gaze a little distant. "Maybe not, but my big brother Wilder used to hog it every time it was served at a meal. Grandma used to be able to bribe him to do extra chores the day it was on the menu."

She flicked through the cards. "Irish Stew. Cornmeal

Oven Fried Chicken. Jelly Thumbprint Cookies. Dutch Apple Pie. Wait—Turkey Gravy? Dried Apple Stuffing? You know how to make all of this?"

"I . . . uh . . ." He cleared his throat. "I helped Grandma do holiday meals or anytime my brothers or one of the workers had a birthday."

"Archer." She set a hand on his upper arm, the muscle hard underneath. The center of this big, strong man was soft, caring, and loving—a dangerous combination that she found herself powerless to resist. "This box is really special. Thank you for sharing it with me. I've always had this funny little picture in my head of someday having a big homemade holiday dinner with many of these same dishes you grew up preparing."

His gaze searched her face. "I'd love to do that, spend Thanksgiving or Christmas cooking for you."

The image in her head, the vague one of a man next to her at a family table, sharpened into clear focus, his face an identical match to the one staring down at her.

"Hey, you look a little tired." He said gently. "Why don't you take a shower? I've got the dinner handled."

Good idea, if only to have some alone time to calm her racing pulse. When she emerged twenty minutes later, a faint burning smell clung to the air.

"Everything okay?" she asked, opening another window.

He grimaced. "Turns out I'm a little rusty. Maybe it was performance anxiety."

The plate next to the stove was filled with blackened dough.

She giggled.

"I wanted to impress you."

"I'm impressed," she answered truthfully, touched he cared to make the effort. "Want me to take over?"

"No!" He held up a hand, a look of determination crossing his face. "I want to do this for you."

She glanced over at the other ingredients he had on the counter. Powdered sugar. A canister of whipped cream. Old Eden would never suggest the idea occurring to her.

Old Eden could suck an egg.

"Come here," she murmured.

He cleared his throat. "What about dinner?"

"I said come here."

"I came over to show you that I respect you."

"And I appreciate the sentiment." She unbuttoned her top button. "Now, kindly start disrespecting me immediately."

"Damn it," he growled. "I knew this about you the first time we met."

She paused, uncertain. "What's that?"

His eyes darkened. "You're trouble." He crossed the room and hiked her against him so they were belly to belly. "You're not hungry?"

"On the contrary, I'm starving." She worked open his belt buckle, undid the waist button, then the next and paused. "Oh. You go commando?"

"Most of the time."

She popped the last button. "That's . . . convenient."

"That's what I thi—aw, fuck."

She fell to her knees, taking hold off his shaft. He was hard, and the way his abs flexed when she touched him sent a surge of excitement through her. She held him steady and licked his tip, enjoying the flavor of warm clean skin and the faint hint of salt.

"You taste good," she said.

"Bet you taste better," he ground out.

The idea of his mouth working between her legs made her grind her thighs, her silk panties suddenly slick. "Here's something you should know about me." She grabbed the can of whipped cream, popping the lid with a naughty smile. "I'm an eat-dessert-first kind of gal."

She squirted a dollop along his shaft and his laugh was a hoarse bark. This was fun. And it was about to get a whole lot more so. She wrapped her mouth around his head and sucked slow, letting him fill her mouth inch by inch. The cream was sweet and she took her time licking him clean, trailing her tongue along his thick vein. She glanced to his face, and he stared down through hooded lids, his features tight.

"You look fucking gorgeous doing that." He had the exact same expression people wore when at the Met enjoying priceless works of art.

She removed her mouth long enough to say, "You look gorgeous getting it."

He was big so it was hard to reach his base, but she wanted to, she had an overwhelming need to take as much of this strong yet strangely vulnerable part of him as far inside her as possible. Never had she understood the appeal of giving head before, but it all made sense now. This wasn't a passive act, the mindless and demeaning role of letting him ram her face. Instead, she was in charge, had the power to actively deliver pleasure. Slowly, her confidence grew as his head rocked back, the thick powerful chords in his neck standing in sharp relief through the day-old scruff.

Farther she sank, until his abdominal muscles flexed against her forehead and she breathed deep, inhaling his deep, rich male scent. As she pulled back slowly, he returned his gaze to her face, his eyes dark.

He reached and took her by the shoulders, pulling hard enough that she got to her feet in one quick move. His thumbs hooked into her yoga pants, yanked them down, and she kicked them off soundlessly, before removing her camisole.

"No bra," he said with approval.

She glanced down at her bare chest. "Nope."

"You're killing me here."

"Sorry. Not sorry." She couldn't restrain the grin, or the shameless, lovely warmth lapping between her legs like a slow-moving wildfire. She was naked, utterly exposed while he was mostly dressed, except for his open low-hanging jeans, framing his immense erection.

"You sure you want to do this?" he asked.

Her hand went out and embraced his thick, hard warmth. "Yes," she murmured, drunken, dazed. "So much."

He spanned the small of her back with one hand and drew her close, his other hand reaching down, fingers sliding into her wetness. "You're not lying."

She shook her head shyly. "I liked what I did to you before. It turned me on." The act had flipped a switch inside her, the lingering jolt of electricity still sparked through her nerves.

"I more than liked it, I fucking loved it." He braced her face between his hands, giving her a searching look. "What are you doing to me?"

She knew then, that despite any doubts she might have later, about him and other women, there was something happening here, inside her, inside him, unlike anything either of them had experienced. Her brain's circuitry rewired as he removed a leather wallet, plucking a condom from inside.

She tugged on his Western-shirt's metal-clasp buttons, a bit of pressure and they popped open, revealing pecs dusted with dark hair. More buttons yielded hard abs, a narrow, trim waist, and at last a thick arrow of hair extending all the way down.

After he sheathed himself, he looked up, chest rising and falling. His strong features were surprisingly vulnerable.

She looped her arms around his neck. "I want it. You want it."

He hiked one of her legs, settling it next to his thigh. She urged him higher, with enough flexibility to half circle his waist. He held most of her weight and the position brought him into easy contact. From the way his jaw clenched and his ragged breath caught in his throat, he must be trying to go slow, take his time here, with this, with her. But this wasn't the moment for anything measured or gentle. She loved that he offered it, but right now the barriers needed obliterating. She wanted to reduce herself to pure need.

"Don't hold back," she whispered.

Something shifted in his features, his straight brows contracting over his bright deep-set eyes as if he understood, with those three small words, exactly what she asked for.

He claimed her and her mouth in one swoop. Her fingers dug into his hard bicep and the cool silver from his belt buckle pressed into her hip. There was a warm, pleasurable pressure inside as she adjusted around his thickness, and she squeezed as if to grip him closer. He grunted and she did it again, loving she could do this, drive this passionate, wild man to the brink. His kiss grew increasingly hungry as she arched her spine, sliding him that last fraction of the way home. It was the same instinct as when he was in her mouth, of needing him, all of him. She could die from this greed maybe, and she wouldn't regret a thing. That's how he made her feel. As if she needed more, even as he gave so much. With every thrust he pushed her closer to the point where she couldn't take any more, only craving to be sent flying over the side.

He changed rhythm, less urgent, slower, relentless strokes.

"Look at me," he ground out.

His gaze was fierce concentration, every line on his face hard. Sweat beaded his hairline as he dipped, set his lower lip on the sensitive skin between her jaw and ear, and slid toward her chin. She shook, and so did he, their

bodies trembling against each other. He grabbed a fist-
ful of her hair, tugging her head back enough to mouth
her collarbone, sucking her skin as if she was a delicious
thing he'd never get enough of.

And there it went, the last shred of her self-control. *Oh
God. Oh God.* "Oh God," she cried out when he slammed
into her harder. Then, he flipped her around, running his
arm over the counter, clearing a space in one fell sweep.

Things fell on the ground. A crash. She didn't care.
He bent her against the cool tile and was back, warm,
inside her. His thrusts grew erratic, but when he slid his
hand around, and rubbed her clit, that tempo was even,
designed to drive her forward with him. He leaned closer,
not enough to crush her with weight, but to let his bare
skin skim hers, and she tossed her hips back, desperate,
restless, needing them both to fall apart and see what was
inside.

The pleasure built and this was it, the point of no-
return, the absolute peak of pleasure, she couldn't take
any more, not a single bit, until she did, and then everything burned down to a pure white heat.

Chapter Fifteen

EDEN RESTED ON the sofa, safe and silent in Archer's strong arms, reveling in this moment of perfect peace. Her body was shaped as if it had been designed for him, her swells and dips fitting into his hollows. In sleep, his face looked even more boyish, an innocent openness. This wasn't the guy who tore through women like Kleenex, discarding them once used. She knew the stories, but how he looked at her, touched her, moved inside her told a different tale, one of a guy hungry for love and a real, intimate connection.

Her phone buzzed on the coffee table and she reached to turn it off. She didn't want any interruption detracting from this moment. She turned it over to run her thumb over the screen and power it down before freezing. It was a text from Reggie.

Maybe you think I'm playing games. I'm not. Call to discuss payout terms otherwise this photo will be online by the end of the week and attributed to you. Just like old times?

There was a picture of a naked woman on all fours. Her long red hair hung over her face, masking her features. Reggie smiled into a mirror as he held up a camera phone, getting both the angle of his penetration and his smug face into the shot. It wasn't Eden, but a close approximation. She'd never done . . . that.

Never even considered doing *that*.

He threatened her with humiliation, knowing her past with that awful MySpace photograph from high school.

The hard-won precious peace from a moment ago vanished in a foul flash. She gripped the phone, weighing the impulse to hurl it against the wall, smash it into a thousand pieces. But that wouldn't make this situation stop. Why did Reggie need to stoop to this level? She'd never been anything but kind to him, believed they were friends, was prepared to make him her life partner at one point. Now that idea held only horror.

Archer stirred in his sleep and the small shift allowed the evening air to enter between their bodies, spreading cool fingers along her spine. She had trusted Archer to take her from Vegas, not to cause her harm in the seedy motel, trusted him later with her friendship and now her body. But was this wise? It appeared her Trust-O-Meter had a serious malfunction.

She punched out a quick response—*Why are you doing this?*—and hit send before she could debate whether or not such a course of action was wise. Perhaps engaging was a mistake, but Reggie wasn't a man off the street. A stranger. Even so, it didn't matter. He still threatened to destroy her life with a false image.

None of this made sense. If he needed money, why hadn't he ever asked? She would likely have helped if he was in real trouble, that is, if he wasn't involved in anything illegal or immoral. Which now appeared highly suspect.

The phone buzzed. *$5,000,000 by Friday or the photo is online. Show anyone and the photo is online. You may tweak your name but you can't hide. I'll make sure everyone knows it is you. When you're ready to do the wire transfer contact 555-423-4956 for the bank account.*

She dropped the phone on the floor. Suddenly, Archer's body behind her was too much, as was the smell of sex clinging to their bodies. Reggie found a way to spoil everything. She couldn't lie here another second. Sliding out from under Archer's bracing arm, she stood and padded to the shower. As hot as she got the water, for as long as she scrubbed, she'd never be able to cleanse herself from the situation's stink.

ARCHER STIRRED, OPENING his eyes. The apartment was quiet. During their crazy monkey sex, he'd tipped a bag of flour that had split on impact with the floor. A light dusting of flour spread across the kitchen floor, following them to the couch. He smiled and stretched. Jesus, each muscle felt newly made. No ache in his back or his heart. Never had he had sex like that, sex tied to deeper feelings, to the powerful question "what if this is a game changer, the woman that you'll fall in forever love with?"

Such a heavy idea didn't scare the shit out of him. In fact, there was nothing scary about being close to Freckles. He couldn't get enough.

He smiled, hearing the shower run. Soon, she would be out, nice and clean, and he'd have to go make her dirty again. He nestled into the pillow, remembering the breathy noises she made, the wicked gleam in her eye as she pulled out the whipped cream. He'd called it all right. She was a wild one at heart. He chuckled and closed his eyes as sleep rose and dragged him back down into vanilla-filled dreams.

He woke with a jerk. Freckles walked into the kitchen, opened a closet and grabbed a broom. She gripped the handle so tight her knuckles were white. She startled, glancing toward him and then away, like she was ashamed of his nakedness, as if it were unwelcome.

What the hell?

He stood and slid on his jeans, buttoning the top button as he crossed the room.

"Let me do that," he said, reaching for the broom.

"That's fine." She jumped when his fingers grazed her hand. "I don't mind."

"Okay, I'll cook those crepes again."

"Don't worry about it."

She was shutting down right and left, and just after they'd cracked open to the point he wasn't sure he'd ever be the same again. This didn't make sense. "Hey . . ." He set a hand on her cheek, turning her face to his. "What's up? Talk to me."

She zeroed her gaze somewhere past his ear. "I—I—

look, that was good. Amazing. But let's keep things on the surface for now, okay? Don't feel like you need to stick around or anything. Let's keep to your regular routine."

My regular routine? "I don't feel like I need to do anything. I want to be close to you. We made love."

She flinched.

"Eden," he said intently. "What happened between us wasn't just sex and you know it."

She stepped free and began to sweep in furious strokes.

"Eden—"

"I didn't know." She whirled around, eyes misted. "I didn't know it would be like that. I didn't know it could be like that."

"So let me get this straight"—he stalked to his abandoned shirt and boots, shoving them both on—"you are freaking out because what happened was too good?"

"Good is fine. I was ready for good. I wanted good. But that, that was . . . mind-blowing. I can't keep my life simple with a blown mind. It's too much. You don't understand."

"Help me to see because this is all talking in circles."

"Things are too complicated." Her voice faltered and she swallowed hard. "I need to . . . be myself and sort a few things out." What if he saw that terrible picture and turned away? She thought she'd moved on from the trauma in her childhood, but all it took was one photograph to let her know the pain beneath the scars was still real. As much as she wanted to reach out to Archer, she was scared to trust him.

"What's complicated? There is no one else for me. There's not going to be anyone else. This is simple. Me. You. It works."

"Not everything is about you," she threw back. "I—I used you tonight. I wanted sex and got more than I bargained for. But now it's time for you to leave." Big words but she couldn't deliver them while holding his gaze.

She was lying. He knew in his bones these words were untrue. But why? "Leave?"

She walked to the front door and opened it. "I had a lot of fun, thanks for stopping by."

"Don't do this." *Please*. "Don't pretend this didn't mean anything."

"Go." She closed her eyes. "Don't make me beg you to go home. I can't bear to have you here."

"So to be clear, you are accusing me of being a player, but want to play me?"

She looked at him then, her silver eyes bright with pain.

Archer flinched, hating to see her in pain and unable to do nothing. "What is going on?"

"Please, go. Go!" she said louder. "Leave now. This was a mistake. I don't want to be in a relationship. You can't want to be in a relationship with me."

"I'll be the judge of that. You aren't giving me a chance or telling me what the hell happened. We've gone from the best sex I've ever had, to you throwing me out on my ass. I missed a memo along the way."

"The best sex . . ." She paused.

"Ever." He stepped forward. She was out of his league

but that fact couldn't keep him away. Nothing would stop him from trying to close the distance.

"Let me in," he said, reaching out. "Let me see inside. Tell me what's bothering you."

Her lips parted and for a moment it seemed the answer would be yes. Then her gaze shuttered and he felt like a kid, wanted to throw up his hands and say, "Please don't hurt me." Instead, he stood there, aware he was a big guy, and big strong guys aren't supposed to show weakness.

Fuck that. He kissed her forehead, then both her cheeks. Let her see he wanted to be the guy for her, the best guy, the guy that would help her carry whatever load threatened to crush her.

She turned away. "I'm sure you have someone else on your speed dial you can go to."

Whatever had split open inside his heart, iced over. "This isn't fine. Not by a long shot. This is a bunch of bullshit." He wanted to give Eden his best, but it didn't look like his best was good enough. "I'll go, but I'm only going to say this once more. Eden, I'm crazy about you. I'll wait. But the next time, you come to me. I can't do this again."

"Good night, Archer." A good night that sounded more like a goodbye.

It had been, but now the goodness was gone, replaced by the cold grip of disappointment. As the door shut there came a muffled sob.

All he could do was punch the wall. The hard brick split his knuckles and did nothing to dull the pain inside his chest.

He drove home in silence. Not listening to music, just

the low run of the engine. Maybe he should go talk to Sawyer. His older brother knew about women. At least more than he did. He'd been spending a lot of time with Annie Carson, their old flame reignited. No. He twisted his hands on the wheel.

Things went right for his brother, the same way they always did. But because Archer worked hard didn't mean he'd win. He could try his guts out, leave everything on the field and still lose. There were no guarantees. No promise that everyone could be a winner.

Outside, the moon reflected on the peaks. What did his ancestors think when they arrived in Brightwater, having crossed the Rockies, the desert, and the White Mountains to end at this insurmountable granite wall? Did they give up? No, they looked around at the new reality and made the best of the situation. They thrived despite the hardships.

Edie pushed him away but she had her reasons. And he was going to show her that those reasons were wrong. He might be the wrong guy, but she was wrong to think he'd walk away without a fight.

And maybe, just maybe, two wrongs would make a right.

"It is a fact universally acknowledged that the harder one tries not to think about Archer Kane, the more one can't help but think of Archer Kane," Edie murmured to herself, thrusting another dirty pan into the sink and giving it a vicious swipe.

She had wonderfully stupid sex with him, the most intense, magnificent, glorious sex. The kind of sex that made her look back on the sex she'd had previously and wag her finger saying, "Sex, you were doing it all wrong."

Talk about a recipe for disaster.

The only recipes she needed were the ones that would keep Haute Coffee bustling.

It had felt right, she had felt right, he had felt . . . exactly right, the part of her that she'd been missing. But then there was the threatening photo that was going to leak unless she paid the blackmail. She had that kind of money. She had that kind of money many times over, but there were lots of worthy places that could put that kind of sum to better use than padding slime-bag Reggie's pockets.

Her internal world might be a mess but at least the outside one was humming along nicely. The whir from the milk frothing up front made her smile. Tonight a live band would be playing, a popular indie bluegrass act called The Foggy Stringdusters that was en route to Los Angeles. People had been calling to check on the show all day from as far away as Reno.

With the busy night expected, she'd hired her first employee, Margot, Annie Carson's sweet stepdaughter, fresh out of high school. She'd worked at a coffee shop back in Portland and slotted in behind the counter as if she'd been there forever. Edie hadn't realized how great it would be to have the extra help until she didn't have to rush around like a chicken with her head cut off.

Maybe she could speak to a counselor at Brightwater

High School about setting up a work-training program with students once the fall term started. Local kids often hung around the one gas station in town, the Kum & Go where the K was predictably defaced on a regular basis. They needed more to do.

Her thoughts drew to the money sitting in her trust. Hmmm. She was in a lucky position to accomplish real good. Quincy's connection with media had potential too. In this remote location, perhaps also connecting kids with technology and media had potential. Annie Carson had been in earlier. She was a blogger and a nice, open-minded person. Perhaps she'd have ideas.

But would anyone talk to her if Reggie's photo leaked? She wasn't famous, but her family name was well-known and tabloids were attracted to salacious stories like mosquitos to fresh blood. It wouldn't take Sherlock Holmes to realize Eden Bankcroft-Kew was Edie Banks.

What if everyone stopped coming to the store? Laughed? Called her terrible names?

Stop.

Stop it.

Reggie wasn't going to win. Good would beat evil. She had to believe that even though it sounded like a fairytale. Quincy's work commitments took him to Europe and then on to Asia. Reggie made it clear he'd post the picture if she tried to get help. If he was stooping to such sleazy tactics, he must be getting desperate, but did that also mean more dangerous?

Archer might listen, but what if he didn't believe her? What if he saw that woman in the picture and it burned in his brain, warping his views? Right now when he looked at her, it was as if she were rare and special. The feeling was unique. Never in her life had she had such a relationship.

Even if she had consented to the physical act shown in the image, which she never would have done with Reggie, never in a million years, not in a billion, the idea of risking a change in Archer's view of her was scary. Did she really want to risk losing the magic, the idea he'd finally see there was something wrong with her? Judge or, worse, sneer?

But then, if he was that sort of guy, wouldn't it be better to know the truth despite the hurt?

Yes.

And no.

A sob hitched in her throat. Oh God, what was she going to do?

Someone screamed. There was the sound of a dish breaking.

"Edie!" Margot screamed out. "Quick, the mayor!"

Edie fled from the kitchen and there in the middle of her store, Thomas King, the mayor of Brightwater was choking. His hands grabbed his throat, eyes bulging. There were a handful of patrons but no one reacted, everyone stared in muted horror.

Edie didn't think, but moved fast, wrapping her arms around the mayor's midsection and joining her hands to give an in-and-up jerk. Nothing. Go again. She'd done a first-aid course during college but this was the real deal, not pretending with a partner or a dummy. Again, she tried, and again. On the fourth compression a piece of pie projected halfway across the shop and he doubled over coughing.

"Margot," she called. "A glass of water, please."

"I'll call for an ambulance," her assistant said, rushing around the counter with a glass of water.

The mayor cleared his throat. "I'll be fine, don't fuss. That pie was delicious and I ate it fast. Thank you, you saved my life."

"Please take a seat," Edie said. The few remaining patrons gawked.

"I'm fine," he said, shaking her off. "I'm more embarrassed than hurt." He left with a quick wink and a step that suggested a new lease on life.

Outside, a small crowd gathered by the front door. Marigold Flint crossed the street, a suspiciously pleased expression on her face. "What happened? I heard someone got food poisoning."

"No, there was an accident," Edie replied, coming outside.

"Sounds like Haute Coffee might be hazardous to your health."

A few people murmured, whether for Marigold's assertion or against was impossible to say. Too many eyes were on her. It was like in her youth, when she'd been ganged up on, people staring, jeering. She hated it.

Hated it.

"Why can't you leave me alone?" she said, her voice rising.

"Was it something I said?" Marigold threw her hands in the air, batting her eyes, the picture of false innocence.

"There is nothing wrong with the food I serve. The mayor choked—"

"Your food is so good that people are choking when they eat it?" Marigold's smile was triumphant.

"Please don't twist my words. That's not what I meant."

"The country fair is in a few weeks. May the best baker win." Marigold looked around at the crowd. "Must say, no one's ever choked in my establishment. Guess Haute Coffee is so amazing people are dying to get in."

Something snapped in Eden as quiet as a twig breaking in two. It was her self-control. "Why wait for the fair? I challenge you to our own bake off. You, me, right here on Main Street."

"A duel?"

"That's right." Dear Lord, did she really want to reenact a kitchen version of the O.K. Corral? No. But given the chance, bullies stomped all over you. Time to dig in and hope for the best. "You in?"

Marigold's jaw took on a determined lift. "You know it."

No choice but to saddle up and ride this scenario to the end. "One week from today, at high noon."

"How will we decide the winner?"

"We need judges."

"Impartial?" Marigold's eyes narrowed.

"You pick one. I pick one. And then there can be a wild card."

"Okay, okay . . . I nominate you." Marigold pointed at a blond older gentleman in the crowd. "Hank King." The local bigwig real estate agent and mayor's brother.

"Okay, I pick . . ." Eden scanned the crowd, but then

her gaze fell behind it to a woman walking up the street, regarding the crowd with a curious expression, holding a small child's hand. "Annie Carson. Are you okay with that?"

Annie pointed at her chest with a small smile. "What am I agreeing to?"

"Will you be a judge for me in a pie bake off?"

Annie didn't bat an eye at the strange request. "I've never met a dessert I didn't like. Sure, why not?"

"Who will be the wild card?" Marigold asked.

"Me!" came a voice from the back of the crowd. The bodies parted, or rather they were thrust aside by a steely-faced older woman, the same woman who had leveled such a scowl at Edie, the same woman she now knew was . . .

"Grandma Kane," Marigold's voice rang out victorious, clearly pleased to have another longtime Brightwater resident on her side. "Welcome to the bake off."

"I plan to be fair and impartial," Grandma said, folding her arms. "Should be easy, seeing as I don't particularly like either of you."

Marigold gasped, affronted, hand over her heart.

"Don't you play the innocent with me. I don't forget a slight against my family."

Vague intimations circulated hinting something once happened between Kit Kane and Marigold but Edie had no idea what. From the shuttered look on Marigold's face, she didn't want that particular cat getting out of the bag.

"As for you, missy." Grandma whirled on Eden, finger raised. "I don't like outsiders. I don't trust outsiders."

"Well, thank you very much for participating in the event." Edie forced a smile.

Grandma strode away and the crowd dissipated as Marigold stalked back toward The Baker's Dozen.

Edie stood, settling a hand against her neck, pulse racing beneath her fingers. Way to go with that big mouth. She'd built her own coffin. By publicly challenging Marigold to a duel next week, she had made herself more public. This was a small town but people used their computers and with the influx of LA types, there was a rising interest in celebrity news and online sites. People chatted in the shop about who was dating who, or who had recently been seen scouting for property in the valley.

What would they say if that sex picture went live? When the bake off rolled around would everyone come to throw eggs? Call her a whore? Or worse? As friendly as people had been, she was still firmly an outsider. And after Reggie's stunt, they might slam the door in her face permanently.

"Hey there, you okay?" Annie stood a few feet behind her.

"Yes, I'm fine." Edie's shoulders stooped. "Actually, no. I'm not."

Annie flashed a sympathetic smile. "I do the same thing. Why do women always say they are fine, no matter how cruddy their day is going? Is it that we don't want to burden each other with the truth or that we're supposed to be perfectly pleasant at all times?"

Edie sighed. "Both maybe?"

"Well, I hope you know you can be honest with me. I'm not perfect, never have been, and never will be."

"But you are perfectly you." Edie admired her yellow Peter Pan–collared tank top, high-waisted shorts, and retro sunglasses.

"What a sweet thing to say." Annie beamed. "Between you and me, sometimes I think I'm a perfect mess."

"Aren't we all?"

"I hope so." Annie threw back her head and laughed. "It would make me feel so much better."

"Can I ask you a question—a personal one?"

"Shoot." Annie's gaze turned curious.

"Grandma Kane—does she scare you?"

Annie looped her arm with Edie's. "Terrifies me, but I wonder if she's more bark than bite. Still, we women need to stick together. All we need is friendship, trust, and a little bit of the ol' pixie dust."

Edie smiled to herself. Maybe Annie was spot on. The trouble was that as much as she wanted to trust Archer with Reggie's terrible photograph, there wasn't enough pixie dust in the West to give her the courage.

Chapter Sixteen

ARCHER ARRIVED NEAR the end of The Foggy String-dusters set. The coffee shop was packed. The tables were cleared away and people on the dance floor jumped like hot cakes on the griddle. Edie and her new assistant, Margot, stood behind the counter, their heads bobbing to the quicktime beat of the upright bass. Archer leaned against the wall, taking the opportunity to enjoy Freckles unobserved. A stray lock of hair escaped her headband and she idly blew it away. His hands itched to take her lithe frame into his arms and lead her around the dance floor.

"For our last number we're going to slow things down," the lead singer crooned as a guitar started an intro.

A couple swayed a few feet away as the rest of the band joined in, the song a love ballad. Envy sucked. He wanted to share so much more than his bed with Edie. He wanted quiet moments too. He'd grown up without parents. His big brothers and Grandma loved him, but he'd never had the one thing Edie brought to his life. Tenderness. Peace. The kind that only comes when someone believes in your potential.

Edie didn't want him just for a good time, she saw deeper down to the man he was only now beginning to recognize inside. The man he'd been running from for years, scared as hell, which was stupid. What was frightening about stepping up and shouldering responsibility? Meaningless fun grew empty after a while.

A leopard might not be able to change its spots, but it could quit running aimlessly around the jungle, chasing any tail in sight. He wanted purpose. And the person who'd grown to mean more to him than anyone was right there.

Her gaze shifted, scanning the crowd, her left eyebrow raising a fraction as if sensing a stare. When her eyes finally locked on his, he started walking in her direction. Margot's mouth dropped and she turned away, busying herself with wiping down a spotless counter.

"Can I talk to you?" he said to Edie. "Alone?" When Grandma called to say that a package arrived in the mail, he took it as a sign to stop screwing around. He collected the small box, saddled up Philomena, and drove into town to go get the girl.

Her pupils dilated even as her spine stiffened. "I can't. I'm working."

Looked like the girl didn't want to be caught. The cold tone didn't match the hot flash in her gaze though. Something didn't add up.

He braced his hands on the counter. "It's important."

Her next breath lifted her small, sweet breasts, and she bit the corner of her lower lip before turning away. "Tomorrow is a big day. And . . . and . . . and . . ." She rubbed her temples. "I have a migraine coming on. I need to rest."

Margot glanced over. "You don't feel good? I was going to stay with you tonight, but if you're feeling sick, I'll go home."

"It's okay," Edie said glancing between them uncertainly.

Archer's jaw tightened. Edie was a terrible liar. There was no headache. Why was she doing this? This wasn't just withdrawing after sex. Something else was in play, but what? He'd fallen asleep with her wrapped, warm and willing, in his arms and woken to her frozen and shut down.

"Can you give me a ride home?" Margot asked him. "I live right by you and don't want to put out Edie if she's not well."

Shit. That's the last thing he wanted to do. "Uh—"

"Yes," Eden forced a bright smile. "That sounds like a great idea."

The band finished and began dismantling the stage as the crowd faded with happy laughter, disappearing into the night.

Margot grabbed her bag and approached. "I'm all set."

"Great," Archer said as Edie waved goodbye to them both, refusing to make eye contact. He couldn't linger, not now that he had a responsibility. "Let's roll. And, you,

I'll call you tomorrow." And from the way Edie flinched, it sounded like she took it as a threat.

He placed the small white box on the counter between them. "This is for you."

"What is it?" She reached out, almost but not quite touching the package.

He leaned in and said, so low that only she could hear, "You deserve only good things in life—this is just a small reminder."

"Archer." She pleaded with her eyes. "I'm sorry if it seems like I'm blowing so hot and cold. It's just that there's a lot going on for me at the moment."

"And I'm here, the minute you are ready to let me in. Say the word. You don't have to face anything alone." He tapped the box. "I hope this helps you see that."

MARGOT DIDN'T SHOW up for work the next morning. "Strange," Edie muttered to herself, checking her phone for the third time. No new messages. With her wayward curls and expressive brown eyes, Margot was very pretty, but only eighteen. Archer wouldn't have . . . no that's impossible. But then who'd stuck up the big "Keep Out" sign? Yes. She'd essentially gone and made herself the old lady who shouts, "Get off my lawn." And all because of Reggie.

Wait a second . . . because of Reggie?

What a stupid notion. Why throw away a chance at something that made her happy because she had given someone else power? Her ex-fiancé was a thousand miles away and here she was, dancing to his tune, causing herself misery because she was afraid. Afraid that Archer wouldn't believe her. Afraid that he would judge her and find her lacking. Afraid that in the end, he'd turn away, think she was deficient, realize that despite everything she was still Eden the Ew. Unworthy of love.

Eden took a cherry pie out of the oven and slammed it on the cooling racks. She'd run so far from her old life, yet hadn't gone in a different, better direction. Instead, it was like she was on a track and circled back to places she never wanted to be again.

It was time to stop letting other people define her. She settled down in Brightwater because she craved a simple life.

When did simple get so hard?

Sure, maybe Archer would judge her if the photo came out, but she'd already judged him by not being open and for his own sexual past. Shouldn't he at least have an opportunity to be the good guy, the guy that she knew in her heart he was, the kindhearted man who gave her a Lifesaver in a diner and a ride when she was lost?

She stared at the wall clock, thinking, and not thinking, just feeling. From the start, her gut trusted Archer; it was her head that kept messing things up. Why couldn't she believe her instincts? Every time she did, they pushed her in the right direction. It was her head that had said "Marry Reggie." Her heart had said, "Um, this seems like a terrible idea."

It was her heart that said, "Go to Brightwater." And, "Start a coffee shop."

On both accounts she had no regrets.

The shop was set to open in ten minutes and still no sign of Margot. She couldn't be with Archer, but still, she'd seemed responsible and eager. Hopefully nothing was the matter. Edie called the girl's phone and it rang and rang. Just before hanging up, she answered, a little groggy. "Hello?"

"Margot? It's Edie." There was a pause. Edie gripped the phone harder. "Margot?"

"Oh crap, the time! I'm sorry, I'm still in bed." She sounded more awake, and more than a little alarmed. "Last night was so crazy. There was the accident, and then with the medication I slept way later than I thought, but the—"

"Accident?" Edie said sharply. "What accident?"

"Didn't you hear? We were hit, Archer and I on the drive home. A drunk driver ran a four-way stop near the farm."

"What? Are you . . . is he?"

"We're both fine by some miracle. I sprained my arm. My face looks worse, but it will be better."

"Margot, I'm so sorry. And Archer?"

"I think he bruised a few ribs, but I'm not sure, I was pretty out of it. His brother Sawyer got me checked out and then took me home. Annie is pretty angry with me. She thinks I was out messing around with Archer or something. But I wasn't, you know that, right? I mean, the guy is crazy about you. Totally bonkers."

"I . . ." Edie stared ahead, unseeing. Strange to hear another person confirm what her heart had known for some time.

"He can't even take his eyes off you for a second if you're in the same room."

"I . . . I well I'm glad you are okay. That all sounds terrifying. Please don't worry about the shop. Everything will be fine, focus on getting yourself better."

"I'm going to be in a sling for a bit so I can't work the espresso machine, but I can bus tables and wipe counters with one hand."

"Let's see how you feel after a couple days."

"Okay." Margot let out a big yawn. "Sorry, the codeine has done a number on me."

"That's fine. Get some sleep."

"M'kay," Margot murmured, sounding drowsy again. "And you should prolly go see Archer. I'm sure he feels bad too and doesn't have anyone to look after him."

"Good night, or morning," Edie said.

Hanging up, she walked slowly to the front door. The sign was still set to closed and it was two minutes before opening. Instead of flipping it over she pulled the blinds.

Her heart said, "What are you waiting for?"

She locked up, turned off the lights, and went upstairs. She opened her underwear drawer and her heart said, "Don't even think about the cotton. Lace. Matching set."

She went with white, classic and delicate. Doing up the bra clasp felt like she was preparing for battle. And she was in some ways—with herself. Her head was not happy, it made loud disapproving noises, ready to say "I told you so" if this went badly.

She found a light summer dress, again in white, with capped sleeves, a slight flare in the skirt and a fitted waist.

Paired with sandals and a lightweight wrap to keep away any chill, she was ready for anything.

Enough of this seesaw. Time to see Archer and figure out once and for all, if she was going to be in or out. Because otherwise this tug of war within her would drive her mad.

The small white box was on the coffee table. She'd chickened out of opening it last night. What could it be? All night she had tossed and turned, wondering what could be inside, but dreading it as if it were some sort of Pandora's Box—a ridiculous notion. "After all," she huffed to herself, sitting on the couch to tear open the packing tape, "what was at the bottom of that box?"

Hope.

The same hope alighting inside her as she lifted the lid, peering inside. What nestled in the tissue paper was beyond anything that she could have imagined. A king's ransom couldn't mean more.

She pulled out a small carved ballerina, the exact match to the one that had long ago gone missing. How did he find her? She rose and walked to her old music box, opening it up and screwing her in. The fit was perfect. Winding the box, the tune "Edelweiss" filled the quiet room as the ballerina slowly spun.

Archer hadn't just given her hope for the future; he'd helped her find a shred of peace with the past.

Chapter Seventeen

ARCHER ROLLED OVER with a grimace. He'd been advised to breathe deeply but fuck did it hurt. Black and blue mottling spread across his rib cage. He rubbed his face with a groan. Last night all he'd wanted to do was reconnect with Edie. Instead, his ass nearly got sent packing to the Pearly Gates. Do not pass Go. Do not collect $200. Here's a harp and halo—try not to swear.

Shit.

If anything good came out of last night's accident, it was the realization that life is fragile and can be snuffed out at any second. Was he making the right choices? Yes and no. Working the ranch was good, better than good. Great. But he needed more in his life than work.

A quiet knock came on the door. "Archer?"

Edie? He bolted upright. Here at his place? He stared around his small bare studio. The walls were plywood and looked half assed. This was a bachelor flop house, a place to crash when he wasn't couch surfing with buddies or bed hopping with random one-night stands. No one but him ever spent any time here.

The door cracked opened. "Hey," she whispered. "Are you—oh . . ." She covered a hand over her mouth. "Oh God. Look at you."

"Don't want to." He breathed hard, hard enough it caused a stabbing pain and yet a rush of pleasure. She was here.

She held up a pie and thermos. "I decided to keep the store closed after hearing about the accident. I brought you a pie and some fresh coffee."

"Great." That was a typical sweet Edie gesture, and probably goddamn delicious. But right now he hungered for one thing. Her touch.

"Set that stuff on the table and come closer," he said.

She glanced uncertainly at the pie tin. "It's bourbon pecan, your favorite."

"Sounds good, but you're my favorite."

She set the pie and coffee down, fidgeting with her skirt.

"Hey you, what's up?"

When she raised her gaze, her eyes were wet with unshed tears. "Your gift."

Shit. What had he done? "I'm sorry. Don't cry. I didn't mean to—"

"Sorry?" She wiped her eyes with the back of one hand. "That was the nicest, sweetest, most thoughtful gift I've received in my whole life."

A two-inch wooden ballerina? Damn. He couldn't wait to really knock her socks off.

"Where in the world did you find it?"

"I wrote to a specialty music-box shop on the coast. After giving a description, they emailed a few pictures and once I saw yours it was straightforward." It had actually been a rare stroke of luck according to the shopkeeper. The man had been chuckling at the serendipity.

"You are a good man, Archer Kane. The best of men." She reached out and lightly stroked his cheek. "What this is between us, when we're together, when you touch me, I didn't know it could be this way, at least in real life."

He reached up and held her wrist. "What we share is the simplest thing in the world, Freckles. And maybe the most complicated."

"Before anything else, I have to show you something." Her smile faded. "Something bad."

His stomach took a nosedive. "Is this the nothing that is something? What's made you freeze me out the last few days?"

She nodded, lines cutting across her forehead. "It's bad and has the potential to go really bad. Possibly nuclear."

"Then come snuggle up and tell me everything." He patted the mattress.

Her eyes narrowed. "Will I hurt you?"

"I've had worse." He laughed, wincing. "Not holding you hurts worse than a bruised rib."

"What if I get you something? A pain reliever? A glass of water? A cup of tea?" She cocked a brow, examining his nearly bare counter. "A shot of Jack Daniel's?"

He scooted over on the mattress and plumped the adjacent pillow. She'd feel better once she got whatever was eating at her off her chest. "You. Here. Now. No bullshit."

Edie crawled in beside him and couldn't restrain a deep inhalation. The bed smelled incredible, like the man who was beside her. Woodsy. Spicy. Undeniably male. No cologne in the world could come close to capturing it.

He turned to face her and his features softened, hard to put a finger on exactly how, because the strong jaw and bold features remained the same. No, it was the eyes. His bright green gaze was overwhelmingly caring, grateful even. She didn't deserve it, not given her recent behavior.

"Come in close," he murmured, gathering her in, brushing his lips over the top of her ear.

She had to do it. She *had* to tell him the awful truth, reveal herself as a subject of mockery. "My ex-fiancé, Reggie, threatened me."

The tenderness extinguished. Archer was a powerfully built man, but in this moment, he felt like a giant. Six feet of pure muscled anger. "What the fuck has that asshole done?"

She sniffled and removed her phone from her purse, handing it over. "The first text came the day you and I made love."

His gaze locked with hers and she held it, even as the blush tore across her cheeks. They had made love; there was no better description. It had been hot, dirty sex, but so much more. She'd made herself more vulnerable than she'd ever been in her life. And it seemed like he did too.

When he looked at Reggie's image, what would he think, what would he say? There were the reactions she feared, disgust and revulsion, but what did she hope for? When his eyes dropped to the screen, it was impossible to get a handle on his response. His normally expressive features shuttered into an impassive mask.

Her pulse pounded out the seconds, twelve . . . thirteen . . . fourteen . . . *What is he thinking?*

Finally, after an eternity, he raised his gaze to her. "I've never wanted to kill a man. Never understood how a person could get to that point. But I do now. All I want to do is get my truck from the shop, drive across the country nonstop, find that scumbag, and throw him off a bridge."

She reached and set her hand over his clenched fist. "The woman in the photo, that's not me."

He gave her a surprised look. "Of course not. I have your body memorized. That woman doesn't have a single one of your gorgeous freckles." He opened his hand and encircled hers. "And even if that had been you, it wouldn't have mattered. Not to me. Not in a million years. A woman is entitled to do what she likes in the bedroom with the man of her choosing, and not be photographed and threatened by the situation."

Hot tears gathered in her eyes. This, this was the reaction she hoped for, that she had convinced herself wouldn't be possible.

"Thank you," she said. "But I'm not going to give him the money, and I think that he's going to make good on his threat."

"Fuck him," Archer said fiercely. "I don't know how,

but the truth will come out. He won't win. Guys like him never do."

"Guys like him win all the time." Edie's voice quavered. "That's why Wall Street is such a cesspool."

"He won't win this time," he said. "Whatever it takes, I'll protect you. You don't deserve a single one of those little lines on your forehead. You deserve nothing but the best life has to offer. And in the future, if you ever need me, don't hide—tell me and I'll be there. I'll always be there. I'll always trust you."

She should say thank you. She should say what a relief it was to hear him say everything that made her heart beat faster. But words wouldn't do in this moment. Instead, she kissed him with every inch of her body and soul.

He stifled a moan and slung an arm around her pulling her close, dragging his hand in her hair, hauling her against him until their teeth knocked and they laughed in each other's mouths. Seconds past, or maybe they were lifetimes. The sun could have exploded and the solar system ended in this infinite moment.

"I can't get enough of you," he murmured. His desperate lips wouldn't stop and hers couldn't. She couldn't quit him now if she tried.

She stroked his tongue, sweet madness tangling through her. "Me too."

He released her, sat, and fisted his tight grey t-shirt off in one yank. "Now you."

"Are you sure?" She reached out and rubbed his hard chest, gentle, right above a nasty fist-sized bruise.

"I'm not sure about most things in my life. Never have

been. But that's all changing. I'm sure about you. And I'm sure if I don't get you naked in the next five seconds, I'll kick my own ass." He made quick work of her clothes, and rolled her onto her back, whispering, "So fucking beautiful."

Never in her life had Edie been so comfortably naked. No shame. No embarrassment. He bent and licked her nipple, roamed her breast with his lips, stubble grazing the sensitive skin. "You like this, don't you?" he muttered, moving to suck her other tip, adding a light tug with his teeth.

Any coherent reply was lost in a soft moan.

He sat on his knees and positioned her legs on either side of him. "I love you here." He stroked his hand over her belly to cup her mound. "Like fire. Soft, silky fire." His finger slid across her slippery skin and her next moan filled the room.

"Sorry." She clapped a hand over her mouth.

"Never apologize for your pleasure. Now wrap those sweet legs around my neck and let's see what other sounds you can make."

Laughing, she threw her legs on his shoulders, careful not to give him too much of her weight. It didn't matter. He grabbed her thighs and hauled her close. He pressed his face against her, inhaling, enjoying, savoring. She couldn't look away and as he parted her folds, he glanced up, his green eyes locking with hers as his tongue flicked to circle her clit.

Her eyes closed on instinct, pure pressure radiating through her hips.

"Watch me." His breath brushed across her slick heat. "Watch me love you." He feathered her with his tongue, his mouth increasingly fervent. How could she feel him through her entire body, strange when he only touched one place? Every limb tingled. He needed to be here too, feeling everything she did.

She pulled away and he growled, actually growled, grabbing her ass. "No. Let me give you this."

"Yes, don't stop," she said. "But I'm doing you too."

He paused, brow creasing.

She crawled around to his side, grabbed his strong thigh, and slid on her back between his legs, his cock hanging thick and full above. "There's no reason we can't both enjoy it." She craned to run her tongue along his long, hard shaft.

"Jesus, woman," he ground out.

She grabbed him at the root and angled his length between her lips as he crushed his mouth between her spread legs. If he'd been hungry before, this time he consumed her like a man starved. He circled her clit, kissed her folds, but even as she took him deep into her throat, he wouldn't go where she needed him most. She writhed, rocking her hips in pleading thrusts, until realizing he toyed with her.

He knew what she wanted. What she begged for with her body. And he withheld the reward until the build was unreal. Her thighs trembled so much that the bed shook and the noises tearing from her chest were inhuman. Her nails dug into his perfect hard ass and she moved back to lick his sac. That seemed to do the trick.

"Fuck." He fixed his lips on her clit and sucked, wild and strong, almost as strong as she sucked him, and it was like going from sixty miles an hour to hurtling at the speed of light. He did it again and her mind blanked. The pressure built, not just in her pelvis but throughout her stomach and thighs. Her heart buzzed as nerve endings grew extra sensitive, pulsing with ever increasing intensity.

She couldn't bear another second, she couldn't breathe, or whimper. Never had her mind been so empty while every sense was honed, brighter, and more aware than ever before. A gasp, one last suck, and she screamed her release with his cock between her lips, pleasure and adrenaline coursing through her.

Then he was gone and she couldn't move. She tried. She struggled to open her eyes but nothing would cooperate. She'd run hard in her day. Pushed her body over miles, to paces that left her lungs burning and legs on fire. But never had she been this worked.

Foil tore. She couldn't . . . how could she take him when so sensitive . . . it wouldn't work, and then he was inside her, one solid thrust and she was full. Her hands fisted his hair. It was like he'd always been there, a part of her, and her body found a reserve it didn't know it had.

"Edie," he ground out. Again, and again, he rumbled her name as if it were a holy word, a prayer, a blessing. In and out, he moved deep and slow.

"Don't stop," she begged. "Don't stop, don't stop."

"Never stopping." Faster he went, hips pumping in a

mind-blowing rhythm. "You like this?" he asked when she offered a soft whimper.

"I like it all," she responded. "What you do, how you move."

"What about this?" he swiveled his hips in a slow circle, hitting new places.

She arched. "Yes, that too."

"I want what's best. I want to give you the best orgasm of your life."

"You just did," she gasped.

"I can beat it."

"No, you can't, it's physically impossible."

"Nothing's impossible with you." He buried himself to the hilt, grinding his pelvis against her clit. A minor adjustment of speed and everything shifted, became more.

"Yes?" He groaned.

She bucked. "Yes. God, yes."

It didn't take much, this time there was no slow build. This was dropping in a bucket over Niagara Falls, the world receding to a thunderous roar. He cried out and as her quick-fire pulses receded, he brushed his mouth with hers.

Falling onto his side, his arm slung over her waist, they stared at each other, in shock, in wonder, as if seeing each other for the first time. The same world spun on but suddenly shined with strange magic.

"The best?" he said at last.

She laughed, and once she started, couldn't stop. "So much better than the best."

And in this golden moment, in Archer's bed, a shaft of sunlight pouring through the window, all was right with the world.

Maybe, just maybe all would be well.

And if everything burned, she'd fiddle in the flames, as long as she had Archer standing by her side.

Chapter Eighteen

ARCHER PEEKED INTO his bar fridge and back at Edie, blinking from the bed, wrapped in his sheets, wearing his cowboy hat. Her wild red hair spilled over her bare freckled shoulders and for the eight hundred and second time in the past few hours a feeling of pure dumb luck socked him in the chest.

"Besides your pie, I don't have much to offer as far as food goes," he said apologetically. "I usually grab dinner at The Dirty Shame."

She raised a brow. "Every night?"

"Sometimes I go to the Save-U-More for a roast chicken or deli sandwich. That old recipe box hadn't been touched in a long time."

"Archer, that's not okay." She looked equal parts confused and concerned. "You need meals cooked with love."

"Haven't had a lot of love before meeting you, sweetheart. These cupboards are bare. I got a six-pack, a half a pack of Twizzlers, and a bottle of ketchup." He glanced to the dusty can on the counter and his lips twitched. "Oh, and Dinty Moore beef stew."

She made a disapproving sound. "We need to go do some serious shopping. But tonight we should go back to my apartment so that I can look after you. At this rate, you'll have scurvy by the end of the month."

"What do you say I do a quick town run and grab some supplies? Seems a shame to make you cover up all that pretty with clothes."

"But you are injured."

"I need to move, it feels better than being cooped up in bed."

Edie glanced down at herself. "I can't sit around your room naked by myself."

"You absolutely can. It will keep a smile on my face."

"How will you drive? You truck is in the shop because of the accident."

"Can I borrow your car keys? Before you say anything else, let me get in another sentence. Let me do this, spoil you." He pulled out the Twizzlers, walked to his shelf and grabbed his iPad, fiddling with the screen. "You cuddle up on the pillow and watch a chick flick."

"Are you serious?"

"I'll be back before you know it."

"Um, okay. I feel really spoiled." She looked a little bemused, but also thrilled.

His heart gave a funny double beat at the notion that licorice and a show made her this pleased. How the hell had she been treated in the past? From now on all he could do was treat her like a queen. "So what will it be . . . *The Notebook*?"

She gaped. "You're a Nicholas Sparks fan?"

"Okay, confession, it's the only girlie movie I know. Don't all women love that one? It seemed like a safe bet."

"Most women at least love Ryan Gosling making out in the rain."

He gave her a playful glare. "In the rain? Hmmm. Maybe not that one then."

"What about *North & South*?"

He typed that into Netflix with a frown, peering at the thumbnail of a woman in a flouncy dress. "A Civil War movie?"

"No!" She giggled. "Victorian costume drama starring Richard Armitage."

"Who?" He stared blankly, no bells ringing.

She placed a hand over her heart in mock dismay. "Only the most yummy British actor who has ever existed. His voice alone is pure sex."

"That English accent does it for you?"

She mashed her lips together. "Are you getting jealous over an actor in a BBC drama?"

"An actor who has a voice that's pure sex?"

She crawled to the edge of the bed, leaving the sheet behind. He approached and she took off his hat and set it on his head. "Did you know that I used to think cowboys weren't my type?"

"Is that a fact?"

"Yep. I never could figure out the big attraction."

"And now?"

She looped her arms around his neck and pulled him on top of her. "I was blind but now I see."

After another thirty incredible minutes, Archer threw his shirt back on, stomach growling. "We keep this up and I'll have to go grab an animal from the ranch. I'm starving."

"Me too," she admitted. "I could probably demolish a burger with bacon."

"That's my girl." He handed her the iPad. "Okay, make do with your Dick Armitage and I'll be back in two shakes." He gave her forehead a kiss and then one more for each cheek. "Will you stop being so damn cute? You make it impossible to leave."

"Thank you," she said, taking his hand.

"What for."

"For everything." She kissed his knuckles. "I . . . I . . ."

A distant crash occurred.

"What was that?" Edie snapped her head around.

"I don't know. It sounded like it came from the ranch house."

Edie jumped up and threw on her clothes. "I'll come with you."

Together, they ran down the stairs. Inside the barn horses whickered uneasily. Night settled into the valley and the main house was dark.

"Hello?" Archer cupped his hands over his mouth. "Grandma? Sawyer? Who's out there?"

Silence followed.

"Maybe it was a raccoon or something?" Edie whispered. "Could it be a bear?"

"Doubtful. Anyway the sound didn't come from over near the garbage bins."

He scanned the dark windows. Grandma was usually still up at this hour, but maybe she turned in early. If an eighty-year-old wanted to go to bed with the sun, God-speed, she had every right.

"Wait." Edie pulled up short. "Did you hear that? Was that a cow or . . . ?"

Archer cocked his head, only wind rustled in the trees. In the distance, a truck backfired. Then it came again. A low moan. "Shit, that's no animal." He ran around to the front of the ranch house. Grandma was crumpled in a heap at the bottom of the porch stairs.

"I'll call an ambulance," Edie said, turning toward his apartment.

"Here, take my phone." Archer dug it out of his back pocket. "Call 9–1–1 and then Sawyer. He's probably at An-nie's next door." He ran to Grandma's side and dropped to his knees. "Can you hear me? It's Archer."

"I know who you are." Grandma's eyes fluttered open. "I broke my hip not my brain."

"You think it's your hip?" Shit, what should he do? She looked so frail, far more fragile than he was used to.

She nodded, flinching. "Tripped down the steps like a damn fool."

He wanted to kick himself. He'd focused so much on proving himself on the ranch; he hadn't paid attention to the obvious fact staring him the face. While Grandma's wit was sharp as ever, should she be rambling around this big old house alone? He and Sawyer lived close by, but that wasn't good enough. If he hadn't been home to-night . . .

"You're going to be fine, just fine. Sawyer will arrive any second." His big brother was her favorite. She'd be happy once he got here and reassured her everything was under control. "Right now you're stuck with me, but I'll do my best." He took her hand in his, the skin paper thin, bones jutting in sharp relief, like a baby bird.

"Such a good boy," she murmured. "Always such a good boy."

Shit, she was starting to get delirious.

"Funny and charming. So like your grandfather."

Damn it. How do you check for a concussion?

"I need you to try and focus. How many fingers am I holding up?" He held two in front of her nose.

She grimaced. "What are you doing?"

"Seeing if you hit your head."

"I told you, it's my hip."

"Just doing a quick examination. You're not acting like yourself. You thought I was someone else."

"Archer James Kane, who the heck did you think I thought you were?"

His shoulders caved. "Dunno. Sawyer."

"What would I think that?"

"Because . . ." Hell, this wasn't the time for his hang-ups.

"Listen to me good." She gripped his leg. "If some-thing should happen to me, Hidden Rock, it's to go to you. My will has it all laid out. You're the one meant for the place. You always have been. Born to it."

"Okay, Grandma," he patted her hand. Yeah, maybe

she hadn't hit her head but she was certainly not right in the head.

Headlights appeared. Not the siren of the ambulance but Sawyer's truck. His brother pulled up on the lawn, jumping out, keeping the lights trained on the house.

"Have you checked for signs of shock," Sawyer asked Archer. "Rapid weak pulse, confusion, irritability?"

"Haven't checked her pulse, man, but I'm worried. She's confused, keeps saying things that don't make sense. And irritable? That's not out of the normal."

Sawyer gave a tight smile before crouching to turn his attention to Grandma. "Do you know where you are?"

Her brow wrinkled. "My ranch."

"Do you know what happened?" Sawyer pressed.

"I saw a strange car by the barn and went out to investigate. Someone could have been messing around with the horses. Or my grandson."

"What day is it?" Sawyer continued.

"Quit your horse and pony show. You're as bad as your brother." She glared at Edie. "It's you, the redhead from the coffee shop. You're together with my grandson."

Sawyer glanced up, his normally stoic face lit with surprise. "She is?"

Archer set a hand on Edie's shoulder and gave a reassuring squeeze. "She is."

Grandma moaned.

"Shit, I hope the ambulance gets here fast. I don't have a PASG with me," Sawyer muttered to himself.

"A *huh*?" Archer said.

"It's an airbag that wraps around the pelvis and in-flates."

The siren of an ambulance sounded in the distance, growing incrementally louder. Somewhere a dog howled. Then a coyote joined in.

"What a bunch of fuss and nonsense," Grandma said through gritted teeth.

The ambulance pulled up and Sawyer ran to greet them. As sheriff, he knew all the local first responders. Archer stayed next to Grandma, still gripping his hand, and Edie stayed huddled beside him.

The paramedics approached, carrying a stretcher. They carefully put her in a collar that immobilized her neck and then got her onto the board, administering oxygen. "Archer." Her hand fumbled in the empty air. "Archer James. Where are you?"

"Grandma, I'm here, right here."

"Ride with me," she whispered. "Don't make me go alone."

"I'll fetch Sawyer."

"No. You." She gripped his hand. "I want you."

Sawyer clasped a hand on his back. "Stay with her, there's not much more these guys can do now except give her diesel therapy."

"What the hell is that?" Archer muttered.

Sawyer's smile was grim. "Drive fucking fast."

Edie stepped beside him. "Go. We'll meet you at the hospital."

Archer nodded, gave her a quick kiss, and climbed

into the back of the ambulance. He wasn't sure why he was the one Grandma wanted, but he'd do his best to look after her.

"Everything is going to be okay," he told her again, crawling inside the back of the ambulance.

Her face grew pale. "How many dead people do you think have been in here?"

"Let's not worry about that. You're going to be around for a long while yet."

Grandma gripped his hand. "You're a good man."

And Archer realized that he was finally starting to live up to the word.

Chapter Nineteen

THE AMBULANCE SIREN disappeared into the night. Sawyer turned to Edie. He was taller than Archer and didn't sport the dimples, but they obviously were closely related, those hooded green eyes a family trait. But whereas Archer's face held mischief and humor, Sawyer was unruffled, letting little show. A perfect sheriff. "Things are going well between you and my brother?"

She smoothed a hand over her hair. "What makes you say that?"

"Your dress is on inside out," he muttered.

"Oh no!" She blushed as he broke into a kind smile, one that changed his whole face, made him more human, less like a serious man of the law.

"My little brother has been acting like he's got a bee in his bonnet for months, it's good to finally know the cause."

"And how do you know that I'm the bee?"

"I see how he looks at you. It's like he's never seen anyone else."

"Well," she said, ducking her head, embarrassed and undeniably pleased. "You should get on to the hospital. My purse is back up in his room. I'll follow along."

"I'll give you a ride."

"Oh, you don't have to."

He simply stared at her. It was the same as when Archer wouldn't let her pay for the motel.

"I guess Kane men are uniformly stubborn."

Sawyer's laugh came out in a surprising boom. "We can be, yes."

"Okay, hang on. I'll only be a second." She ran back to Archer's bachelor pad above the barn. For so long he'd been settling for this clean but sterile space, just a bed, kitchenette, couch, bookshelf, and television. It didn't feel like a home, more like a place to pass through. Except for the bed. The mattress was half off the frame and the sheets looked as if a tornado had touched down.

She quickly righted her dress and ran down the stairs. "One last thing," she said as they walked to his truck. "Archer hasn't eaten all day and his kitchenette cupboards were beyond bare. We have to pass my shop on the way to the hospital. If we can stop at my apartment, I can run in and get him something to eat, leftover pasta or a sandwich. This might be a long night."

"Sounds like a plan," Sawyer said, opening her door.

Her phone buzzed as they drove down the driveway. Quincy's name flashed on the screen. "I'm sorry, I have to take this."

"Fine by me," Sawyer responded easily, eyes on the road.

"Hello?" she said. "Where are you? London or Paris? Let me guess—"

"The more pressing question is where are you?" Quincy's posh voice was concerned.

"On the way to the hospital."

Quincy cursed. Strange. He never swore. "Did he find you then?"

"Did who find me?" Edie asked. "I'm with Sawyer Kane, we're on our way to the hospital. Archer's grandmother broke her hip."

"Reggie's in Brightwater."

Her blood ran cold. "What?"

"You're with the sheriff?"

"Yes."

"Good, that's good," Quincy sounded relieved. "Stay with him."

"How do you know he's here?"

"I got back to town early, went by your shop, and saw it had been closed all day."

"I went to see Archer. He was involved in a car crash last night."

Quincy heaved a heavy sigh. "This does seem like a day for calamities."

"He's okay, but yes, it scared me." It was nice for her cousin to be so concerned.

"As I was saying, I stopped by the bakery to check on you. Found your apartment ransacked."

"What?" Her voice rose.

"Yes, I'm here now."

"Why do you think it was—"

"The photo Reggie threatened you with has gone online," Quincy said gently. "Your computer was open and the image was set to the homepage. As far as I can tell it's only on a few sites so far. I have my people working to remove it, but these situations are notoriously difficult. It's like playing Whac-A-Mole. There's a good chance the damage is permanent."

"Did you call the police?" She stiffened as Sawyer glanced over. Sharing this situation with her boyfriend's brother wasn't something she looked forward to.

"No, I called you first. When I saw the condition of the space and that you were missing, I'm afraid I rather assumed the worst."

"I'll tell Sawyer now."

"Tell me what?" he said quietly as she hung up the phone.

"It's kind of a long story," she said.

"I'm a good listener," he responded.

ARCHER TOSSED ASIDE the magazine he wasn't reading and stared across the emergency waiting room. A framed poster of a beach scene hung on the wall in a cheap pastel frame. Who decided that's the sort of picture to have in a hospital? Maybe the idea was that the tropical image could relax people. Instead, it felt like shitty mockery, the idea that somewhere life was all mai tais and warm water instead of the cold creeping fear about a loved one's condition.

He pounded back the last of his disposable cup of watered-down coffee as Edie rushed through the sliding doors, staring around wildly as she made her way to the triage desk. He threw up a hand and she veered in his direction, her mouth turning into a sympathetic smile.

"You're here," he said, standing to pull her into a bear hug. "Where's Sawyer? Parking?"

She kissed his cheek. "First, how is your grandma?"

"Grumpy as ever. In addition to the broken hip, the paramedics said she looked to have pneumonia too."

"What?"

"Yeah," Archer clenched his jaw, before burying his face into Edie's hair, inhaling her rich, comforting scent. His pulse slowly returned to normal for the first time in hours. "As much as Grandma is a pain in my ass, that tough old bird loves me, my brothers, and that ranch something fierce."

"I know," Edie crooned, rubbing his back with small circles. "Of course she does."

"I doubted it for a long time." His insecurity came from a weak place, one he wasn't going to visit any longer.

"When can you see her?"

Archer shook his head. "I'm not sure. No one has been out since she went into surgery."

She gripped his hand and pulled him back to sitting. The plastic chair was hard and uncomfortable, but everything seemed better with Edie here, more positive, like maybe things might work out for the best.

"You starving? I was going to bring you something to eat, but I can go see what's in the cafeteria at this hour. Might be scary but better than nothing."

"That's okay," he said with a shrug. "My stomach is in knots."

Edie gave him a long look. "She's really special to you, isn't she?"

"I feel like shit that I never recognized it. We all grumble about the way she rides our asses, but yeah, she's special. Maybe not your typical sweet grandma knitting socks and baking cakes, but I've never had a mom or dad, at least for as long as I can remember. She's been my parent. And all that ass-riding, it was a push for me to step up and take more responsibility. When I didn't believe in myself, she knew I could do it." He broke into a wry smile. "Of course, she never said any of this straight out. But that's just not her way."

He was honored that she chose him to continue the legacy and would do his level best not to disappoint.

"It's not hard to see your potential," Edie said. "You have it coming out your ears. Seriously, you are amazing, and the only person who doesn't seem to see it is you."

"Thank you." Edie had a caring heart and he wanted to treasure it. As much as he understood Grandma's love for him, he still craved a different love. The affection he never got growing up, that of a gentle word and a soft touch.

He slung an arm around the back of Edie's chair and rested his head against hers. Her scent steadied him. Maybe that's why he'd chased women the way he had.

Always searching for a human connection, a moment to be held, loved even for a few passing minutes of pleasure. Shit, he must be exhausted. Chasing this train of thought wasn't his usual MO, but when faced with a person's mortality, deeper thoughts seemed to bubble up.

Edie fidgeted in her seat, doing her nervous tapping eyebrow thing.

"What is it?" he asked, frowning down at her face. Something else seemed wrong. She was pale, each freckle standing out in sharp relief.

"It's nothing," she answered quickly.

"Damn it, I thought tonight we agreed to quit the run around. Here you are, not a few hours later making that closed-door face."

"You have so much on your plate right now." She sighed, holding his hand tighter. "I don't want you to worry."

"I'm going to worry why you aren't being straight." He angled his body toward her and nudged her shoe with his boot. "Come on, let me in."

She took a deep breath. "Yes, you're right. Honesty, right?"

"Please," he said. "In all things."

"Sawyer isn't parking his truck in the hospital lot. He let me take it after he stopped at the sheriff's office. He can't come . . . because . . . it appears Reggie broke into my apartment."

Archer sat straighter. Hot anger and a grim happiness took root deep in his stomach. "You're telling me that shitty-ass excuse for a human is in my town?"

Edie took a moment before responding. "Quincy came by to check on me as the shop was closed all day, and my little home was destroyed." Her voice cracked. "There weren't many trinkets I'd had sent from New York, but the few I asked for were important to me. We're not sure it was him, or if he's acting alone, or what exactly he hopes to achieve. The motive is unclear. I know he wants money, a lot of money, but why does he need it? He makes a seven-figure salary."

Archer's trigger finger twitched. He was ready to go hunting. Wouldn't be hard to rustle out a yuppie weasel in a town this size.

"No! Don't think of going vigilante," she said quickly, sensing his intentions. "Stay here. Your grandma needs you."

"But—"

"I need you too. Your brother has the law on his side. This is his job."

His mind was a blur of red rage. "If you think I'll sit on my ass while someone is out there trying to cause you—"

"Mr. Kane?" A doctor stepped through the ER door with a serious expression.

"That's me," he said, rising to his feet. He was pulled in so many different directions that he might rip into pieces.

"Your grandma is in recovery and asked you to come sit with her. In addition to the hip, she is suffering from pneumonia. Not unusual for someone at her age, but serious."

"We'll go right now." Edie took his hand.

The doctor shook her head. "I'm sorry, it's immediate family only."

Archer readjusted his hat and rolled his shoulders. "My grandma needs me and I need my girlfriend. That's final. Go on and speak with your supervisor but that's how this is going to go." With that asshat on the loose, no way would Edie be out of his sight. Not for two seconds.

The doctor looked between them, frowning before consulting the chart. "I think we can make an allowance in this case."

When they got to Grandma's room, she was resting as machines clicked and whirled. She looked smaller in the hospital bed, more fragile than ever.

There was a faint buzz and he glanced sideways. Edie subtly checked her phone.

"What is it?" he murmured.

"The photo." She held up the picture posted on a porn site. "Quincy sent it. It's on five sites and counting."

"Reggie's lies won't go anywhere."

"Even if they do, the fact you are with me makes this a million times easier to bear."

Grandma stirred on the bed, her eyes fluttering.

Archer settled a hand on Grandma's toothpick arm. "She isn't going to like being laid up or off Hidden Rock. She's never even taken a proper vacation away."

"Can I ask a random question?" Edie murmured, pulling up a chair. "Something I've been curious about."

"Shoot."

"Why is the ranch called Hidden Rock?" she asked.

Grandma stirred, her eyelids fluttering again and her mouth working soundlessly. No clear communication yet, but a good sign her vitals were okay.

"Hidden Rock?" Archer shifted his weight. "Huh. I don't actually know. Funny, I grew up on the ranch and never once asked how it got that name. I've heard time and time again about the legend of Five Diamonds Farm, and how it was won off a Kane in a poker game a hundred years ago, but I've never wondered about our own name."

Grandma's eyes snapped open, sharply focused. "You don't know the legend?" she wheezed.

"Hey, welcome back. You're awake," he said, eyeing the call button. Should he page the nurse or—

"How can you run the ranch if you don't know its history?"

"Shhh." He crooned, rubbing her arm. "Settle yourself, won't do any good getting yourself worked into a twist. Just rest."

"I'll rest when I'm dead," she rasped. "The whole story is written plain as the nose on your face in *Brightwater: Small Town, Big Dreams.*"

Archer wrinkled his brow.

"Don't tell me you never read the town history."

"I . . ."—he scratched the back of his neck—"didn't know there was a town history."

A small alarm sounded and a nurse rushed in. "Mrs. Kane, is everything all right?"

"No, it's not all right. My grandson is going to take over my ranch and doesn't even know its history."

The nurse glanced at Archer as Grandma's blood pressure spiked on the machine.

"Is the book at home?" Archer asked quickly, ignoring the nurse who fussed with the IVs and oxygen.

"In the living room, on the same bookshelf it's been since you were born."

"I'll read it as soon as I get home."

"You will, and you'll both hear it now."

"Grandma, you need to rest."

Edie shook her head at Archer. "If this helps her, it's a good idea."

"Thank you," Grandma said frostily. "Good to see one of my grandsons has fallen for a woman with a lick of common sense, even if she is a brazen hussy."

Archer resisted the urge to face palm.

"Excuse me?" Edie said, horror crossing her features. She must think Grandma knew about the picture.

"She saw you and me in the truck, the day you arrived in town," Archer mumbled.

"But why does that make me a brazen hussy?" Edie said, looking puzzled.

"What else would you call a woman who engages in fellatio on Main Street?"

The nurse dropped the chart in a loud clatter.

"Aw, hell, Grandma—"

"Don't you swear around me, boy."

"But I never—I didn't—I don't understand—" Edie stammered.

"Nothing happened," Archer cut her off gently.

The nurse leaned against the wall, riveted, as if she were watching a daytime talk show.

Archer chewed the inside of his cheek, resisting the urge to offer the woman popcorn. "If everything is okay with my grandma, do you think you can give us a few moments in private?"

"That's fine. Mrs. Kane, the doctor will be in to check on you shortly." The nurse spoke a little too loud, her voice a little too cheerful.

Archer was pretty sure that vague crunching sound was his grandma gnashing her teeth.

"Mrs. Kane, I'm not sure what you thought you saw," Edie said.

"I got this," Archer said, setting a hand on her leg. "Grandma, this is a woman I deeply care about."

Edie startled and he glanced over. "It's true. I do. And Grandma, I care about you too. I know we aren't a big huggy kissy sort of family but sometimes these things need to be said. Like when you're in the hospital or when you run your mouth about my reputation." He held up a finger. "That all needs to stop now. I'm going to ask once, this once, and be nice about it. This woman is my everything and I won't sit by and hear a single negative thing said about her in my presence, and that goes for when I'm not there too. You will give her, and me, that respect from here on out. She deserves nothing less. Do you understand?"

Grandma eyed him for a moment. "Yes." She nodded. "I was right to go with my gut. You are the man to run Hidden Rock. I'm still not sure about you." Grandma scowled at Edie. "I'm not sure what to think about you and your fancy coffee. That's not my way. That's not what I know. But if my grandson sees fit to defend you, then this stops now."

Archer's shoulders loosened. That was about as good a peace offering as he could hope for.

"And you're ready to hear the story of Hidden Rock." Her whisper was fainter.

"It can wait for another time. You should rest."

"Don't worry about me. I'm so full of painkillers I could jog down the backroads like your little girlfriend," she said. "Now this story doesn't have a happy ending, mind."

"Why am I not surprised?" Archer murmured.

Grandma ignored him. "Once upon a time, back when Brightwater was just the founding families . . . your great-great-great-grandfather, Fielder Kane founded the ranch . . . before his damn fool son lost part of it on a cockamamie hand of poker." She held up a hand. "I promised Sawyer I wouldn't speak ill of that old story either, and this is me honoring my word. Anyway, Fielder Kane had nothing but his boots and a hat. Not even a pot to piss in. Legend has it he was hard drinking, hard living, and came West for the adventure and to seek his fortune. But, as Brightwater grew, a merchant arrived in town, and he had a beautiful young daughter, and Fielder knew the first time he saw her that she'd be his. That he'd do whatever possible to win her hand. Her father made it clear that his girl wasn't going to any wild cowhand. So Fielder put his head down. For five years he worked and gathered a sizeable herd, working men, land, power, and position. And when, at long last, he had more of the above than anyone, he bought a ring and went to town to make his proposal. She accepted, having waited for him too and they were married. Soon she bore three fine sons.

"But . . ." Grandma grew quiet. "This is where the story takes a sad turn. The girl grew ill with consumption. When she died, Fielder was encouraged to marry a widow, plenty had their eye on him, a woman to raise his sons and warm his bed. He wouldn't hear of it. Instead, he took that engagement ring and hid it on the property, never telling a soul where. And that's the hidden rock."

Edie's phone rang. She glanced at the screen. "I'm sorry, I have to take this. Let me step out into the corridor."

Grandma shifted on her pillow. "You think Jimmy Fallon's on now? This is past my bedtime, but he's so handsome. It would be a treat."

Archer shook his head, was it possible to wipe the idea of Grandma's Fallon crush from all memory? "And where's it now?" he asked.

"Where's what?"

"The ring. The hidden rock."

"Only Fielder Kane knows and dead men tell no tales."

"Are you saying the rock is missing?"

"Hidden. Wouldn't have quite the same ring if it was Can't Find the Ring No More Ranch."

Archer shook his head. "This isn't Middle Earth, Grandma. Rings don't just disappear from memory in real life, do they?"

"Middle huh?"

"We're getting sidetracked."

"No one's ever found the ring. According to *Brightwater: Small Town, Big Dreams*, it's a good thing too. Fielder's good for nothing gambling son, Wild J, tore up the place trying to find it to gamble off. He's the one that lost the land that became Five Diamonds Farm, not that I'm saying anything bad anymore about the current occupant, Annie Carson. So don't run your mouth tattling to your big brother."

"Wonder where it could be," Archer said, half to himself. Hidden Rock was a large working ranch and a diamond ring was no size at all. It would be like searching for a needle in a damn haystack.

"What do you need a ring for?" Grandma asked suspiciously. "Don't tell me you have any ideas about—"

"Excuse me, Archer?" Edie cracked the door and peered inside. "I am going to have to go see Sawyer."

"I'm coming too." He stood. "I'll be back soon, Grandma. You won't even notice I'm gone."

Grandma clicked on the TV with a grunt. "Jimmy's on. Don't hurry."

In the hall, Edie's cheeks matched the stark white halls. Each freckle clearly defined.

"What is it?"

"They've found Reggie."

Chapter Twenty

WALKER WAS THE next village over, a fifteen-minute drive from Brightwater. It hadn't seen the same recent influx of money and out-of-town investment so it remained quieter, a sleepier cousin. The town's main claim to fame was the Walker Inn, a quaint B&B in a Victorian house that was featured on the town postcards.

Archer parked his brother's truck down the road from the inn and killed the lights. Sawyer waited in his patrol car with his deputy, Kit.

"Stay here," Archer said to Edie. "I'll find out what's going on."

"Absolutely not," Edie said, scrambling after him. "This is about me, I need to be involved."

Archer bit back a response. That might be true but he'd keep her safe tonight, no matter what happened.

Sawyer gestured to the back of the vehicle, popping the locks. "Get in."

They climbed onto the backseat's hard bench, where the criminals were normally held.

Edie leaned forward and hooked her fingers through the bars. "You said you found him?"

Sawyer nodded once. "He's here all right."

"This guy's a regular Sherlock," Kit said, clapping a hand on Sawyer's shoulder. "A+ character profiling. I couldn't have done better myself."

Archer gritted his teeth. As much as he was relieved Sawyer had tracked down Reggie's whereabouts, Edie was his woman. This was a dumbass territorial instinct—and he was genuinely grateful that the scumbag would be feeling the heat he'd so readily inflicted on Edie—but damn it would be nice to be the hero for once.

Sawyer turned. "I thought about what you told me about him, Edie. This guy has money, comes from money, if that's the case, he's not going to hole up just anywhere. He's going to look for the best place in the area. And for now, that's still Walker Inn. I know the owner and gave her a call, described Reggie, and she said a man checked in yesterday fitting the description. He's using the name Richard Weatherby."

Edie gave a humorless snort. "Oh, that's a good one."

"What so funny?" Archer asked.

"Richard Weatherby is an uncle on his mother's side. A Catholic priest."

"I hope he likes confession," Archer snapped. "When do we roll?"

"Not we," Sawyer said firmly. "In the interest of Edie's privacy, I'm keeping this operation small. Kit and I have it handled. We're doing it on the up and up—no vigilante justice."

"Are you serious?" Archer said. "This guy has terrorized her. I'm beating his ass into next Tuesday."

Sawyer opened the door. "You stay put. I'm dead serious."

Kit exited with a sympathetic look and opened the back door. "For fresh air," he said. "You can't open the doors from the backseat, but do us a favor and stay put, huh? If this goes south, we'll have our hands full." He turned, jogging after Sawyer and they were alone.

Archer held her hand and said nothing. He hated being weak and worse than useless, stuck in a cage, letting other men fight his battles.

After a few minutes the sound of whistling started up the street behind them, an old tune, "Mac the Knife."

Edie recoiled. "It's Reggie, he always does that."

Archer turned and there was a guy in the dark, his face briefly illuminating as he inhaled a cigarette.

"He said he quit too," she murmured.

"He's going down."

"Wait," Edie said. But too late . . . Archer couldn't hold back. He was out of the car's open door, and face-to-face with the asshole himself.

"Good evening," Reggie said, moving to step around him.

Good evening? Who actually spoke like that?

"Not really," Archer said softly. "At least not for you."

The asshole's face looked bemused.

Edie flew out. "Don't touch him. He's not worth it."

"Eden?" Reggie said, tossing his cigarette to the ground and grinding it under his wing-tip shoe, gripping the leather satchel he had slung over his shoulder. "Fancy seeing you here."

Archer would give the guy one grudging compliment. He kept his cool like a goddamn psychopath.

Okay, not so much of a compliment.

"I want to know one thing," Eden said. "Why? Why would you do this to me?"

"Why?" Reggie's tone was a high-pitched mock. "Why, Reggie, why?" His hand snaked out, his long fingers wrapping around her throat. "You're like an unwanted kitten begging to have the life choked out of you." He pulled her close, the stale alcohol on his breath washing over her face. "Why? Because I could. And so I did."

Archer slammed his hand down on Reggie's wrist, breaking his hold on Edie. "You sure did. And now I'll do this." He swung hard and true, connecting his fist to the underside of Reggie's smug jaw. The man flew off his feet and sprawled on the lawn beside the sidewalk.

"I hope that was worth it to you," Reggie spat. "I'll have you know that my lawyers are the best, and your ass is grass, pal."

"That a fact?" Archer grabbed him by the white collar. "You started this whole mess, and escalated it by putting your hands on Edie. Right now I only see one ass in the grass, and it ain't mine."

Reggie fumbled in his leather satchel.

Archer pinned his arms behind his back. "Grab that bag, please," he directed Edie.

She leaned close. "You always have loved your man purses, huh, Reg?"

"Fuck you," he snarled.

"Hey now, mind your manners." Archer made a low, dangerous noise in the back of his throat. "Otherwise you're going to be eating those filthy words."

In his peripheral vision, Edie gasped, peering into the satchel.

"What's in there?" he said.

"A pistol or handgun." She glanced up, eyes wide. "Is there a difference? I don't know if it's loaded. I've never touched a weapon."

"Don't start now." Archer lowered his nose to touch Reggie's. The other man breathed unevenly. He stunk of desperation and cheap wine. "What does a guy like you need a gun for?"

Reggie tried to head butt him but Archer moved fast so he only whacked his face into empty air.

"Please," Edie said, touching his back. "Don't get into trouble over me."

"Listen to her," Reggie sneered. "She's right. She's not worth it."

"Funny," Archer gripped him tighter. "To you, it seems she is worth a hell of a lot. Even for a Wall Street fat cat, five million dollars isn't something to sneeze at."

"What happened to your money?" Edie asked. "You inherited a fortune when your grandfather passed away. Mother said—"

"Gone," Reggie snapped, a little breathless because Archer was twisting his shirt.

"But how?"

Reggie pressed his lips together, shaking his head.

Archer shook him again, harder this time. "She asked you a question. After everything you've done, the least you can do is give her the courtesy of an answer."

"What the fuck?" he gasped as Archer squeezed tighter. "I can't breathe."

"If you can talk, you can breathe," Archer snapped.

"Investments went bad."

"You mean you overreached," said Edie.

"You can never overreach," Reggie bit back. "That's what a person like you can't ever understand. You're wired to play it safe. Sit on the sidelines and watch people like me take what's ripe for the plucking."

"That's what you think? You honestly thought that I'd do nothing while you tried to ruin my life because you felt entitled to money that wasn't yours?"

"Five mill is chump change to you."

"Five million isn't chump change to anyone unless it's a chump like you," she fired back.

"Well, we both lose," Reggie grunted. "I might not have the money. But you'll be chased by that photo for the rest of your life."

"Of course I won't be, don't be ridiculous."

"Your cousin won't be able to scrub it off the internet. Once an image like that is out there, it stays forever. It'll turn up time and time again like a bad penny. I hope it's worth it."

Edie bent into his face. "The only person that photo damaged is you. Yours is the face everyone can see and you're the one holding the camera. And what's worse, you conned your lover into compromising herself for your dirty plot. But as for me, even if the world pointed a finger, the person I care most about is right here, and he isn't bothered by any of this. He knows the real me and that's enough."

"Is that what you told her?" Reggie leered at Archer, his teeth streaked red with blood from the earlier punch. "That's a good one. Got to say, you're playing a clever game."

Archer's neck muscles tightened. "What's that supposed to mean?"

"If I'm the bad cop in this situation, you're the good. Buttering her up. Acting like her mousy attitude is something that doesn't make you want to punch yourself in the face. Stick with it and I guess it will pay dividends. You a cowboy or something? Well good for you, you can probably score a couple of horses off her, plus a few rides. Although she's no bucking filly, more like a dead fish—"

Boom! Archer's punch landed square in the nose with a sickening crack. Reggie fell flat on his back.

"Holy shit," came a shout down the street. "What the hell happened?" That was Kit. Sawyer hot on his heels.

"I leave you alone for five minutes and you're committing assault?" Sawyer snapped.

"Trust me, bro." Archer shook out his wrist. "He had it coming to him."

Sawyer groaned. "Fuck. Are you saying that's the suspect?"

"That's Reggie," Eden said, passing over the man purse. "He had a gun."

"Do you always have to do the opposite of what makes common sense?" Sawyer muttered.

"What's that supposed to mean?" Archer said.

"I give you one simple order and you break it. Was it on purpose? Or are you hardwired to make bad decision after bad decision? What if he presses charges? Am I supposed to lock you up too? My own brother? Give me a second," Sawyer said to Kit, who turned to flash Archer a quick "oh shit" look. Kit and Archer raised hell throughout their youth. Whenever it got too out of hand, Sawyer got that tone, the one he used now. Archer stiffened as his brother drew near.

"You should have let him go. Kit and I had it handled."

"He walked right by us," Archer fired back. "I don't see how I stole your thunder."

Sawyer stilled, his face a mask. The only sign his temper was growing was the quick tick in his jaw. "My thunder? Are you crazy? You punched him."

"Twice. No regrets."

His brother uttered a muffled curse. "It's late so I'm going to get this bastard in lockup." Sawyer hauled up Reggie's limp body. "Reginald Winter, you are under arrest. You have the right to remain silent. If you say anything it can be used against you in a court of law."

Reggie groaned. "I demand to speak to my lawyers."

Kit cuffed him. "You have the right to have a lawyer present during any questioning. If you can't afford a lawyer, one will be provided for you."

Reggie spat on the ground. "I can afford enough law-yers to bury you and your entire shithole town."

"Not if you are needing to blackmail me for cash," Edie muttered. "My guess is you are flat broke."

Reggie kicked out in her direction.

"You're drunk and you've been caught doing a stupid thing," Edie continued. "I'm more sorry for you than angry. You're pathetic. A guy like you had the chance to be anything he wanted. The fact you've blown it is no one's fault but your own."

Sawyer and Kit hauled Reggie to the sheriff's vehicle and got him inside.

Archer stepped forward, addressing Sawyer's broad back. "Hey, I'm sorry about what I said, about stealing your thunder, but not for having given the bastard what he deserved."

Sawyer turned to Kit. "Hey, man, can you give us a second? I need to have a word with my little brother."

Archer winced at the word *little*. What that really meant was "no-good, impulsive fuck up —"

"What if this asshole counters with an assault charge to screw with the investigation?" Sawyer snapped the minute Kit shut the car door. "The law is there for a reason. You should have worked within it."

Archer pushed his shoulders back. "There is no law in this country that's going to make me stand by and watch some sleazeball psycho put his hands on my girl. I'm sorry to have gotten my hands dirty and caused you extra hassle, but this had the potential to go to the worse kind of bad. You can say I did the wrong thing, but I know in my bones that my actions were right, even if they do cause a few headaches."

Edie settled a hand on his chest and turned to Sawyer "If a guy blackmailed Annie, threatened to destroy her life, then called her foul names to her face before trying to choke her, what would you have done?"

Sawyer was quiet for a long time. He stared out into the darkness before turning back with a shrug. "Honestly?"

"Yes, please."

"I'd have done exactly what Archer did."

Archer exhaled one slow long breath.

Sawyer shook his head. "Look, it wasn't the right thing to do, but it was also the exactly right thing to do. I'm sorry I came down hard. The fact he had a gun, it scared me. You're my brother. I can't have something happen to you."

Scared? Sawyer was scared? "I never thought you were scared of anything."

His brother laughed then, a low rumbling chuckle. "You're kidding yourself, man. When it comes to the people we love, we're all vulnerable. I love Annie and her son. I love you. I love Grandma. I love Wilder, although Christ knows what he's up to. When it comes to those people facing harm or hardship, sure I get scared. Absolutely. And sometimes I act like a shit. It's because I care, but that doesn't excuse it. I'm sorry."

And like that the years of private jealousy, the bubbling fear that Sawyer was beyond human, too perfect, popped. His brother was just a man. A good man, one of the best, but not better than him. They all were going through life trying to do the best they could for the people that mattered most.

"Come here, you," Archer tugged him into a bear hug and thumped on his back. Sawyer did the same in turn.

As Sawyer drove away, Edie reached out a hand.

"How are you?"

"Forget me," Archer said. "How are you?"

"I was scared," she said. "Scared you'd get hurt. But I'm not going to forget you. How you feel is important and that conversation with your brother seemed to mean a lot."

"It did," Archer admitted. "I hate to admit it but I get jealous of that guy. He just always has seemed to do better."

"He's not better, just different. He's a good man and so are you."

"Thank you for believing in me, for not thinking I'm a big joke."

She smiled. "You make me laugh sometimes, but no, you're not a joke."

"I love you," he said.

"You love me?" she said as if tasting the words, a bewildering flavor.

"To the moon, but that's only getting started. I love you to wherever the universe ends."

"But the universe doesn't end."

"Exactly," he replied, taking her hand in his and kissing it.

She was quiet for a moment; a moment that dragged

on long enough that his heart began to pound. He hadn't said what he said because he expected her to reciprocate, that's not what this had been, but damn it, when they'd been together, she had to have felt what was between them. What was undeniably right.

And if she didn't. Fuck. It would hurt like nothing he'd known, but no regrets. He meant every word, come hell or high water.

"I've never had anyone tell me that. I mean no one who's not obligated to, like Mother or Daddy. In fact, I'm not sure if they ever said the words. They did love me, of course they did, but they weren't demonstrative and now I'm babbling."

How had no one told this lovable, wonderful woman she was worthy of all that was best in the world? His heart broke even as his mind couldn't conceive of the fact. It just didn't make sense. "The first time we met, I told you that the man who wins your heart needed to tell you how beautiful you are every night as you fall asleep and every morning when you wake. I don't know why you've been surrounded by people who are blind or stupid. I've got to say I never trusted city slickers much and this only confirms my suspicions."

"You really mean it."

"I mean it so much that saying it doesn't even feel right. It's too big. It's too much. But it's all I've got, no other fancy words."

"Archer." She sniffled. "I love you too."

And those words might not be enough, but to hear her say it, they were everything.

He wrapped his arms around her middle and picked her right up off her feet. It hurt like a mother, his ribs were sore as hell. Maybe it was a bad idea, but he wasn't ever going to be the kind of guy who made all the responsible choices. Right now he needed his woman up and against him.

"All I want to do is be the kind of guy who is worthy of someone like you."

Her toes pressed into his shins as she wrapped her arms around his neck. "And just who do you think I am?"

"Beautiful on the inside, in a way that shines through and makes your pretty outside something amazing. You are brave. Look at you, moving to the other side of the country, becoming a business owner. You could be a spoiled brat chewing out maids and testing out the limits of your credit card and no one would bat an eye. You chose another path and I have so much respect for you."

Edie rested her forehead on his. "Thank you for saying all these things. Thank you from the bottom of my heart. But I'm not perfect either and I've done things I'm not proud of. And I need to make amends too."

Chapter Twenty-One

EDIE PARKED OUTSIDE a cheerful yellow cottage a few blocks off Brightwater's Main Street. Well-planned garden beds encircled the house bursting with blossoms of every imaginable color. She had to be at the sheriff's office in an hour to give an official statement. Reggie was going to be released on bond but the charges of blackmail and possession of an illegal firearm would follow him. Not to mention the fact that revenge porn was illegal in California. The area was grey since she wasn't specifically in the photograph, but still . . . the decision to post such an intimate image to cause harm wouldn't do him any favors when he had his day in court, never mind the assault charges.

Sober, Reggie acted more ashamed than cocky, Sawyer said. Good. Let him return to New York with his tail between his legs. He was also being investigated for involvement in a Ponzi scheme so it might well be a case of out of the frying pan and into the fire. It sounded like Suki had taken off for greener pastures when the money dried up.

Sad to have so much and to lose it all.

But Reggie had made his own bed and the person she'd once been was gone. She still loved that Old Eden—sad, insecure, expecting people to dislike her, lurking in the sidelines of life. But that wasn't her anymore.

She was Edie Banks in Brightwater. But to move forward in this new chapter, she needed to clear the air.

With a deep breath, she got out of her car and walked up the zinnia-lined path toward the house.

Inside was silent. Maybe no one was home.

She knocked and waited.

Marigold opened the door. "What do you want?"

"I don't want to go through with the bake off," Edie said. "I should never have challenged you in the first place. It was the wrong move. I'm new here and while I don't want to be walked all over, I don't want to be unnecessarily adversarial either."

"Unnecessarily adversarial?" Marigold rolled her eyes. "Who talks like that?"

"I do," Edie said simply. "But I want to come here and make peace. It doesn't benefit you, me, or our respective businesses to have a public disagreement."

"Is this because of that dirty picture?"

Edie froze. "Excuse me?"

"The one online. I heard about it and found it this morning."

"No." Edie's shoulders slumped. "That's not why I'm here."

Marigold gave her a long look. "Why don't you come inside?"

Edie glanced behind her. The sidewalk was empty. No one was in their yards. Not a single witness would see her enter Marigold's house. The place looked cute and from what she could glimpse through the open door, it seemed neat and tidy, not a torture den, but still, uncertainty caused her heart to beat faster.

"Can I get you something, a glass of water, cup of tea, crappy coffee?"

Edie blushed and entered. "Look, I'm sorry for what I said my first morning here about your coffee. It had been a long twenty-four hours and while that's no excuse, I wasn't at my best either."

Marigold waved to a couch. "Take a seat." She perched on the edge of a chair opposite. "The photo—"

"It wasn't me."

Marigold wrinkled her nose. "Of course not. Your hair color is unique, so many different shades. The woman in that picture is wearing a wig, or box dyed it. Anyone can tell."

Edie wasn't sure whether to be relieved or not. Marigold's intense stare gave away very little. "This happened to me once," she said.

"It did?" Edie's hands formed two fists. "A photograph?"

"I moved to LA for a year after high school." She rolled her eyes. "I thought about getting into modeling or acting."

"You are very pretty."

"Thanks." Marigold's smile was tight. "I wasn't pretty enough. But I got a few small time swimsuit model gigs, and found an agent who became my boyfriend. It got murky. Anyway, he took some images of us . . . together. I was stupid and young, trusted that he loved me, that he'd never hurt me. Bad decision."

"He posted them." Edie's blood chilled as her heart clenched in sympathy.

"Eventually. I got homesick and wanted to come back to Brightwater. My mom wasn't well and she couldn't manage The Baker's Dozen all on her own."

"So you moved home."

"Yep, and got stuck. My mom died and I got her shop, kept it going in her memory. He didn't like my decision and posted pictures of me as revenge, emailing me the link. I don't know who, if anyone, here has ever seen them. But they are out there floating around on the internet somewhere. Men must occasionally look at them. Do things while looking at me." She shuddered.

"That should never have happened—you didn't deserve it."

"I haven't trusted anyone since. Sure, I date sometimes. But I can't take it farther. Ever. Plus, I don't know . . . I want to leave sometimes. I love Brightwater, I do. But there's a whole world out there and I feel like it's all going to pass me by. Most of my friends from high school left, or if they stayed, they are married with kids. They don't have time for me. I'm by myself most of the time and . . . I'm lonely."

Edie blinked. Suddenly Marigold didn't seem like such

a mean girl. The cold face was nothing more than a mask to keep the world from seeing how much she hurt. She lashed out at others because she was insecure herself. Was that how it was for the bullies that attacked her when she was younger too? It was too late to know, but maybe so.

Here she had taken all of Marigold's attitude and made the situation about her. It was never about her. Marigold was sad and lonely, but none of it was about Edie.

Compassion swelled Edie's heart. "You don't love the bakery?"

"No," she shook her head, rubbing her eyes. "I don't. I never have. I don't like to cook. It's not my passion. But I love my mom and that place is my last connection to her. I can't bear to sell it."

Edie sat for a long moment. "What would you do if you didn't have the responsibility of running The Baker's Dozen?

"Seriously?" Margot stared into space with a dreamy expression. "I'd like to travel to France and visit Monet's Garden or the grounds at Versailles. I've always loved gardening and flowers."

Edie leaned forward. "I might be able to help you."

ARCHER FINISHED WORK for the day, the last of the ranch hands headed home. Grandma was still in the hospital but she'd been steadily improving. He dug out his phone and hit "Wilder." A robotic message told him to leave a message. It didn't even have his real voice. He and Sawyer had been trying to contact his brother since Grandma went into the hospital last week, but so far nothing. They'd be forced to call him at work. He'd probably be pissed, but Jesus, no man could be an island.

Edie was out for a run. The half-marathon was coming up and she wanted to make a good time. The fact she could still stand after twelve miles impressed him, but she was determined and that was the thing that got him about Freckles, lassoed his heart and squeezed. When she put her mind to something, she did it.

And it rubbed off. Inspired him to dig in and try harder.

Hidden Rock chugged along fine under his new management and soon he'd be moving into the big house. Grandma couldn't be there alone. Not anymore. And besides he needed room for a wife.

His heart squeezed even tighter, enough that he got light-headed. Yeah. Shit. Look at him. A steady career. A house. Thinking about marriage.

But, as impossible as it seemed, he wanted to do it right. Any guy could buy a ring for the woman he loved. But this was Freckles. Only a legend would do.

Over the mountains came a low rumble of thunder. The clouds were building and the wind shifted. Temperatures dropped quickly and when he breathed deep, the scent of ozone hung heavy in the air. Thunderstorms weren't common in the Eastern Sierras, but any water was welcome. It had been an unseasonably warm winter and river levels were approaching record lows. Fires were a real and present danger and any water would decrease the risk.

Besides, something about a good storm quickened his blood. It always had, ever since he was a kid. Grandma would let him go out on the porch and watch lightning strike the high peaks of the range. Watching the overwhelming power of nature unleash itself made him feel small, but in a good way, like he was part of something bigger, not inconsequential, but in tune with the landscape. He didn't have a good way to voice the feeling then and he still didn't. It was a sense that anything could happen.

He didn't mind getting wet so he reset his hat and walked past the old barn. Maybe he'd go and say hi to Sawyer, Annie, and her son, Atticus. They were all living in Sawyer's cabin now and it wasn't far, about a half mile walk if he cut across the rise.

He walked and idly mulled the many places Fielder Kane might have buried the ring. There weren't any buildings from his era still standing on the ranch. They'd been torn down for firewood over the years, or replaced with new, stronger structures.

The house dated back to just over a century.

There was an old cemetery on the property, no doubt Fielder Kane's wife was laid to rest there. Archer hadn't visited it in a long time. He switched directions from Sawyer's cabin to head that way. Even if the ring was hidden there, he wouldn't be digging around his great-great-great-grandmother's grave, but his parents were laid to rest there, and it had been a long time since he'd paid them respects.

The first heavy drops of rain fell as he reached the

family cemetery. It was a quiet place, set beneath a grove
of trees a discrete distance from their grazing lands and
ringed by a black wrought-iron fence.

The place didn't have the abandoned look he expected. The closest grave was covered in cut roses, the
same yellow ones that bloomed near the ranch house.
This is where Grandfather was buried. The words on the
headstone were simple.

A good man, husband and father.

Grandma must still visit him. The roses didn't look
more than a week old, only just beginning to lose their
freshness. He'd cut some more and tell her. She'd like
that he did that while she was in the hospital.

A little farther away was another, bigger headstone.
This one had two names and more flowers. Bridger and
Lynn Kane. His father and mother. They'd died in a freak
house fire when he was four years old. He couldn't remember anything about that night and no one ever spoke
of it. All he knew is that he and his brothers survived.

How long has it been since he visited them?

Too long.

"Hey, Dad. Hey, Mom," he said, kneeling. Rain pelted
his back and shoulders but he wouldn't melt. This was
important. "It's me. Archer, your youngest." As if they
might not know. "If you've been watching me all these
years, I don't think I've done a hell of a lot to make you
proud. Thinking back on it, I didn't give much of any
thought to the fact you might be watching. Lately, I'm
turning over a new leaf. Getting my head screwed on
right. Grandma wants me to take on Hidden Rock and

I met a woman, Edie, Eden. But I call her Freckles, and she's the most beautiful thing I've ever seen. When I'm with her I feel like the ideas that scared me for so long, of settling down, having a family, things I didn't know if I was cut out for, are within reach. It's different with her. It doesn't feel hard. It feels like the natural next step. I don't think she'll go easy on me but I do think she'll always love me. And I aim to love her too."

He reached out and touched the cold marble. "I'm sorry that I haven't been up here to see you. I bet Sawyer comes a lot. But that's going to change too. I'll stop by again soon and plant some pretty things. I'll bring Edie too.

"I wish . . ." His throat tightened, it was hard to get out the next words. "I wish you guys were here. I feel like I'm getting closer to the age you were when you died, and I can't imagine leaving my kids behind. I hope you didn't suffer. I hope it was quick. And you must have saved us because we kids all made it out. I haven't talked to Wilder in too long, but I'm trying to change that too. At the end of it all, family is the most important thing, nothing else—money, land, jobs—matters if you don't have that. A tree can't grow without roots and mine have been shallow long enough."

Thunder boomed, echoing up the valley.

"That's my cue," Archer said, pushing himself up to stand. "I want to ask Edie to be with me always, but I wanted to find that ring. The Hidden Rock ring. If I'm going to ask her to move here and live with me, it seems fitting. I'll probably never find it but, hey, worth giving it a try."

Lightning flashed. He stared at the big old tree opposite, gnarled with age. The storm turned fierce, the wind nearly sending his hat into the air. He clapped a hand on the brim and again lightning flashed. His eyes could be playing tricks but he walked forward, patting his parent's gravestone as he passed. He got to the iron gate and hopped it easily. There, in front of him, was a big old tree trunk. Overhead the branches swayed wildly, scratching, cracking, and knocking together. But in the bark, carved deep with a pen knife, were initials. "F loves M," Archer muttered. "F loves M."

From here, there was a vantage point down the valley. The mountains, mostly locked in storm clouds were hidden but on a clear day you could see for miles. It would be a romantic spot for a picnic. Perfect for courtship. A place where he'd like to bring Edie.

Above the initials was a hole. Archer started to reach forward and then stopped himself with a laugh. "You are being a fool," he said to himself.

And maybe he was. But who cared? He was a fool in love.

He reached inside and his hand closed on a small box. "I'll be damned."

Pulling it out, he peeked inside and whistled. Then he glanced back to the cemetery beyond. Who knows if this was a sign, or luck, or pure dumb coincidence, but it felt like he had his parents' blessing.

Chapter Twenty-Two

THE CROWD STARTED to gather an hour before noon. Margot kept going to the window of Haute Coffee and peeking. "Four new people," she called.

Edie wiped her forehead. "Do you mind stepping away? I'm getting more and more nervous."

"Why? You decided not to duel Marigold Flint at high noon."

"Yes, but the town doesn't know that yet. They don't know what is going to happen. Only that there is a big announcement."

"I don't even know the big secret," Margot said with a little pout. "Oh, look, Annie just got here."

Margot banged on the glass window and gave a cheery wave. "Hey there!" she called through the glass before looking over her shoulder with a sheepish grin. "Sorry! Sorry! I know, back away from the window. It's just that this is her first week with the new job, editor in chief of the *Brightwater Bugle*. It's a really big step."

"Of course, I'm so excited for her. I invited her myself. It's just . . ." Edie reset her headband and smoothed invisible wrinkles from her A-line skirt. She'd chosen her outfit with more than the usual care. Who knew who in this small town had heard the rumors about what happened, and she wanted to look like the furthest thing from a sex scandal possible. Quincy had called and advised her to dress like a Sunday school teacher or a kindergarten teacher. "Basically like you usually do, darling, except add a cardigan."

She'd taken his advice.

"You look cute," Margot said. "And I'm wildly curious about what you are going to say."

"Not long now," Edie looked at her wristwatch. "It's almost time."

The back door opened and loud footsteps moved through the kitchen. Before she could turn around, two big hands braced her hips, and hiked her backward.

"Archer," she squealed. "Put me down."

"How'd you know it's me?"

"I'd know those hands anywhere," she whispered low enough that Margot wouldn't hear. Turning around, she kissed him on the cheek. "Thanks for leaving the ranch to come hear this. I know you are so busy."

"Anything for you. And, Freckles, you got to eat more of your pies. You're running so much that soon you'll weigh as little as a feather."

"The half-marathon is in forty-eight hours. I know it's

the same day as your Grandma gets moved to the rehab center so it's fine to miss it. Hopefully I'll live to pavement pound another day."

Outside, the town clocked struck twelve.

"Wish me luck," she said, taking his hand. "Outside of Quincy and Marigold, you are the only person in the know."

"And it makes me feel so proud of you I might burst."

"You really don't mind? It's a lot of money. Money that could go to the ranch."

"Hidden Rock will carry on the same way as it always has. Through hard work. What you are proposing to do is something I have never seen. Giving back to a town you barely know."

"I hope it's the town I'll grow old in," Edie said simply. "I really love it here."

"Okay, okay, I can see you are raring to get the show on the road, but first, one kiss for good luck."

She crooked her lips. "As if I can turn that offer down."

He slanted his mouth over hers, and not for the first time did she marvel at the perfect way that they fit together. She parted and let him tease her tongue with his, just a hint of promise, that tonight, and tomorrow, and every other day would be theirs, full of kisses that made her blood quicken and limbs heat. He started to pull away but she sunk her fingers into his hair and held him firm, pushing her breasts against his hard chest, loving the way her softness fit against his hardness.

And he was hard in other places.

"Oops," she said with a wicked giggle.

"You aren't the least bit sorry," he said with his easy grin. "Now I'll have to think about baseball or accounting software or—"

"Leeches?" she batted innocent eyes.

"Done and done. That does the trick. Almost. As good as this whole shop smells, your vanilla scent drives me wild, Freckles."

She cupped a hand over his ear, whispering, "I bought some honey vanilla bubble bath from Bab's Boutique. I'm thinking you and me and a bath for two later."

He groaned. "Shit. Leeches won't cut it."

"Thank you," she said, lacing her fingers with his. "I feel less nervous."

"You've got me standing beside you always."

She squeezed his hand. "I know. Thank you."

Archer let Edie lead him out of the front of the shop to where a small crowd gathered on the sidewalk. In the front, Marigold stood, her features as strained as Edie's. Both women were clearly uncomfortable in the spotlight. Still, this was their moment so he took a step away, but Edie gripped his hand. Making it impossible to move far.

"Marigold, would you mind joining me up here?" Edie asked. Marigold stepped forward and turned to face the crowd, wiping her hands on her dark jeans. Quincy was there alongside them.

"As you may have gathered—" Edie began quietly.

"Speak up, we can't hear in the back," someone shouted.

"Marigold and I aren't here for a public bake off at high noon," Eddie said louder. "While we have had our differences over the past few months, we have also learned that we both have things in common too. Just like anyone. Isn't that part of what makes living in a small town special? We can drive each other crazy but then be there to lend a helping hand. That's what I'm learning at least. I come from New York and it's very different, but I'm finding my way, and appreciate the fact so many of you have opened you hearts to support the shop and make me feel at home.

"This leads me to an exciting announcement." She turned to Quincy. "Bankcroft Media will be facilitating a large anonymous donation to the Brightwater School District. There are many opportunities for young people in the valley for life skills and job training, but to date the resources are not matching the need. This donation will see a state-of-the art media lab installed at Brightwater High School, plus work-study opportunities throughout the town, including The Baker's Dozen. The bakery will be closing shortly and reopening as an affiliate of Haute Coffee where students will be allowed to study culinary arts and gain valuable customer service skills. Doing is the best teaching, and we look forward to providing young people with opportunities normally only offered in large population centers.

"Now I have spoken a lot, I'm going to pause and open it up for questions."

Annie raised her hand. "Marigold, where will you go if the bakery closes?"

Marigold cleared her throat. "I will still own the space and am not releasing that interest. My mother loved that bakery and was proud of it. I think she'll be more than gratified to know that her legacy is living on. As for me, I plan for Brightwater to always be my home. It's where I was born and where I expect to live my final days, hopefully far far in the future. For now, I'm off to do a little traveling. I've never left the United States and would love to travel to Europe—see Ireland, go to Italy or France. Maybe all three, who knows?"

Laughter rippled through the crowd.

"Where did the money come from?" someone piped up in the back of the crowd.

"An anonymous donation," Quincy said. "I am sorry, but I am not at liberty to disclose any information about the donor."

"What about the bake off?" someone else called out.

Marigold and Edie traded glances. "Do you want to tell them?" Edie asked.

"No, you go ahead," Marigold answered with a giggle.

"To celebrate this recent turn of events, both The Baker's Dozen and Haute Coffee are going to be offering complimentary pie and coffee for the next hour. Please stop by both locations. Plans for the bakery remodel will be on display at The Dozen, including a look at the new classroom space."

People split into two groups, each pouring into the shops eager for the free pie and fellowship. Archer hugged Edie to him. "I am so proud of you. That went off without a hitch—you did fantastic."

"Thank you," Edie replied. "I was nervous someone would say something about the—"

"Doesn't concern you," Quincy said, stepping beside her. "The best revenge you can have is to never let the image you weren't in enter your head again."

"Reggie is up to his neck in trouble," Archer reassured her, smoothing away the worry lines on her forehead. "All you need to do now is figure out how fast you can serve the people in there. Margot must be sweating bullets."

"Oh dear, I should get to her," Edie said as Annie approached.

"I do have one more question," Annie said with a grin.

"Tell you what," Archer said. "You talk to Annie and I'll go and serve the pies."

"The question is more for the two of you."

"What's that?" Archer asked, pulling up short.

"Are you really a couple now?"

"As real as real can be," Archer replied right as Edie said, "Oh yes."

Annie clapped her hands. "I am so thrilled. Welcome to the family."

"Whoa now, I am not officially in the family yet or anything."

"Oh sure you are," Annie said waving her hand against inconsequential details. "In all the ways that matter at least. Sawyer and I are still living in sin. Who knows, maybe we can have a double wedding."

Edie glanced shyly at Archer who felt his ears burn. "We haven't talked about any of that yet."

Annie slapped her forehead. "And here I am putting my big mouth into it. I'll let you get to work and will invite you all up to the cabin soon for dinner."

"That sounds great," Edie said.

"Now all you guys have to do is find your brother," Annie continued. "Have you had any luck getting him on your phone?"

Archer shook his head, trying to hide his unease.

Annie pushed back her short bangs. "Same with Sawyer. He's starting to get really worried."

"There's got to be a reasonable explanation," Archer said. But shit, the facts were, Wilder hadn't returned a single message and with Grandma in the hospital, something wasn't passing the smell test.

Annie waved them both to the shop. "I can't wait to write this story up for my first feature. As for Wilder, Sawyer will give the smoke jumper office a call later today. Figure out what's going on."

They watched her walk away. He took Edie's hand. How had he ever lived for so many years without her touch? "I love you," he said.

She glanced up, surprised. "What's the occasion?"

"You're alive. The fact it's a Tuesday. Because I'm the luckiest guy in the world. Are those good enough reasons?"

Her eyes danced. "Works for me."

He kissed the side of her forehead. "And you better get used to hearing me tell you, because I'll never get sick of saying it."

Chapter Twenty-Three

EDIE'S LEGS WERE leaden. The rest of her didn't feel anything at all, except for a vague stinging sensation from her eyes as sweat dripped off her forehead. "Almost there. Almost there," she chanted. This last mile turned out to be a killer, but head down; soon she'd be able to say she'd run a half-marathon. This sport couldn't be simpler, all she needed was her two feet, and it couldn't be harder, all she needed was sheer will—the unwavering faith to push through pain, doubt, and the overwhelming need to stop, lie in the soft grass, and devour an entire tray of brownies.

It was a conscious choice, to keep moving when you didn't have to, when you didn't even want to. Keep going. Break through. She'd run from her old life, and now she ran toward her new life, one where she was in control, not weighed down by rules and expectations, but free to be who and what she needed to be.

With such a truth behind her it was a wonder she didn't fly.

"You run fast. Didn't think I'd ever catch up."

Edie glanced over her shoulder and nearly tripped. "Archer? What are you doing here?"

He was dressed in a pair of black athletic shorts and . . . that's all. His bare chest was slicked with a sheen of sweat and his abs bunched and flexed as he pulled alongside her.

"Got to say, Freckles, my brain feels about to burst and I can still think of twenty things more fun to do than run. You're a masochist."

She laughed as they rounded the final bend, the finish line ahead.

"I didn't think you'd be able to make it."

"Grandma had a good night. That tough old bird will live to peck us all another day," he said with obvious affection. "But Annie agreed to stay with her for the move to rehab so I could come here. She and Grandma have a tense relationship, but they'll figure it out. I wouldn't miss this for the world. It's not every day my girl completes her first half-marathon."

Sudden tears burned Edie's eyes. Mount Oh-Be-Joyful was doused in morning light and the air held a crisp tang, hinting of the coming autumn. Ahead would be cozy autumn nights, drinking hot apple cider and cuddling before a bright fire with this amazing man beside her.

Almost there. Her legs were officially aching. All she wanted was to give Archer a big kiss, and pound a Gatorade, in that exact order. The crowd let out a cheer as the runners came down the final pipeline, the announcer broadcasting runners' names and hometowns. In another minute it would be her turn, and she'd be Edie Banks from Brightwater. She was also still Eden Bankcroft-Kew, and would always love that girl she'd been. She was also Freckles, who loved the man beside her, body and soul.

"Here we go," she whispered.

"Hey, hold up." Archer grabbed her elbow and she halted.

"What's the matter? Let's go!" The finish line was calling her name. They were right there. So close.

"Edie Banks."

She glanced, startled as the loudspeakers boomed her name.

"Edie Banks, this man beside you has a very important question to ask."

"What's going on . . ." Her voice trailed off as she turned to Archer who wasn't standing. No. He knelt.

"There are so many ways to have fun in life," he said. "But I've never had more fun than since I met you. I promise, no one, *no one*, will ever work harder to make all your dreams come true." He pulled out a small box from his shorts, and opened it, the diamond catching the sun. It wasn't two carats, but it was the most beautiful thing she'd ever seen.

"Oh my, oh, oh my God," she whispered, as he reached out and gently took her hand.

"This is the Hidden Rock ring. I want you to wear it, to have the ranch, and to have my name. Everything that is mine is yours, especially my heart. Will you marry me?"

"Yes," she said. "Yes, yes, yes, a thousand times yes." Despite the cheers exploding from the sidelines, her world shrank down to her and Archer, even as her heart grew bigger and more expansive than the surrounding landscape.

He slid the ring on her finger and pulled her in for a soft, thorough kiss. "Did I mess up your finish? I know how hard you've trained."

"Are you kidding me?" she said, laughing and crying. "This is the exact right moment." She laced her fingers through his. "Let's cross together, Cowboy."

Hand in hand, they crossed the finish line together, heading toward a bright new future.

Can't wait to read more of Lia Riley's
Brightwater series?
The next fantastic book in the
series drops in October!

BEST WORST MISTAKE

SMOKE JUMPER WILDER Kane once reveled in the rush he got from putting out dangerous wildfires. But after a tragic accident changed his life, he's cut himself off from the world, refusing to leave his isolated cabin. When a headstrong beauty bursts in, Wilder finds himself craving the fire she ignites in him, but letting anyone near his darkness would be a mistake.

After her glamorous LA life went up in smoke, Quinn Higsby decided to leave Tinseltown behind and returned to Brightwater to care for her ailing father. Spending her days in a small bookstore, her peaceful existence is upended by a fascinating but damaged man. Quinn is determined to not to be scared off by Wilder, not once she's experienced the heat of his passions.

But when an arsonist targets the community and Wilder is framed for the crimes, he must confront the ghosts of his past. Will his desire for Quinn flame out or will he be able to tame the wildness inside and rekindle a hope for the future?

**And keep reading for an excerpt from
the amazing first novel in the series!**

LAST FIRST KISS

A kiss is just the beginning. . .

PINTEREST PERFECT. OR so Annie Carson's life appears on her popular blog. Reality is . . . messier. Especially when it lands her back in the one-cow town of Brightwater, California, and back in the path of the gorgeous six-foot-four reason she left. Sawyer Kane may fill out those Wranglers, but she won't be distracted from her task. Annie just needs the summer to spruce up and sell her family's farm so she and her young son can start a new life in the big city. Simple, easy, perfect.

Sawyer has always regretted letting the first girl he loved slip away. He won't make the same mistake twice, but can he convince beautiful, wary Annie to trust her heart again when she's been given every reason not to? And as a single kiss turns into so much more, can Annie give up her idea of perfect for a forever that's blissfully real?

Available Now from Avon Impulse!

An Excerpt from
LAST FIRST KISS

THE KNOCK CAME as the last ice cube melted into her scotch.

What the . . . ? Annie Carson slammed against the chair, adrenal system upgrading from zoned out to Defcon 1. The vintage pig cookie jar stared back from the Formica counter with a vaguely panicked expression. Nothing arrived after midnight except lovers and trouble.

Annie didn't have a lover. And the biggest trouble she had tonight was trying to finish this blog post while forgetting all the reasons she fled from here in the first place. On the surface, Brightwater boasted a quaint Ye Olde West appeal. Nestled under the shadow of Mount Oh-Be-Joyful's fourteen-thousand-foot peak, the historic main street boasted a working saddlery instead of Starbucks, the barbershop offered complimentary sideburn trims, and tractors caused the only traffic jams.

Then there were the cowboys. Some women—fine, *most* women—would consider the local ranchers to be six kinds of swoon-worthy, but she'd learned her lesson ten years ago.

If you meet a cute guy wearing a Stetson, run in the opposite direction.

The next knock rattled the front door's hinges; whoever was out there meant business. Annie sneezed before drawing a shaky breath. Drinking wasn't a personal forte, but chamomile tea didn't do much to blunt the first-night-back-in-my-one-cow-hometown blues, even with extra honey.

Maybe if she took her time, whoever was out there would go away.

She closed her laptop's lid, stood, and walked to the sink, setting the tumbler under the leaky tap. Water drip, drip, dripped into the brown dregs. Dad's radio above the fridge, tuned to a Fresno classical station, piped in Mozart's *Requiem* on the scratchy speakers, hopefully due to coincidence rather than cosmic foreshadowing.

More knocking.

This could very well be an innocent mistake. Someone had confused directions, taken a wrong turn, driven up a quarter-mile driveway to an out-of-the-way farmhouse . . . to where she sat wearing a *Kiss Me, I'm Scottish* apron with a sleeping five-year-old upstairs.

She hadn't missed Gregor in months. Her ex-husband might be a metrosexual philosophy professor, but at least he stood higher than five feet in socks. Why, oh, why had she enrolled in yoga instead of kickboxing last summer in Portland? No way would a sun salutation cut the mustard against a crazy-eyed bunny boiler. An alarmed buzz replaced the hollow feeling in her chest. Brightwater was a sleepy, safe backwater. Had it grown more dangerous since she tore out of here on her eighteenth birthday? Meth labs? Cattle thieves? Area 51 wasn't too far away, so throw in possible alien abduction?

Well, she was alone now and would have to deal with whatever came.

As a rule, killers and extraterrestrials didn't announce themselves at the front door. Still, this was no time to start taking chances. She grabbed her father's single-malt by the neck and padded into the living room. The change from bright kitchen to gloom skewed her vision as blood shunted to her legs. Shadows clung to the beamed ceiling and brick fireplace. If the rocking chair in the corner moved, she'd pee her pants. That old gooseneck rocker starred in more than a few of her childhood nightmares—ever since her sister had mentioned that Great-Grandma Carson had died in it.

"Hello?" she called, her voice calm—but, darn, an octave too high. "Who's there?"

Silence.

The door didn't have a peephole. This was the Eastern Sierras, a place where shopkeepers left signs taped to their unlocked front doors saying "Went to the bank, back in five minutes."

Think! Think! What's the game plan?

Retreat not a choice. But more whisky was definitely a viable option. She opened the bottle, and the gulp seared her throat. At least the burn helped dissipate the cold fear knotting her stomach. She pressed her lips together while screwing the cap back on. *Here goes nothing.* Brandishing the bottle like a club, she flung open the door.

A light breeze blew across her face, cool despite the fact it was early July. Five Diamonds Farm sat at four thousand feet in elevation. She glanced around the porch. Empty. Unable to stand the suspense, she stepped forward, her bare toes grazing warm ceramic. A baking dish sat on the mat. Annie knit her brow and crouched—a neighborly casserole delivery? At this hour? Fat chance, but one could hope. She removed the lid, and an invisible fist squeezed her sternum.

If hope was a thing with feathers, all she had was chicken potpie.

Literally.

A toothpick anchored a Post-it note to the crust.

> *Caught your hen in my tomatoes.*
> *Chicken #2 will be nuggets.*
> *Welcome home.*

She tightened her shoulders. No name, but none was needed. This had Grandma Kane's fingerprints all over it. The crotchety old woman ruled the spread next door, Hidden Rock Ranch, like it was her own personal empire, and she regarded the Carsons as unwelcome squatters.

Annie smashed the note in her fist and hurled it as far as possible. Crud, such a crappy toss—the wadded paper barely cleared the bottom step. She couldn't even throw right. Three seconds later litterbug guilt struck, and she scrambled to retrieve it.

An engine roared to life near the barn, brake lights illuminating the ponderosa pine grove. Tires kicked up gravel and the horn tooted twice before turning onto the main road.

Enough was enough. The Kanes had once made her life a living hell, and that old woman's capacity to nurse a grudge went beyond anything remotely sane or reasonable. The one-hundred-and-fifty-year-old feud had to end. This was the twenty-first century, time to leave behind the kerosene-lit dark ages once and for all. After the last terrible year, she was due a little peace.

She tucked her chin to her chest and strode around the house to assess the poultry situation. Five Diamonds might have become a farm in name only, but at least the chicken coop remained operational. As a girl, she loved collecting the eggs, selling them for a few bucks a dozen. The money went to her college fund, but that wasn't the reason she took over the chore. She loved how when she appeared with cracked corn, the flock approached at warp speed, offering nothing but cheerful clucks. The comical sight never failed to induce a giggle.

Tonight, the hens were quiet in the brooder box and nothing appeared amiss. Relief drizzled through her veins. Grandma Kane must be playing a joke. She probably shopped the poultry specials at the local Save-U-More and—

"Oh, no." A corner of rusty wire bent at an awkward angle. Annie yanked it as her groan rose to the moonless sky. Nearby, a coyote joined in, harmonizing with a single, mournful note.

There was more than enough wiggle room, even for the fattest hen, to escape. The back fields were overgrown, the orchard was a gnarled jungle, and the house was more weatherboard than paint. Backbreaking chores stretched in every direction. Couldn't Dad at least have kept the coop in one piece? She fought back a sniffle, dropped the whisky bottle, and wiped her nose before twining the wire around a nail, shaking it a few times to ensure the quick fix held. A better shoring of defenses would have to wait until morning.

In the distance, atop the low rise, a light flicked on. Grandma Kane must have been arriving home. She probably sat on a throne of chicken bones and gnawed drumsticks like a wrinkled Genghis Khan.

Annie clenched her jaw, eyes narrowing. As much as she wanted peace, all necessary recourses were on the table if that woman so much as inched a toe on her property again. There were laws, and they existed for a reason, such as protecting respectable people from bloodthirsty octogenarians. Five Diamonds and its inhabitants were now her responsibility.

Dad packed up his painstakingly restored '68 VW van and left for his artist residency in Mexico yesterday. He was ready to sell the farm and move on. Before leaving, he mentioned that offers had started to come in for neighboring properties last year—unsolicited and mind-bogglingly high. Brightwater was on the map after *Tumbleweeds* filmed in the valley, won an Academy Award, and captured the public's imagination. *Sunset Magazine* followed up with a feature, "Last Best Secret in the West," and local property values skyrocketed, LA types snapping up second, third, even fourth homes.

Chest caving, she trudged to the front porch to gather what remained of the wanderlusting hen. A committed vegetarian for years, choking down even a single bite was out of the question. It was hard enough to swallow the fact that with Dad off to Puerto Peñasco and her sister, Claire, running a food truck in San Francisco, Annie was the only person left with the time to deal with Five Diamonds.

Her summer could be distilled to one simple goal—get the old farm ready for sale. With her share of the profit, she would be able to afford the astronomical housing in the Bay Area and move Atticus closer to his beloved aunt. Her mother died not long after Annie's birth, and Dad wanted to retire south of the border. This was a way for her and her son to have a taste of family life.

The city also had a vibrant tech scene, perfect for an ambitious blogger ready to re-enter the workforce. Atticus would start kindergarten in the fall, and at last she could blow the dust bunnies off her journalism degree. Perfect timing, as *Musings of a Mighty Mama* exploded this year, going from a hobby mommy blog to pulling in five figures in advertising revenue—low five figures, but a more than promising start. Gregor was legally committed to providing child support, but she needed to figure out a way to stand on her own two feet. A robust blog presence could open the door to a syndicated column on a national website, or a book deal, or—

Something.

But right now what she needed was more coffee cake. After scraping the potpie into the garbage, she snagged the last slice from the Bundt pan. Cinnamon sugar dusted her front as she trekked upstairs to bed. The bathroom's toilet ran while she brushed her teeth. Wonderful. Add another bullet point to the near-biblical-length "to do" list. Everything in Five Diamonds was leaky—including her.

No! No tears. She practiced water conservation as a rule.

"Nature doesn't deal in straight lines," Dad said once, while taking her on one of his "scouts" as he called it, hunting for inspiration. He'd spend weeks trolling river bottoms for just the right stones to place in just the exact swirl, or days creating an elaborate nest from twigs. People called him a genius, and perhaps they were right. He certainly didn't inhabit the same world as others, floating past broken chicken coops, leaking toilets, and dripping faucets as if they were background static. Reality didn't interest him, only the beauty and possibility hidden in flotsam and jetsam.

"Look at that tree branch, see the jags and bends?" he had muttered. "Or how about the groovy arc to that pebble? The world isn't a perfect Point A to Point B, Annie. Life's infinitely more complex."

It sounded nice the morning he said it beside the river bend, under cottonwoods starting to change color. But alone, in the dark, when you're almost thirty, divorced, without a clue where you're going—perfect lines, simple and clear-cut, were infinitely more appealing.

Growing up wasn't magical; it sucked.

Annie tiptoed into her childhood bedroom and quietly slipped into her pajamas so as not to wake her son. She could always crash in the master, but this room felt right. The matching brass beds, hers and Claire's, were still covered by the same nine-patch quilts they'd sewed during one long winter in their teens. Atticus slept in one, curled on himself, butt in the air, the awkward pose no adult would find comfortable but kids returned to time and again. She glanced at the empty bed and back to her little one. Not even a question, really. Crawling in beside him, the big spoon to his little, Annie inhaled his scent, a comforting blend of hot chocolate, fabric softener, and boy. The perfect antidote to the farmhouse's forlorn mustiness.

But the night was an honest time.

She was lost.

The pressure to keep a brave face and feign optimism since the divorce threatened to buckle her knees. But who wanted to hear that story? No one. She needed to be Mighty Mama, the superwoman who taught Atticus a hundred infant signs, ensured there was always a seasonal décor project on the go, and cheerfully concocted homemade laundry powder.

The suitcase against the far wall didn't hold thongs or sexy lace. It was time to hike up her practical cotton briefs, grab a glue gun, and get back on track. Her career, and more importantly, her son, counted on it.

"I'm going to take care of you, little man." Atticus stirred at her whisper, murmuring a few jumbled syllables. Outside, the coyote yipped again and the air seemed to vibrate from the melancholy pang. "I'll take care of everything."

Tomorrow she'd figure out how.

About the Author

After studying at the University of Montana-Missoula, LIA RILEY scoured the world armed with only a backpack, overconfidence, and a terrible sense of direction. She counts shooting vodka with a Ukrainian mechanic in Antarctica, sipping yerba mate with gauchos in Chile, and swilling fourex with station hands in Outback Australia among her accomplishments.

A British literature fanatic at heart, Lia considers Mr. Darcy and Edward Rochester her fictional boyfriends. Her very patient husband doesn't mind. Much. When not torturing heroes (because, c'mon, who doesn't love a good tortured hero?), Lia herds unruly chickens, camps, beach combs, daydreams about as-of-yet unwritten books, wades through a mile-high TBR pile, and schemes yet another trip. Right now, Icelandic hot springs and Scottish castles sound mighty fine.

She and her family live mostly in Northern California.

Discover great authors, exclusive offers, and more at hc.com.

Give in to your Impulses. . .
Continue reading for excerpts from
our newest Avon Impulse books.
Available now wherever e-books are sold.

CLOSE TO HEART
By T.J. Kline

THE MADDENING LORD MONTWOOD
THE RAKES OF FALLOW HALL SERIES
By Vivienne Lorret

CHAOS
By Jamie Shaw

THE BRIDE WORE DENIM
A SEVEN BRIDES FOR SEVEN COWBOYS NOVEL
By Lizbeth Selvig

An Excerpt from

CLOSE TO HEART
by T. J. Kline

It only took an instant for actress Alyssa Cole's
world to come crashing down . . . but Heart Fire
Ranch is a place of new beginnings, even for
those who find their way there by accident.

Justin stared at the woman across from him. As familiar as she looked, he couldn't put his finger on where he might have seen her before. Alyssa wasn't from around here, that much was certain. There weren't many women in town who could afford a designer purse, impractical boots, and a luxury vehicle more suited to city jaunts than the winter mountain terrain. But there was something else, some memory niggling at the back of his mind, teasing him, just out of reach.

Her waifish appearance reminded him of a fashion model. She was certainly lovely enough to be one, but the idea didn't suit the woman standing in front of him. Justin assumed models would be accustomed to taking criticism and judgment, and this woman looked as if she'd crumble if he so much as raised his voice.

That was it, he realized. Behind her sadness, he recognized fear. Justin felt the uncontrollable instinct to protect Alyssa swell in his chest. She might not be his responsibility, but he couldn't stop the desire to help her any more than he could have let the dog die. When she glanced up at him again, his mouth opened without acknowledgment from his brain.

"D'you know anything about accounting or running an office? You did pretty well with these guys. You could work here for a while, at least until you get your car fixed or figure something out, since my regular help doesn't seem inclined to answer her phone."

"I guess, but I couldn't let you fire her ..."

What the hell are you doing? He knew she came from money, since she wore a huge wedding ring. Hell, that ring alone should have been enough reason for him to keep his mouth shut, since she was another man's wife, but his lips continued to move.

Justin laughed out loud, but he wasn't sure whether it was at himself for his stupidity or her comment. "I can't fire her; she's my cousin. But maybe this would be a wake-up call to be more responsible."

Alyssa gave him a slight smile before ducking her head again. He didn't miss the fact that she wasn't able to meet his eyes for more than a few seconds.

"My sister has a ranch with a few guest cabins. I can see if she has one empty. I'm sure she'll let you stay as long as you need to."

Her eyes jumped back up to meet his. He could easily read the gratitude, and a hopeful light flickered to life in her eyes. But there was more—a wariness he couldn't explain and that had no reason to be there.

"Why are you being so nice? You don't know me."

Justin shrugged, as if car crashes and late-night emergency puppy deliveries were commonplace for him. "It's the right thing to do."

The light in her eyes darkened immediately and she frowned, not saying anything more. He reached for the runt, still in front of the oxygen and barely moving. "I don't know if this little guy is going to make it," he warned, slipping the dropper into the puppy's mouth. He wasn't surprised when the puppy didn't even try to suck. It wasn't a good sign.

"We have to help him," she insisted, her voice firm as she set the puppy she was feeding back into the squirming pile of little bodies.

Justin looked up at the determination he heard in her voice, the antithesis of the resignation he'd seen there only moments before. His gaze crashed into hers, and he felt an instant throb of desire. He cursed the reaction, especially since she was right, he *didn't* know her or her story.

"*We?* Does this mean you're staying?" The corner of his mouth tipped upward in anticipation of spending some time with her, finding out how a woman like her ended up in the middle of nowhere like this.

Easy, boy. You're allowed to help and that's all. That ring on her finger and that belly say she's committed to someone else.

Yeah, well, that sadness in her eyes and the fact that she's alone say something completely different, he internally argued with himself. Justin wondered what happened to his "no romantic entanglement" resolution and how quickly this woman was able to make him reconsider it. But he couldn't just leave a damsel in distress to figure things out on her own. His father had taught him better than that.

An Excerpt from

THE MADDENING LORD MONTWOOD
The Rakes of Fallow Hall Series
by Vivienne Lorret

Lucan Montwood is the last man Frances Thorne
should ever trust. A gambler and a rake, he's
known for causing more trouble than he solves.
So when he offers his protection after Frances's
home and job are taken from her, she's more than a
little wary. After all, she knows Lord Montwood's
clever smile can disarm even the most guarded
heart. If she's not mindful, Frances may fall
prey to the most dangerous game of all—love.

"You've abducted me?" A pulse fluttered at her throat. It came from fear, of course, and alarm. It most certainly did not flutter out of a misguided wanton thrill. At her age, she knew better. Or rather, she *should* know better.

That grin remained unchanged. "Not at all. Rest assured, you are free to leave here at any time—"

"Then I will leave at once."

"As soon as you've heard my warning."

It did not take long for a wave of exasperation to fill her and then exit her lungs on a sigh. "This is in regard to Lord Whitelock again. Will you ever tire of this subject? You have already said that you believe him to be a snake in disguise. I have already said that I don't agree. There is nothing more to say unless you have proof."

"And yet you require no proof to hold ill will against me," he challenged with a lift of his brow. "You have damned me with the same swift judgment that you have elevated Whitelock to sainthood."

What rubbish. "I did not set out to find the good in his lordship. The fact of his goodness came to me naturally, by way of his reputation. Even his servants cannot praise him enough. They are forever grateful for his benevolence. And I can find no fault in a man who would offer a position to a woman who'd been fired by her former employer and whose own father was taken to gaol."

"Perhaps he wants your gratitude," Lucan said, his tone edged with warning as he prowled nearer. "This entire series of events that has put you within his reach reeks of manipulation. You are too sensible to ignore how conveniently these circumstances have turned out in his favor."

"Yet I suppose I'm meant to ignore the *convenience* in which you've abducted me?"

He laughed. The low, alluring sound had no place in the light of day. It belonged to the shadows that lurked in dark alcoves and to the secret desires that a woman of seven and twenty never dare reveal.

"It was damnably hard to get you here," he said with such arrogance that she was assured her desires would remain secret forever. "You have no idea how much liquor Whitelock's driver can hold. It took an age for him to pass out."

Incredulous, she shook her head. "Are you blind to your own manipulations? It has not escaped my notice that you reacted *without* surprise to the news of my recent events. I can only assume that you are also aware of my father's current predicament."

"I have been to Fleet to see him." Lucan's expression lost all humor. "He has asked me to watch over you. So that is what I am doing."

What a bold liar Lucan was—and looking her in the eye all the while, no less. "If that is true," she scoffed, "you then interpreted his request as '*Please, sir, abduct my daughter*'? I find it more likely that he would have asked you to pay his debts to gain his freedom."

"He declined my offer."

She let out a laugh. "That is highly suspect. I do not think you are speaking a single word of truth."

"You are putting your faith in the wrong man." Something akin to irritation flashed in his gaze, like a warning shot. He took another step. "Perhaps those spectacles require new lenses. They certainly aren't aiding your sight."

"I wear these spectacles for reading, I'll have you know. Otherwise, my vision is fine," she countered, ignoring the heady static charge in the air between them. "I prefer to wear them instead of risking their misplacement."

"You wear them like a shield of armor."

The man irked her to no end. "Preposterous. I've no need for a shield of any sort. I cannot help it if you are intimidated by my spectacles *and* by my ability to see right through you."

He stepped even closer. An unknown force, hot and barely leashed, crackled in the ever-shrinking space. She watched as he slid the blank parchment toward him before withdrawing the quill from the stand. Ignoring her, he dipped the end into the ink and wrote something on the page.

Undeterred, she continued her harangue. "Though you may doubt it, I can spot those *snakes*—as you like to refer to members of your own sex—quite easily. I can come to an understanding of a man's character within moments of introduction. I am even able to anticipate"—Lucan handed the parchment to her. She accepted it and absently scanned the page—"his actions."

Suddenly, she stopped and read it again. *"As soon as you've finished reading this, I am going to kiss you."*

While she was still blinking at the words, Lucan claimed her mouth.

An Excerpt from

CHAOS

by Jamie Shaw

Jamie Shaw's rock stars are back, and a girl from
Shawn's past has just joined the band. But will a
month cooped up on a tour bus rekindle an old
flame . . . or destroy the band as they know it?

"That was a hundred years ago, Kale!" I shout at my closed bedroom door as I wiggle into a pair of skintight jeans. I hop backward, backward, backward—until I'm nearly tripping over the combat boots lying in the middle of my childhood room.

"So why are you going to this audition?"

I barely manage to do a quick twist-and-turn to land on my bed instead of my ass, my furrowed brow directed at the ceiling as I finish yanking my pants up. "Because!"

Unsatisfied, Kale growls at me from the other side of my closed door. "Is it because you still like him?"

"I don't even KNOW him!" I shout at a white swirl on the ceiling, kicking my legs out and fighting against the taut denim as I stride to my closed door. I grab the knob and throw it open. "And he probably doesn't even remember me!"

Kale's scowl is replaced by a big set of widening eyes as he takes in my outfit—tight, black, shredded-to-hell jeans paired with a loose black tank top that doesn't do much to cover the lacy bra I'm wearing. The black fabric matches my wristbands and the parts of my hair that aren't highlighted blue. I turn away from Kale to grab my boots.

"*That* is what you're wearing?"

I snatch up the boots and do a showman's twirl before plopping down on the edge of my bed. "I look hot, don't I?"

Kale's face contorts like the time I convinced him a Sour Patch Kid was just a Swedish Fish coated in sugar. "You're my *sister*."

"But I'm hot," I counter with a confident smirk, and Kale huffs out a breath as I finish tying my boots.

"You're lucky Mason isn't home. He'd never let you leave the house."

Freaking Mason. I roll my eyes.

I've been back home for only a few months—since December, when I decided that getting a bachelor's degree in music theory wasn't worth an extra year of nothing but general education requirements—but I'm already ready to do a kamikaze leap out of the nest again. Having a hyperactive roommate was nothing compared to my overprotective parents and even more overprotective older brothers.

"Well, Mason isn't home. And neither is Mom or Dad. So are you going to tell me how I look or not?" I stand back up and prop my hands on my hips, wishing my brother and I still stood eye to eye.

Sounding thoroughly unhappy about it, Kale says, "You look amazing."

A smile cracks across my face a moment before I grab my guitar case from where it's propped against the wall. As I walk through the house, Kale trails after me.

"What's the point in dressing up for him?" he asks with the echo of our footsteps following us down the hall.

"Who says it's for him?"

"Kit," Kale complains, and I stop walking. At the top of the stairs, I turn and face him.

"Kale, you know this is what I want to do with my life. I've wanted to be in a big-name band since middle school. And Shawn is an amazing guitarist. And so is Joel. And Adam is an amazing singer, and Mike is an amazing drummer . . . This is my chance to be *amazing*. Can't you just be supportive?"

My twin braces his hands on my shoulders, and I have to wonder if it's to comfort me or because he's considering pushing me down the stairs. "You know I support you," he says. "Just . . ." He twists his lip between his teeth, chewing it cherry red before releasing it. "Do you have to be amazing with *him*? He's an asshole."

"Maybe he's a different person now," I reason, but Kale's dark eyes remain skeptical as ever.

"Maybe he's not."

"Even if he isn't, *I'm* a different person now. I'm not the same nerd I was in high school."

I start down the stairs, but Kale stays on my heels, yapping at me like a nippy dog. "You're wearing the same boots."

"These boots are killer," I say—which should be obvious, but apparently needs to be said.

"Just do me a favor?"

At the front door, I turn around and begin backing onto the porch. "What favor?"

"If he hurts you again, use those boots to get revenge where it counts."

An Excerpt from

THE BRIDE WORE DENIM
A Seven Brides for Seven Cowboys Novel
by Lizbeth Selvig

When Harper Lee Crockett returns home
to Paradise Ranch, Wyoming, the last thing
she expects is to fall head-over-heels in lust
for Cole, childhood neighbor and her older
sister's long-time boyfriend. The spirited and
artistic Crockett sister has finally learned to
resist her craziest impulses, but this latest trip
home and Cole's rough and tough appeal might
be too much for her fading self-control.

Thank God for the chickens. They knew how to liven up a funeral.

Harper Crockett crouched against the rain-soaked wall of her father's extravagant chicken coop and laughed until she cried. This time, however, the tears weren't for the man who'd built the Henhouse Hilton—as she and her sisters had christened the porch-fronted coop that rivaled most human homes—they were for the eight multi-colored, escaped fowl that careened around the yard like over-caffeinated bees.

The very idea of a chicken stampede on one of Wyoming's largest cattle ranches was enough to ease her sorrow, even today.

She glanced toward the back porch of her parent's huge log home several hundred yards away to make sure she was still alone, and she wiped the tears and the rain from her eyes. "I know you probably aren't liking this, Dad," she said, aiming her words at the sopping chickens. "Chaos instead of order."

Chaos had never been acceptable to Samuel Crockett.

A *bock-bocking* Welsummer rooster, gorgeous with its burnt orange and blue body and iridescent green tail, powered past, close enough for an ambush. Harper sprang from her position and nabbed the affronted bird around its thick, shiny body. "Gotcha," she said as its feathers soaked her sweater. "Back to the pen for you."

The rest of the chickens squawked in alarm at the apprehension and arrest of one of their own. They scattered again scolding and flapping.

Yeah, she thought as she deposited the rooster back in the chicken yard, her father had no choice now but to glower at the bedlam from heaven. He was the one who'd left the darn birds behind.

As the hens fussed, Harper assessed the little flock made up of her father's favorite breeds—all chosen for their easygoing temperaments: friendly, buff-colored cochins; smart, docile, black and white Plymouth rocks; and sweet, shy black Australorps. Oh, what freedom and gang mentality could do—they'd turned into a band of egg-laying gangsters helping each other escape the law.

And despite there being seven chickens still left to corral, Harper reveled in sharing their attempted run for freedom with nobody. She brushed ineffectually at the mud on her soggy blue and brown broom skirt—hippie clothing, in the words of her sisters—and the stains on her favorite, crocheted summer sweater. It would have been much smarter to run back to the house and recruit help. Any number of kids bored with funereal reminiscing would have gladly volunteered. Her sisters—Joely and the triplets, if not Amelia—might have as well. The wrangling would have been done in minutes.

Something about facing this alone, however, fed her need to dredge any good memories she could from the day. She'd chased an awful lot of chickens throughout her youth. The memories served, and she didn't want to share them.

Another lucky grab garnered her a little Australorp who was returned, protesting, to the yard. Glancing around once more to check the empty, rainy yard, Harper squatted back under the eaves of the pretty, yellow chicken mansion and let the half dozen chickens settle. These were not her mother's birds. These were her father's "girls"—creatures who'd sometimes received more warmth than the human females he'd raised.

Good memories tried to flee in the wake of her petty thoughts, and she grabbed them back. Of course her father had loved his daughters. He'd just never been good at showing it. There'd been plenty of good times.

Rain pittered in a slow, steady rhythm over the lawn and against the coop's gingerbread scrollwork. It pattered into the genuine, petunia-filled, window boxes on their actual multi-paned windows. Inside, the chickens enjoyed oak-trimmed nesting boxes, two flights of ladders, and chicken-themed artwork. Behind their over-the-top manse stretched half an acre of safely-fenced running yard trimmed with white picket fencing. Why the idiot birds were shunning such luxury to go AWOL out here in the rain was beyond Harper—even if they had found the gate improperly latched.

Wiping rain from her face again, she concentrated like a cat stalking canaries and made three more successful lunges. Chicken wrangling was rarely about mad chasing and much more about patience. She smiled evilly at the remaining three criminals who now eyed her with concern.

"Give yourselves up, you dirty birds," she called. "Your day on the lam is finished."

She swooped toward a fluffy Cochin, a chicken breed

normally known for its lazy friendliness, and the fat creature shocked her by feinting and then dodging. For the first time in this hunt, Harper missed her chicken. A resulting belly-flop onto the grass forced a startled grunt from her throat, and she slid four inches through a puddle. Before she could let loose the mild curse that bubbled up to her tongue, the mortifying sound of clapping echoed through the rain.

"I definitely give that a nine-point-five."

A hot flash of awareness blazed through her stomach, leaving behind unwanted flutters. She closed her eyes, fighting back embarrassment, and she hadn't yet found her voice when a large, sinewy male hand appeared in front of her, accompanied by rich, baritone laughter. She groaned and reached for his fingers.

"Hello, Cole," she said, resignation forcing her vocal chords to work as she let him help her gently but unceremoniously to her feet.

Cole Wainwright stood before her, the knot of his tie pulled three inches down his white shirt front, the two buttons above it spread open. That left the tanned, corded skin of his neck at Harper's eye level, and she swallowed. His brown-black hair was spiked and mussed, as if he'd just awoken, and his eyes sparkled in the rain like blue diamonds. She took a step back.

"Hullo, you," he replied.